USA TOD…

Dale Mayer

MAGNUS

SHADOW RECON

MAGNUS: SHADOW RECON, BOOK 1
Beverly Dale Mayer
Valley Publishing Ltd.

ISBN-13: 978-1-773366-63-0
Print Edition

Books in This Series

Magnus, Book 1

Rogan, Book 2

About This Book

Magnus arrives in the Arctic for severe-weather training, overseen by an international joint task force, but run by military brass. With multiple countries involved and multiple divisions of the military, it's a wide-open mix of potential trouble. And trouble is what he's here to find. Not to create. However, after meeting the one and only doctor on-site, a female member of the British team, Magnus knows that she needs his help to keep her safe. Yet she can't be his main interest, not when something is seriously wrong at this Arctic training compound. Too bad his heart wasn't listening …

Dr. Sydney Jenkins had been a last-minute replacement for the doctor scheduled to be here. Sydney had been delighted for the new experience, until she arrived to find all hell breaking loose, almost on her first day. Men missing, accidents that shouldn't be happening, and her medical clinic targeted. Not sure who to trust, she's inclined to accept Magnus's protective presence, but … she'd been wrong before.

Making a mistake under these conditions would be fatal—for both of them …

Sign up to be notified of all Dale's releases here!

https://geni.us/DaleNews

PROLOGUE

LIEUTENANT COMMANDER MASON Callister walked into the private office and stood in front of retired Navy Commander Doran Magellan.

"Mason, good to see you."

Yet the dry tone of voice, and the scowl pinching the silver-haired man's face, all belied his words. Mason had known Doran for over a decade, and their friendship had only grown over time.

Mason waited, as he watched the other man try to work the new tech phone system on his desk. With his hand circling the air above the black box, he appeared to hit buttons randomly.

Mason held back his amusement but to no avail.

"Why can't a phone be a phone anymore?" the commander snapped, as his glare shifted from Mason to the box and back.

Asking the commander if he needed help wouldn't make the older man feel any better, but sitting here and watching as he indiscriminately punched buttons was a struggle. "Is Helen away?" Mason asked.

"Yes, damn it. She's at lunch, and I need her to be at lunch." The commander's piercing gaze pinned Mason in place. "No one is to know you're here."

Solemn, Mason nodded. "Understood."

"Doran? Is that you?" A crotchety voice slammed into the room through the phone's speakers. "Get away from that damn phone. You keep clicking buttons in my ear. Get Helen in there to do this."

"No, she can't be here for this."

Silence came first, then a huge groan. "Damn it. Then you should have connected me last, so I don't have to sit here and listen to you fumbling around."

"Go pour yourself a damn drink then," Doran barked. "I'm working on the others."

A snort was his only response.

Mason bit the inside of his lip, as he really tried to hold back his grin. The retired commander had been hell on wheels while on active duty, and, even now, the retired part of his life seemed to be more of a euphemism than anything.

"Damn things …"

Mason looked around the dark mahogany office and the walls filled with photos, awards, and medals. A life of purpose and accomplishment. And all of that had only piqued his interest during the initial call he'd received, telling him to be here at this time.

"Ah, got it."

Mason's eyebrows barely twitched as the commander gave him a feral grin. "I'd rather lead a warship into battle than deal with some of today's technology."

As he was one of only a few commanders who'd been in a position to do such a thing, it said much about his capabilities.

And much about current technology.

The commander leaned back in his massive chair and motioned to the cart beside Mason. "Pour three cups."

Interesting. Mason walked a couple steps across the rich

tapestry-style carpet and lifted the silver service to pour coffee into three very down-to-earth-looking mugs.

"Black for me."

Mason picked up two cups and walked one over to Doran.

"Thanks." He leaned forward and snapped into the phone, "Everyone here?"

Multiple voices responded.

Curiouser and curiouser. Mason recognized several of the voices. Other relics of an era gone by. Although not a one wanted to hear that, and, in good faith, it wasn't fair. Mason had thought each of these men were retired, had relinquished power. Yet, as he studied Doran in front of him, Mason had to wonder whether any of them had passed the baton or if they'd only slid into the shadows. Was this planned with the government's authority? Or were these retirees a shadow group to the government?

The tangible sense of power and control oozed from Doran's words, tone, stature—his very pores. This man might be heading into his sunset years—based on a simple calculation of chronological years spent on the planet—but he was a long way from being out of the action.

"Mason …" Doran began.

"Sir?"

"We've got a problem."

Mason narrowed his gaze and waited.

Doran's glare was hard, steely hard, with an icy glint. "Do you know the Mavericks?"

Mason's eyebrows shot up. The black ops division was one of those well-kept secrets, so, therefore, everyone knew about it. He gave a decisive nod. "I do."

"And you're involved in the logistics behind the training

program in the Arctic, are you not?"

"I am." Now where was the commander going with this?

"Do you know another SEAL by the name of Mountain Rode? He's been working for the black ops Mavericks." At his own words, the commander shook his head. "What the hell was his mother thinking when she gave him that moniker?"

"She wasn't thinking anything," said the man with a hard voice from behind Mason.

He stiffened slightly, then relaxed as he recognized that voice too.

"She died giving birth to me. And my full legal name is Mountain Bear Rode. It was my father's doing."

The commander glared at the new arrival. "Did I say you could come in?"

"Yes." Mountain's voice was firm, yet a definitive note of affection filled his tone.

That emotion told Mason so much.

The commander harrumphed, then cleared his throat. "Mason, we're picking up a significant amount of chatter over that training. Most of it good. Some of it the usual caterwauling we've come to expect every time we participate in a joint training mission. This one is set to run for six months, then to reassess."

Mason already knew this. But he waited for the commander to get around to why Mason was here, and, more important, what any of this had to do with the mountain of a man who now towered beside him.

The commander shifted his gaze to Mountain, but he remained silent.

Mason noted Mountain was not only physically big but damn imposing and severely pissed, seemingly barely holding back the forces within. His body language seemed to yell, *And the world will fix this, or I'll find the reason why.*

For a moment Mason felt sorry for the world.

Finally, a voice spoke through the phone. "Mason, this is Alpha here. I run the Mavericks. We've got a problem with that training center. Mountain, tell him."

Mason shifted to include Mountain in his field of vision. Mason wished the other men on the conference call were in the room too. It was one thing to deal with men you knew and could take the measure of; it was another when they were silent shadows in the background.

"My brother is one of the men who reported for the Arctic training three weeks ago."

"Teegan Rode?" Mason confirmed. "I'm the one who arranged for him to go up there. He's a great kid."

A glimmer of a smile cracked Mountain's stony features. He nodded. "Indeed. An oops on my father's part but a bright light in my often dark world. He's a dozen years younger than me, just passed his BUD/s training this spring, and raring to go. Until his raring to go then got up and went."

Oh, shit. Mason's gaze zinged to the commander, who had kicked up his feet to rest atop the big desk. Stocking feet. With Mickey Mouse images dancing on them. Sidetracked, Mason struggled to pull his attention back to Mountain. "Meaning?"

"He's disappeared." Mountain let out a harsh breath, as if just saying that out loud, and maybe to the right people, could allow him to relax—at least a little.

The commander spoke up. "We need your help, Mason. You're uniquely qualified for this problem."

It didn't sound as if he was qualified in any way for anything he'd heard so far. "Clarify." His spoken word was simplicity itself, but the tone behind it said he wanted the cards on the table … now.

Mountain spoke up. "He's the third incident."

Mason's gaze narrowed, as the reports from the training camp rolled through his mind. "One was Russian. One was from the German SEAL team. Both were deemed accidental deaths."

"No, they weren't."

There it was. The root of the problem in black-and-white. He studied Mountain, aiming for neutrality. "Do you have evidence?"

"My brother did."

"Ah, hell."

Mountain gave a clipped nod. "I'll find him."

"Of that I have no doubt," Mason said quietly. "Do you have a copy of the evidence he collected?"

"I have some of it." Mountain held out a USB key. "This is your copy. Top secret."

"We don't have to remind you, Mason, that lives are at stake," Doran added. "Nor do we need another international incident. Consider also that a group of scientists, studying global warming, is close by, and not too far away is a village home to a few hardy locals."

Mason accepted the key, turned to the commander, and asked, "Do we know whether this is internal or enemy warfare?"

"We don't know at this point," Alpha replied through the phone. "Mountain will lead Shadow Recon. His mission is twofold. One, find out what's behind these so-called accidents and put a stop to it by any means necessary. Two, locate his brother, hopefully alive."

"And where do I come in?" Mason asked.

"We want you to pull together a special team. The members of Shadow Recon will report to both you and Mountain, just in case."

That was clear enough.

"You'll stay stateside but in constant communication with Mountain—with the caveat that, if necessary, you're on the next flight out."

"What about bringing in other members from the Mavericks?" Mason suggested.

Alpha took this question too, his response coming through via Speakerphone. "We don't have the numbers. The budget for our division has been cut. So we called the commander to pull some strings."

That was Doran's cue to explain further. "Mountain has fought hard to get me on board with this plan, and I'm here now. The navy has a special budget for Shadow Recon and will take care of Mountain and you, Mason, and the team you provide."

"Skills needed?"

"Everything," Mountain said, his voice harsh. "But the biggest is these men need to operate in the shadows, mostly alone, without a team beside them. Too many new arrivals will alert the enemy. If we make any changes to the training program, it will raise alarms. We'll move the men in one or two at a time on the same rotation that the trainees are running right now."

"And when we get to the bottom of this?" Mason looked from the commander back to Mountain.

"Then the training can resume as usual," Doran stated.

Mason immediately churned through the names already popping up in his mind. How much could he tell his men?

Obviously not much. Hell, he didn't know much himself. How much time did he have? "Timeline?"

The commander's final word told him of the urgency.

"Yesterday."

DAY 1

Arrived safely. Another man missing as of my arrival. WTF is going on here? Confirmed Mountain is here. Haven't connected yet. Blizzard outside. Tempers are short. Fear underneath. Nothing new to report.

Racing through the harsh wind, Magnus Moureaux entered the large snow-covered building, shaking the snow off his hood and his shoulders. He stepped from what seemed to be a huge music concert of Mother Nature's current storm into absolute silence, just with a *snick* of a door. It had been hard to pull the door open against the heavy winds; closing it wasn't exactly an easy job either. Standing here, sensing the stillness around him in this antechamber entrance room—one step away from the other entrances to separate the harsh cold outside from the heated building inside—he felt the change in the atmosphere.

Continuing on into a second chamber, he took off his heavy hooded parka, hung it on his labeled spot, and put his massive snow boots underneath, taking off his gloves at the same time, as well as his balaclava. It was one hell of a relief. Feeling better with every layer removed, and now wearing his inside boots, he strode toward the double doors, welcoming the warmth of the heated building.

As he stepped inside, men turned to look at him, and several raised their hands. He just nodded and kept on going.

He saw Mountain off to the side. It may be Day One for Magnus here at the training camp, but it was at least Day Three and counting for Teegan, missing out in this tundra.

As much as Magnus wanted to head directly to Mountain, this wasn't the time. Mountain would know that. They had already prearranged signals between them, one if Teegan were found dead, another if Teegan were found alive. No such stealth communication between the two just meant that Mountain continued to search for his brother, regardless of how long it took. Nobody understood the strength needed for Mountain to keep all that angst and anger bottled up, to keep his focus steady on the goal, to not snap from the weight of it all.

Mountain and Magnus knew their big target was to investigate the goings-on at this training center, what with two suspicious deaths and now two men missing—one of them being Mountain's brother. This big target was made messier with the international relations involved among the military members from USA, Russia, Britain, Germany, Switzerland, and other countries represented here.

No matter how global this mess was, Mountain and Magnus were under the gun. While this training program was slated to last twelve weeks—and already three weeks in—Mother Nature overruled that future deadline. Any man or woman lost outside in this frozen tundra, with no help or supplies, would be severely tested to last one day, and Teegan had been missing for three days.

Mountain had been honest with Mason and Magnus, fearing his brother was now dead. And, as part of Mountain's cover as head of Shadow Recon, Mountain would publicly acknowledge that possibility, while openly searching to find his body, yet privately holding on to hope forever.

Yet the camp was not to know that Magnus was part of Mountain's team, apart from the colonel on base.

Magnus cast another glance toward the big man, as Mountain's shoulders were slightly stiffer and his head up. Something about Mountain's size came with certain mannerisms, and everybody had his tells. Plus it was almost as if Mountain could sniff out trouble. Magnus wasn't privy to all the information or to who else was here who may or may not be on the same mission.

He hoped it wasn't just the two of them because, God, Magnus could almost taste the trouble in the air, and under it all was … fear. Mountain wouldn't be easy to put down. Neither would Magnus. He had a lot of aces up his sleeve and certainly dropping him wouldn't be easy, but it would take a rocket to drop Mountain, particularly when he was on the hunt for somebody who potentially had hurt his brother. A brother who was still missing. Truth be told, recovering Teegan's body was the expressed goal, but, knowing Mountain, he wouldn't be giving up on finding his brother alive.

Per the current intel, now they had a fifth incident—counting the dead Russian; the dead German; the still-missing man, Teegan Rode; the second missing man, Terrance Billings; and now the most recent missing man, a Russian, who disappeared during a training event. He went missing so recently that we don't even have his name yet. Magnus had been informed when he flew in last night.

He headed over to the kitchen area, where he grabbed a mug of hot coffee, anything to warm him up inside. Nothing like a good stomp around outside to get your blood flowing, but the cold set in very quickly. Once it did, that chill could be hard to chase away.

He'd been here for less than twenty-four hours, and it

was hard to believe that anything could survive this hostile climate for long. Yet a part of him enjoyed being outside. He loved the outdoors, and he loved the cold. Then at times, such as right now, he wanted to go out and do a long-term search, but the blizzard stopped absolutely everything, and that frustrated him to no end.

If he were stateside, even worse weather conditions and possibly tornados, would stop Magnus from going out and finding someone potentially hurt and in trouble. He'd worked search and rescue with his brother and his father for decades growing up in that coastal environment, but here in these circumstances? Even Magnus knew the human body had limits and what it could handle. Both for rescuers and the rescuees.

Still, that reality just pissed him off.

As he sat down, his temper got the best of him, and the cup landed a little too hard.

The guy sitting next to him looked over and went off on him. "Wow, you're in a fine fettle, aren't ya?"

Just enough of an accent to his voice made Magnus smile. "Yeah, you could say that. I wasn't expecting the storm to last this long."

Jesse, who Magnus thought had been around here for quite a while, laughed and nodded. "Yeah, when she settles in like this, you're not going anywhere. Doesn't matter whether it's coming or going." He chuckled. "Mother Nature rules up here. The sooner you accept it, the better."

Magnus nodded; Jesse had no idea that accepting shit like that wasn't part of Magnus's mandate, but finding answers was. Frustrated he couldn't do his job or move this forward in any way, he glared down at his cup. Sitting around, waiting, definitely was not his ball of wax.

When somebody else sat down beside him, he looked over, and there was Dr. Sydney Jenkins. Magnus had reported to her earlier, soon after arriving, as she needed some medical files on him. He smiled. "Hey, how're you doing?"

Sydney smiled back. "I'm doing well. I don't know how you handle being outside like that though. You were outside for hours and on day one. You sure you're okay?"

He shrugged. "I would prefer to be outside a whole lot more than that storm out there will let me."

"Right, but enough people have been lost here already." She narrowed her gaze, adding, "Let's make sure you aren't added to the list."

"Don't plan on it."

She had been here for three weeks now and was likely to be heading back fairly quickly, but Magnus wasn't sure. She was the only doctor at the site. He didn't know anything about her military background, though generally they came fully trained. However, in these circumstances, he wasn't sure. She was also part of the English team, and multiple international teams were here, with members coming in and out on a regular basis.

Magnus couldn't help but think that everybody else on those teams had better luck with the weather than him, what with planes still flying in and out and Arctic Cats moving across the tundra, while he was stuck doing next to nothing.

She smiled. "That look on your face is priceless."

"Yeah, I get it. I'm broadcasting that I'm not happy."

She just shook her head and patted his hand. "Tomorrow's another day."

"What kind of a day though?" he asked, looking at her. "Another storm day?" He dragged out the word *storm*, and it was enough to make her face light up just a bit.

She nodded seriously. "Yes, maybe another storm day. So, if you do go out, make sure you use the safety lines."

His voice equally low, he grumbled, "Didn't help the last guy, did it?"

She stiffened slightly and then relaxed. "No, it didn't, and that's why we want to ensure you are tied securely to the safety lines, so that you come back."

He just nodded and didn't say anything. Of course he planned on following safety protocols, and he had no intention of getting lost out there. In this situation, it was sure death to throw caution to the wind out there. However, at the same time, it was damn hard to sit here and to chomp at the bit while doing nothing.

She lowered her voice, careful not to lean in, but instead she looked around casually and whispered, "You might want to check inside."

He deliberately stopped himself from showing any shock at her words. Impressed at the thought that she may have pegged him already, he lifted his cup casually and asked in an equally low voice, "What would I be looking for?"

"Missing medications." With that, she stood and smacked him hard on the shoulder. "Maybe tomorrow you'll get out." She turned and walked off.

Behind her, Magnus could only stare, as she disappeared around the corner.

SYDNEY RETURNED TO her clinic and quickly shut the door. Once again, she went back over her medication cabinets, checking that all the locks were secure. The fact that they had been secure before was a little more damning in her mind because it meant that somebody had the ability to pick the lock, or get a key made, or use some higher-order skills, which she had no chance or ability to counteract at the moment. Considering the skill set of the people at this compound, that wasn't a surprise. Thankfully everything was still here.

When the door opened a little later, Magnus walked in.

She gave him a veiled look.

"You want to explain that comment?" he asked quietly.

She shrugged and groaned. "Wish I could."

She motioned at the opened door behind him. He quickly shut the door and locked it. While he turned, she pulled her bug detector from her pocket and did a quick search around.

She glanced at Magnus, but he kept an eye on her, standing here, measuring her as she did so. When she was finally done with checking all over her clinic, she nodded, turned, and looked at him in exasperation.

"Somebody has been stealing medications, very powerful drugs, out of the cabinet. They have somehow made a key, or they've been picking the locks, and I can't seem to catch them. Not to mention that I also found a bug in my clinic," she declared bitterly. "I had to contact somebody else who I thought could handle this quietly, and they managed to get me this." She held up the detector in her hand.

He stared at it silently, still unsure of it all, then, as if parking all other thoughts, focused solely on her. "Who did you contact?"

She winced. "Mountain."

He smiled. "Good choice." Her shoulders sagged in relief. "Mountain's one of the good guys."

"I know that he's here because his brother's gone missing, so I figured he had to be on the right side, though I'm not even sure that we have sides here right now." She crossed her arms over her chest, her fingers rat-a-tatting an impatient staccato on her arm. "I don't know what's going on right now." She tried to minimize her exhaustion, but it was hard; she hadn't slept well in days. Fear was her constant companion. "I feel very much as if I got dragged into this problem."

He looked around. "Where's the cabinet? Is this the only one?"

She walked over and showed him. She didn't have as much here as she would like, but there was always the hope that this would only be for emergency circumstances, and anybody seriously ill would be airlifted out. Still, she had to stabilize any patient and needed a full contingency of equipment and medication.

Magnus studied the lock and frowned, and she nodded.

"It hasn't been picked, as much as I can gather."

"No, it hasn't." He turned to look at her. "Which is definitely a concern, but people here have some pretty impressive skills, so we can't ignore that either."

"They have a freaking scary set of skills," she agreed. "It's daunting to consider how much that intellectual pool out there"—she nodded toward the common area—"has among them. When you consider that, and factor in that maybe we have a big problem at this compound, a problem that no one is admitting to—"

"No *maybe* about it," Magnus confirmed, his voice harsh. "We definitely have a problem." She didn't say anything, just nodded. He studied her for a long moment. "See? The thing is, you may have gone to Mountain, but I don't know much about you."

Her gaze widened at that, and she sucked in her breath, before letting it out very slowly. She hadn't expected that, although she should have. She didn't know why she hadn't. It was normal for them to question her role in all this, if anything. She felt his gaze on her, as she sought to find a way to give him an answer.

"And I don't hear an immediate answer."

"Just trying to figure out what I'm allowed to tell you," she said quietly.

He winced at that. "Isn't that great? You're tasked with a job, but you're not allowed to tell anybody. At the same time, you're in a position where people ask questions."

She burst out laughing. "You're not kidding." She gave him a wave of her hand. "Yet it's true."

He nodded. Hearing the doorknob behind him, he turned and looked at the doc inquiringly.

She nodded. "That will be Joy, my nurse."

With an eyebrow raised, he opened the door and let in the one nurse stationed here.

Joy walked in, eyed them both, and frowned. "Am I interrupting? Shall I come back later?"

Immediately Sydney shook her head. "No, not at all. It's fine."

Joy walked over, set two cups of coffee on the table, and turned to look at her boss. "I wasn't sure whether you'd had enough caffeine already or not."

"I'm pretty well swimming." She laughed, as she looked over at Joy's offerings. "Yet I'm always happy with more. I'll take the cinnamon bun too."

"Didn't you just eat?" Joy asked, with a laugh.

"I did, but being up here in these temperatures makes my appetite second to none."

"I guess that's a normal thing, isn't it? I've never been in these temperatures before." Joy walked to the counter and grabbed a well-used blanket and wrapped it around her shoulders. "Even though it's warm in here, I'm always cold," she admitted.

"When was the last time you were outside?" Magnus asked her.

She shook her head. "A couple days ago … at least. I like to visit the dogs."

He nodded. "It's a pretty big base," he said thoughtfully, "and that's the only reason you could handle it. I suppose, otherwise you would go stir-crazy in here."

"I'm pretty well stir-crazy as it is," Joy admitted. "However, every time I go to the door and look out, that's enough to keep me inside."

He laughed. "How long have you been here?"

"Three weeks now." She flashed a smile at him. "What about you?" she asked curiously.

He shrugged. "Came in earlier with a group."

"That's why I saw so many new faces today." Joy laughed. "I wondered whether I had slept through a complete change of staff or something."

"Is there staff here?" Magnus asked. "It's all a joint training mission, right?"

"What that really means is," Sydney explained, "we have three times the bosses." At that, he burst out laughing, as she grinned at him. "You know I'm right."

"Yeah, you probably are." He smiled. "Everybody had to come with their own hierarchy, didn't they?"

Joy nodded. "It'd be nice to think that they could just come with a small team, and sometimes they do. However, with the level of problems that suddenly seem to be arising, … I'm not sure that's what is happening now."

"If serious problems are happening, you would think that they would just shut it all down." Sydney looked over at Magnus.

He shrugged. "I'm not sure anybody believes it's a problem per se, as much as potentially accidents and more or less stupidity of some who are too cocky for their own good."

"Right," Sydney said, with a dry tone. "You mean, like going outside in this blizzard? Glad you came in when you did."

"I didn't get everything done I wanted to," he said quietly, "yet I stayed an hour past what I had planned."

Joy turned and looked at him in shock. "Outside?" she squeaked.

He smiled and nodded. "Absolutely. Just because a storm hits doesn't mean the world doesn't still need us to turn the crank."

"As long as the heat's still on, and we have supplies that can come and go, I'm okay to just stay inside, thanks. But the minute any of those issues come to my door"—Joy shook her head—"well, I'm on the next flight out."

"Except you just completely ignored the fact that there won't be a next flight out, not if they can't land to get us supplies. If they can bring supplies in, they can get people out." He looked around at the medical facility, surprised at how well equipped it was. "I see you're prepared in any case."

Sydney nodded. "There's always the hope that I won't have to"—she shrugged—"but better to have it and not need it than to need it and not have it."

He smiled and then looked over at Joy. "I just stopped in to get some aspirin."

Sydney walked to the cabinet, pulled out a small jar, opened it up, and gave him a little pill box with a couple inside. He smiled his thanks, then quickly turned and left.

As soon as he had gone, and the door had closed behind him, Joy turned to look at Sydney. "Hey, if you want me to, you know, take a walk because something's between the two of you …"

"Nope, not at all." Sydney laughed. "It's all good."

With that, Joy nodded and headed over to her desk and picked up a clipboard. "In that case, I'll get back to adding in the inventory from this last shipment." Then she headed to the medicine cabinets.

Behind her, Sydney watched Joy, all the while wondering if she could trust Magnus. Or had she opened Pandora's box by talking as freely as she had? Could she trust Mountain? He'd seemed the best bet earlier, and she'd taken to Magnus immediately, but … nothing like realizing everything going on around you was a fabrication of somebody else's manipulation.

She didn't know what was going on, and she didn't dare leave when everybody here was so vulnerable. She was the only doctor in the place, and it was her job to ensure everybody stayed safe, but how the hell was she supposed to do that when somebody was watching her, was stealing from her supplies?

DAY 2, MORNING

THE NEXT MORNING Sydney woke and quickly dressed, shivering at the overnight chill.

The heating cost had to be exorbitant, but it wasn't her problem, and that was a good thing, since she had enough on her mind. Speaking of which, she walked to her clinic next door, unlocked the door, and stepped inside. She stopped at the entrance and stood still, looking to see, feel, or sense if anything was wrong and if things had been disturbed. All appeared well, and, with that, she pivoted, stepped back out, and locked up.

As she turned again, one of the guys, Larry, was standing there, a little too close.

He immediately stepped back. "*Whoops.*"

She gave a half smile, as she fell back slightly as well. "Did you need something?" she asked in a calm voice.

He shook his head. "No, I just saw you stepping out and thought I'd say hi."

She nodded. "Hi." She quickly hooked her keys onto her belt loop, then turned toward the kitchen. "I haven't had coffee yet, and I never talk much before that, if I can help it."

He snorted. "You and everybody else in this place."

She nodded because coffee was an easy answer to avoid people and was glad to see Larry wave and walk away. Coffee was an out for any explanation, such as not being friendly or not even being as friendly as most people would expect in this situation. Sydney had lived in various bases and camps before and knew that it was easy to get into trouble very quickly, just by smiling at the wrong person.

Tempers got short after a while, and sex went into overdrive, no matter how much people tried to shut down either, and a single female in a group could cause all kinds of headaches. Definitely other women were here, and Sydney had already heard of one of them having an affair with one of the guys, then breaking up that relationship and was already into a second. Now it seemed as if guys were lining up already to be her third, which made things here very complicated. Sydney was doing her best to stay away from everybody, but, when the woman in question had come looking for condoms, Sydney had immediately handed them over, with a word of warning.

The other woman had just laughed under her watchful gaze. "Nothing else to do here." And, with that single comment, she'd disappeared almost as quickly as she had appeared.

Not exactly Sydney's style, but she understood, and she'd seen it time and time again. Sex, in the right circumstances, was a great outlet for all that pent-up energy. However, here, where only one, two, or maybe three people were sexually active, issues were bound to arise.

Right now, it wasn't a problem, and she hoped it didn't become one. Yet, with everything else going on, Sydney wouldn't be at all surprised if it led to short tempers. Of course short tempers led to outbursts.

As she walked into the dining room area, she noted no noticeable change in the atmosphere. She had become accustomed to looking over her shoulder—something she found herself constantly worried about now, wondering who and what could have been important enough for someone to put a listening device in her clinic. And now wondering if they knew it had been found and disabled, and, if so, was somebody coming back to fix it?

She constantly kept her bug detector on her and checked the clinic every time she went in. It had become an obsession but a sensible one. Mountain had brought her the device, but he hadn't returned since then, and that surprised her. Surely he would follow up at some point. Unless he was trying to keep it all on the sly and to not let anybody know that she'd gone to him—which, considering the number of accidents and missing people, was a good thing.

That medications were missing scared the crap out of her. Especially drugs powerful enough to knock out a horse. … That was a whole different story. Of course people would ask why she even had such things here, but they were really needed in case of problems, big problems, such as emergency surgeries or any other number of things that would require knocking out some of these big strong men. You didn't just knock out a guy the size of Mountain with a regular dose; it would take a horse tranquilizer for him. She cared about every one of these people and wanted to ensure that they all got treated humanely.

She had been questioned by the brass regarding the serious injuries that two of the men had sustained—after the first two deaths had come up. She hadn't seen anything suspicious about these two subsequent injuries at the time of her examination. Except now, seeing both, neither should have happened here.

Investigating the accidents wasn't her job, and the injuries were unknown to her, until the men had presented at her clinic. Now that two men were missing, two men were dead, and another two had serious injuries, it was all the more upsetting in this Arctic survival training arena.

As far as she was concerned, these situations should be handled proactively—such as using a buddy system when going outside—but now it seemed that they needed the buddy system inside as well. She would normally make recommendations, freely handing out her seasoned advice, except …

The base's colonel was hardly the man to listen to a woman. Probably not the men here either. The colonel was a hardnose when it came to work, not the friendly, sociable type. He kept more or less to himself and showed no emotion over being here. Certainly not happiness or even tolerance. Almost a note of resignation on his face, as if he were heading to or had already reached a retirement he didn't want.

Then, welcome to a mostly male-dominated world. Some of them didn't think women belonged here at all, and some certainly didn't think Sydney should even be a doctor, let alone the doctor here. It's not that she hadn't faced prejudice before because she certainly had, but it felt different in this environment. Was she as comfortable here as she could be elsewhere? No, absolutely not.

She had thought that it would be a good experience, helpful for her own education, and for understanding the injuries and the types of lifestyle challenges that came from living and working up here. The realization that it would be a multinational and multiservice training center had also been exciting. She was always up for learning about new cultures and anyone from different parts of the world. She was not at all sure why people would have anything against that, but some had groused about it.

Cup in hand, she sat down at the far side of the dining room, her back against the wall, her boots up against the chair in front of her, and sipped her coffee, wondering what the day would bring.

A typical day would include minor cuts, an odd pain, ear infections, and of course the normal run of colds and flu. So far, nothing too taxing had happened here, outside of the two serious injuries. Still, she had this sense of waiting, the sense of something brewing underneath the surface, and she just didn't know what that was about.

When Mountain walked in, the noise level dropped, as everybody turned to cast a glance at the huge man. She just smiled because she'd met Mountain before at a survival training exercise in the North Sea a few years back. So he had been the one she'd gone to, when she'd run into trouble here.

He hadn't made it clear what he was doing here, but it didn't take too much deduction to realize that, whatever it was, it had to do with the two missing people—his brother was one of them. She knew the chances were slim of either man still being alive, but she'd seen miracles before so wouldn't assume anything at this stage.

Mountain also kept to himself, making it seem he was a complete stranger to everyone. And a man everyone should avoid.

When he stomped toward her, a big mug of coffee in hand, she dropped her feet from the chair and pushed it out toward him. "Grab a seat."

"Don't mind if I do."

As he sat down with enough force that she winced, he looked over at her with a raised eyebrow. "I haven't broken a chair since I was sixteen."

She burst out laughing, the sound ringing through the small hall, and several other people turned to look at her. Despite the silence falling around them, Mountain just grinned at her, not paying any attention to anything in the background, then added, "Honest."

"There's always a second time," she teased, with a smirk. "And, if you keep eating the way you eat now, … that's just around the corner."

He shook his head. "I've been this weight for the last ten years, so it won't change now."

"Glad you have that faith," she replied. "I wouldn't count on it though."

He shook his head. "How come you haven't got any food yet?"

"Chef was a little bit behind this morning, so I was giving him some space."

"That's a good way to miss out."

"Are we that low on supplies?" she asked curiously.

"Not sure. The weather's clearing out ever-so-slightly today. With any luck we could be getting more supplies soon enough anyway."

"I'm surprised that, when they brought in so many extra people, they didn't bring extra supplies. What is that all about?"

"They did bring supplies, just not enough for the extra people." He laughed. "They were planning a second trip right away and got surprised by the weather."

"Any secluded place should have at least a six-week supply as the standard up here," she murmured, as she rested her eyes and leaned against the wall behind her.

"Did you get any sleep last night?"

"Not much," she murmured.

"Anything new or different?"

"No, not that I know of," she murmured, opening her eyes to look at him, knowing exactly what he was asking about and glad he was checking.

He nodded. "That's good. In some ways, the dull, boring old routine is a good thing."

"Especially here and now," she muttered under her breath.

He shot her a glance and then nodded. "We've got enough new people right now to keep all of us busy too," he noted. "They'll resume some outdoor training today, and I know that the sled dogs are supposed to go out as well."

"Even in this weather?" she asked.

"Depends if it clears. They won't go while we're in the middle of a blizzard obviously, but …" Then seeing her aversion, he grinned at her. "You've been outside to where the dogs are housed?"

She nodded. "Yes, it was a shock when I first got here to note several dogs were outside."

"Oh, they have an indoor-outdoor section out there," he corrected, "and you can bet it's pretty-damn cold for them. But … you'll find many outside by choice."

"But they're okay, aren't they?" she asked hesitantly, hating the note of anxiety in her voice at the thought of the animals suffering.

He nodded immediately. "Absolutely. They're fine, and no way anybody here will hurt the dogs."

"Unless through negligence," she added immediately.

"That won't happen." He glanced over at her and frowned. "I promise. It won't happen. Joe, their handler and owner, won't let it happen. Those dogs are his life."

She nodded again. "Good. I'd just hate that."

"I promise. If it comes to that, I'll bring them inside myself."

"You mean, in here, in the base, versus in their own quarters?"

"Exactly. But their own space is good for them. They're all together, and it's quite warm in there."

"If you say so," she muttered, hating even the thought of one dog suffering in this cold. "I mean, look at how much heat we have to produce here to stay warm."

"Yeah, but we're the idiots, and we don't have fur coats anymore," he quipped, with a half smile. He stood up just then. "Food's coming out. I'll go grab a plate. You coming?"

She grinned. "I'll wait. Go on."

He hesitated and added, "I'm really not sure where the supplies stand."

"That's fine," she replied. "Go eat. I need a hell of a lot less food than you do." He didn't say anything, but his scrutiny was intense. She smiled at him. "Honest to God, … I'm fine. I'll head to the line afterward."

"Yeah, well, in that case you'd better go before me." He grabbed her by the elbow, then gently hauled her to her feet.

She laughed at him. "You're not really planning on cleaning them out, are you?"

"Not planning on it, but I'll be outside for a while today, so I won't chintz out on the grub."

She followed him to the line, where, sure enough, he made certain that she was in front of him. Still, she took a normal-size serving on her plate, then looked behind her to see he had two plates. She shook her head in amazement, as he loaded up with carbs, protein, and lots of fats.

As they headed back to the table, she stated, "You know

that the doctor in me says I should warn you about eating too much of the wrong foods."

He burst out laughing. "Tell that doctor part to just clam it because, up here, all bets are off. It's a completely different environment, and I need these for whatever weather is waiting for the other side of that door."

"I would push the point, but, given the current environment and where we're living, I guess anything I would try to recommend would fall on deaf ears," she admitted quietly.

As they sat down, she noted that Magnus was two tables over. He saw them and stood, as they got close, then nodded politely. "Hey," he murmured, as he walked past them.

Mountain looked at her and asked quietly, "Did you meet him yesterday?"

She nodded. Almost immediately Mountain sat down and tucked into his food. She watched in amazement as the groceries disappeared at an unprecedented rate.

"Do you have any siblings?" she asked and then winced. "Oh, gosh, I'm sorry. You're here for your brother."

"Yeah, and there's just the two of us."

"But he's not the same size as you, is he?"

"No. I always tell him that I was a twin, and I inhaled the second one."

She startled for a moment and then laughed. "You know something? It almost would be believable, given the size of you."

"My father is the same," he added carelessly. "Rock solid and a big man."

"Other family?"

He nodded. "He has since remarried, again, and lives with his new family, two daughters though."

"Are you close to them?"

He shook his head. "No, once you're in the military, … all that tends to slide into the background. Then again, when you realize that he's starting all over again, and this time is prepared to go all in, you get defensive. I mean, I've met them and all, but I don't have a whole lot to do with them."

"Right. I guess that happens a lot too."

"Yeah, I imagine it does." He shrugged. "Whatever. I'm an adult and have been on my own for a hell of a long time."

"Your dad's got to be what, in his fifties? Sixties? Not ideally an age to be starting again."

"Yeah, but he says it keeps him young, and, if he's happy, I'm happy for him."

Not sensing any malice or unusual distress over his father's new family, she didn't say anything more. Quickly she ate her breakfast, then stood. "I'll head to the clinic. If you need anything, stop on by."

"Always," he replied.

Without any further conversation, she turned and walked away.

When she reached the exit to the dining area, she cast a glance back, feeling an odd sensation behind her. As she looked, several people were staring at her. As soon as she caught them doing that, they immediately turned their gazes to their plates.

Such a weird feeling, but, with a frown, she continued back to her clinic, quickly unlocking the door and stepping inside. This was her sanctuary. She was comfortable here and knew what she was doing, although new injuries and new circumstances always concerned her. This place was where she shone, regardless of the situation.

She sat down, pulled out her reports, and started her day.

DAY 2, MORNING

Third man missing now. A Russian. During war game event. Hope this will not be a daily occurrence. Blizzard still here.

Stepping outside in full winter gear, Magnus quickly tied his ropes to the baseline and stopped, getting his bearings through the heavy blowing snow. In these whiteout conditions it was hard to see more than ten feet ahead. Resolutely he headed toward the barn where the dogs were housed. As he went inside the kennel, he heard voices—the two caretakers assigned for the day were already here. He smiled as he stepped in, the dogs giving him a royal welcome. Several breeds were traditionally used as sled dogs—Alaskan Husky, Alaskan Malamute, Canadian Inuit Dog, Samoyed, Siberian Husky—and some were here.

Magnus had already become quite attached to one big male with an odd white streak along his side.

"Hey, Toby. How are you, boy?" Toby woofed and damn-near knocked over Magnus, as the dog sideswiped him with his butt, looking for attention. Magnus looked over at the two kennel workers, changing out bedding and giving the dogs food. "I guess they don't suffer too much here, do they?"

The one guy shook his head. "Honest to God, it's rare for them to even want to be inside during this weather," he shared. "That's why they have a dog door that lets them go in and out."

"Are they all in right now?" Magnus asked curiously.

The owner and trainer, Joe Fibke, looked over at him and smiled. "No, I think about four are still outside, over that way. Take a look."

Magnus walked closer to the doggie door and looked out the window. Sure enough he saw several dogs, one rolling around, scratching his back in the cold, another one lifting his leg off to the side. Two of them came racing in, when they saw him.

He bent down and greeted them with equal enthusiasm. Toby immediately walked over and butted into the middle, looking for more attention.

Joe laughed and said, "You've made quite an impression on them."

Magnus nodded. "Dogs know good people."

"I won't argue with you there," Joe agreed in a serious voice. "You can always tell there's a problem if dogs don't like somebody."

Magnus concurred. He'd seen many instances where the dogs didn't like men who Magnus would have thought were fine.

After greeting the dogs, he looked around and asked, "Are we doing sled training today? I was told that was my assignment, by a staff sergeant—Chester somebody." Magnus still played the role as being one of the attendees. Plus he was excited to get outside and to learn more about this environment.

Joe nodded. "Yes, but only if the temperature out there improves. We don't work in this temperature."

Magnus didn't say anything, hesitated a moment, then

asked, "Were you on the training exercise when the guy went missing?"

"Do you mean the guy named Terrance? Or the one called Teegan?" he asked, with emphasis.

"No, we are now missing a Russian in today's training session. Don't know his name. Plus Teegan who went missing first, then Terrance, who just went missing two days ago."

"Yes," Joe replied, his voice deepening. "I don't know what the hell's going on here, but it seems this place is jinxed."

At that, Magnus winced. "Just don't say that too loud."

"Right." Joe gave a headshake. "Superstition never goes down well, yet it still doesn't change the way I feel."

"No, and it's understandable. What's that, two accidental deaths and three men missing?"

"And that's only the more major events around here. We've had minor kitchen mishaps with knives and even fires. At least two were airlifted out of here, so maybe that's a good thing for them. Hell, better than being stuck here."

"You don't want to be here?" Magnus asked, turning to the trainer. The man appeared tired, fed up. He had to be sixty-plus, and a few wisps of white hair curled around the rim of the woolen hat he always wore.

"Once the first guy went missing, … it was a case of, well, maybe that was an accident," Joe explained, shaking his head. "But, once the second guy, Terrance, went missing, it didn't feel quite so much like an accident. Now? With a missing Russian too? … Hell no."

Magnus took a close look around at the security around them, but there wasn't much. There shouldn't need to be much. This was the joint task force of Arctic Ice Training

Program, a chance for countries to get together and to play war games to a certain extent, but also to learn how to handle this extreme cold and to experience just what it's like to be up here. Magnus glanced at Joe, when the younger of the two workers walked out.

At that, the older man asked him, "Are you part of the investigation?"

Magnus shook his head. "Nope, I'm not."

Joe stared at him intently. "You look it," he stated bluntly. "Others are saying you are."

Of course there would be rumors. With a headshake Magnus bent to scrub Toby behind his ears. "They'd be wrong."

Joe nodded but didn't say too much, neither did the intensity of his gaze lessen.

Magnus could only hope that he might convince him. It was true that he wasn't part of *that* investigation. He looked over at the man and added, "I didn't even think the investigation team was here yet."

"I think they are," he muttered. "At least that's also the rumor. Still, you just never know. People always talk and not necessarily in a good way."

"No, they sure don't," Magnus agreed with him. "Since I got here, I haven't liked a whole lot of anything I've seen."

"And yet," Joe noted in a dark tone, "I bet you can't point your finger at anything specific. There is nothing, … nothing but this feeling …"

Magnus stared at him and then slowly nodded. "No, you called that right." He looked around the warm and cozy barn, filled with happy dogs, as his hand still massaged Toby's ruff. "Why do you stay?"

"US Government contract. These are my dogs. I've got

sixteen dogs here, and no way I'm leaving them to whatever the hell's going on out there." He pointed toward the base. "The dogs are my life and my living. I agreed to the full term, with a huge penalty if I quit early. I've done a couple of these training camps before, but they weren't anything like this one."

"Do you stay here in the shed all the time? Never in the base?"

He nodded. "Yeah, I prefer it here. Easier to stay away from whatever the hell is going on over there, and, at the same time, I can keep a close eye on my animals."

"Understood." Magnus nodded. "What about food?"

The owner shrugged. "I go back and forth—to get what I need and then to confirm the dogs are getting their meals. But, believe me, some things are just not worth getting involved in."

"Meaning that something is happening over there?"

Joe shot him a look and spat out what looked like chew onto the ground. "What do you think?" And, with that, he turned and headed over to deal with some of the dogs. He had clearly said more than he had intended to say.

Magnus waited for a long moment, hoping Joe would return and talk to him more, but it was pretty obvious he was done. With that, Magnus headed out again toward the base, taking a look at what went on and checking out the schedules. It was a jam-packed day, and, as he watched, it appeared the world outside would lighten up and would become one of those beautiful Arctic days that he had seen in the past, but not since he'd arrived.

STANDING OUTSIDE, MOUNTAIN cherished the feel of the wind, the bite of the flurrying snow hitting his skin, reminding him that he was alive. Anything was better than the frozen numbness inside. His brother had to be alive. Anything else was unthinkable. He knew the others all thought Teegan was dead, and these constant searches were strictly recovery missions. But they weren't that for Mountain. He heard someone approaching him.

"Your brother's gone, you know."

He stiffened. "Don't know what you're talking about."

"I heard you were looking for your brother."

Mountain turned to face the newcomer. He didn't recognize him and figured he must have come in on one of the latest flights. "Do I know you?"

"No, you probably don't." The stranger spat on the ground.

Mountain wasn't sure this guy was spitting chew as much as he might be just spitting as an attitude. He gave him a hard look.

"Something fucking weird is going on around this place."

"Yet you're still here," Mountain noted.

"For the moment." And, with that odd comment, he left.

Lots of innuendos, absolutely no accusations, and no interest or proof to point in a certain direction. What the hell went on here? Mountain had no idea at all, and that was the troubling part. The caliber of people here all knew something odd went on here; they felt it in their bones, but nobody really understood what it was or who was involved. That caused everybody to start looking over their shoulders, trying to figure it out, or just keeping to themselves and hoping that whatever the trouble was would bypass them.

If you couldn't get out of this training event, that was a different story. However, here it just bred fear and created lots of accusations, likely in the wrong direction, as people used their pent-up, harbored, and festering issues to cause trouble.

Mountain walked back to the complex, checked out who was working with him for the day, then headed for the winter gear. There he found his partner for the day, a guy named Salmo. When he got up close, the other guy glanced up and then grinned.

"Hey, Mountain."

He looked at him, not recognizing the speaker.

"Yeah, I know who you are."

Mountain shrugged. "Good for you because I don't know you."

"Sure you do," he replied, with a smirk. "At least you used to."

At that, Mountain stopped and stared at him, then shook his head. "Sorry."

The other guy laughed. "I guess I'm not really surprised, but I am a little disappointed that you didn't recognize me," he noted quietly. "Of course I've changed some, so that was expected. But still …"

As Mountain continued to stare at Salmo, the tumblers clicked. "I didn't know you as Salmo though."

"No, most people didn't call me that back then," he agreed, with a nod.

Mountain stared at somebody he did know and rather well. He just didn't look anything like he used to. Mountain swore. "I'm struggling with this. What the hell are you doing here? Last I heard, you were on medical leave."

"Yeah, I was," he stated quietly. "Sometimes medical leaves don't go the way you expect them to."

Mountain winced at that. "And yet you're here, so"—he waved his hand—"hopefully in better health? What's up with your name?"

Salmo shook his head. "Salmo's my real name," he admitted, "but everybody used to call me—"

"Selly," Mountain added quietly. He stared at him, trying to figure out how any of that might fit into this nightmare playing out in front of him. "Are you okay now physically?"

"I'm okay," he hedged. "I won't ever be, you know, great again."

At that, Mountain winced yet again and nodded. "Yeah, I'm pretty sure a lot of us can say that to a certain extent." He gave a stilted laugh.

"Yeah, most likely. Still, it's good to see you," Salmo replied.

"We're supposed to be paired up for the day, I understand."

"I heard that." Salmo nodded. "I checked the schedule, and I couldn't believe when I saw you were here. This is hardly your thing, is it?" he asked, his voice quiet, his gaze watchful.

Mountain smiled. "Yet the bosses seem to think that maybe I could learn something."

"Learn something or are you teaching something?"

"Probably both." Mountain shrugged. "Whatever is needed." Salmo didn't say a whole lot, but something was different about him. "I never did hear exactly what happened to you."

"Yeah, I don't talk about it," he replied, "and I won't be

talking about it now either." And, with that, he tossed snowshoes toward Mountain. "Gear up, big guy." Salmo grinned. "We've got a long run to do today."

Mountain nodded, grabbed the snowshoes, adding them to the pack he carried. Donning his balaclava and the rest of his winter gear, he turned to find Salmo standing at the door, waiting for him.

"You ready?" Salmo asked.

"Let's go."

And together they headed out into the frozen north.

As they walked, Mountain asked, "Do you know exactly what the training is today?"

"Today we're just getting the lay of the land. We're to check on some scientists camped up ahead," Salmo noted quietly. "Asking for help with their generators."

"This is not a place to run into trouble with your generators," Mountain declared, with a watchful gaze. "Why aren't we taking one of the big Arctic Cats then?"

"We'll bring one home apparently," Salmo stated, "but one part of this job is to make sure we're fit enough to walk over."

Mountain just nodded and didn't say anything. Being fit enough to walk over was one thing, but to expend that energy in a frozen tundra didn't make any sense, but he'd realized long ago that you couldn't argue with the brass. By the time they reached the scientists' camp, Mountain had worked up quite a sweat. While he could still breathe at a regular pace, he definitely felt the burn.

Salmo laughed at him. "And here I thought you'd be in better shape."

"Oh, I'm in good-enough shape," Mountain corrected, "just trying to get used to the cold on the lungs."

"That's often a big problem," Salmo agreed, his tone serious. "Make sure you take care of yourself up here. Weird shit's happening," he shared, his tone cryptic, which Mountain found unnerving.

As Salmo went to go inside, Mountain grabbed his arm. "What does that mean?"

Salmo looked at him quietly for a long moment, before murmuring, "You'll find out." And then, as if that weren't enough mystery, he added, "If you live long enough."

Then Salmo bailed and went inside.

DAY 2, NOON

BY NOON, SYDNEY was surprised at the fairly steady stream of patients to her clinic. Always the same complaints. A couple people coming down with colds, which was not something to sneeze at up here, pardon her pun. A cut that occurred in the kitchen but not a bad one. She quickly bandaged it up and gave him a word of warning about taking better care. It's not as if he needed to hear that from her though; he already knew, as he had been working in kitchens for a long time.

When the last of them was done, she looked over at Joy and smiled. "Never seems to be an end to these things, is there?"

Joy nodded. "I'm quite surprised."

"At what?" Sydney asked curiously.

"The steady stream today. I mean, you'd think that, with no outdoor training happening, any medical needs would be fairly mild."

"Some training happened today, but I'm not sure they are back yet. I think the men are bored and came here to check you out," Sydney teased.

Joy flushed and looked over at her boss. "Right. If they're checking out anybody, it's you."

"Ha, they can keep checking then. I'm so not interested."

At that, Joy looked at her. "Seriously?"

"Yeah, seriously," Sydney declared. "Up here? Hell no."

But Joy shrugged. "You know? It's a nice place to meet somebody. You can have a relationship while you're here, then walk away. Short-term, it's a fun time and nothing serious."

"Maybe," Sydney replied. "Still not my thing."

Joy looked at her oddly for a moment, then opened her mouth, as if to question her on it, just as the door opened, and the colonel walked in.

Sydney immediately snapped to attention. The colonel waved her off, looked over at Joy, and said in a businesslike tone, "I believe you have another place to be."

Joy immediately closed her jaw and scrambled. "I can find another place to be, sir."

He smiled. "Good."

She immediately took off.

At that, the colonel—Boring, she thought his name was, or Berring, Burring, she wasn't sure—turned and stared at her intently. "Have you noticed anything unusual in the injuries lately?"

She paused, then shrugged. "Outside of the two already flown out, not much happening since then. We had a minor kitchen cut and a few people with colds today, just the run-of-the-mill stuff. A steady stream of them but nothing very interesting."

"Nothing that would make you suspicious?" he asked quietly.

She pondered that and then shook her head. "No, sir, not at all."

He nodded. "If you hear of anything or if something bothers you, bring it to me."

She frowned at that, but he waited quietly. "Any specific reason for that, sir?"

He smiled. "See? Only because you're on the medical staff do you ask that. If you were any of the men, … you wouldn't even question me."

"Maybe, but you're not the person I report to."

He considered her, as if not expecting any argument, but they kept coming. "That's right. You're one of the British team, aren't you?"

She nodded. "I am." This would be a good time for the colonel to thank her for her service to all the countries represented here, regardless whether she were on the British team or not.

"In that case I'll talk to your boss and get back to you."

And, with that, he quickly left.

Stunned, she was still staring in his wake, when the door opened again, and Magnus walked in. She nodded at the door behind him. "You saw the colonel who just left, correct? He asked me to notify him of anything unusual happening."

He stepped back out of the doorway, checked to see who it was, then returned. "That's pretty interesting. Did he explain why?"

"No, and, when I questioned him about it, he pointed out that I was medical and not part of his team because otherwise I never would have questioned him. Then I explained that I reported to someone else. He seemed quite surprised and then told me that he would speak to my superior and get back to me."

"Interesting." He tilted his head. "You would think he would have already known."

"That's what made me feel strange about the whole interchange. You would have thought that he would have known, and the fact that he didn't …"

Magnus nodded. "You are looking after yourself, right?"

She sucked in her breath and nodded. "Yes," she replied in exasperation. "But you know? … I wasn't thinking I *needed* to be looking after myself, not to mention I don't really know what I'm looking for at this level."

"We never are aware fully, but …" He let his voice drift off. "That is part and parcel of the job, so hang in there." He lowered his voice. "Any new bugs?"

"No, thank God." She pulled the detector from her pocket and stared down at it. "I will keep checking."

"Good, and let me know if you find something."

He left soon afterward, and she wondered just what the hell she'd gotten herself into and how the hell she was supposed to get herself out of it. Even as she sat here, contemplating the question, Joy came running in the clinic.

She cried out, "There's a kitchen fire."

Sydney was all business in that moment. "Anybody hurt? How many?"

"No idea. All I know is that we've got burn victims coming in."

And, with that, Sydney sprang into action.

MAGNUS WALKED INTO the small room. This is where the internal investigations of all the incidences at the center were centered. Only two other men, both dragged into service due to previous experience, were here. Brass had no intention of bringing in someone new to look into these issues. Not when that would go in his file too. Magnus walked over and sat down.

Immediately the others stiffened and glared at him.

He nodded. “Yep, I know you don’t want me here. I get that, and I really don’t give a shit,” he declared, his voice hard. “But something is going down in this place, and we need to sort it out.”

The older man, sitting at the head of the table, nodded. “I can’t say I’m happy that you’re involved, particularly that you get to move in the dark, whereas … we don’t. I’m Ted. This is Jerry.”

“Think of me as your eyes and ears,” Magnus invited. “Now, who the hell’s doing the supplies here?”

“What difference does it make?”

Magnus hesitated to answer but shrugged. “Because I need to know how the system works. Who’s bringing in supplies? How do people get them? Can you request specialty items? When I say this, I really need to know anything and all things such as that.”

“You’re thinking somebody’s bringing in drugs or equipment that aren’t allowed?” asked the boss man, Ted.

“I’m not sure what’s happening,” Magnus admitted, as he pulled out the bug that he’d found in the doctor’s office and put it on the table. “But this is the second one of these I’ve seen.”

Instantly came silence. Ted shook his head. “What the hell?”

“Yeah, what the hell is right.”

“Where did you find it?” Ted asked suspiciously.

“The medical clinic.”

At that, they stared at him, shaking their heads. Again Ted spoke up. “But that makes no sense.”

“No, it doesn’t, but I would like answers, and that’ll be

one of the areas I work on. So back to how do the supplies come in and out? Are we bringing things in, such as this bug, for any training, or is this completely inappropriate, given our circumstances with international groups represented here?"

"I would say not appropriate," replied the second man, Jerry. "No need for bugs here, is there? God, what's the point of having joint training missions such as ours if we'll be suspicious of each other."

"Considering everything that's gone on up until now," Magnus noted, "obviously we are already suspicious of each other."

"That's true." Ted gave a clipped nod. "We've got two men missing, two deaths, two major accidents, and now the fire, so two more men injured," he pointed out.

Magnus pondered that. "And we must consider the fire as part of this."

At that, both their gazes zinged back to the bug. "Do they really expect injured people to say something?"

"They must, if they are planting bugs, right?" Magnus asked quietly. "And all too often the patients talk, not intentionally, but especially when they're drugged or talking to family or trusted allies," he pointed out quietly.

"But still, that's not what trained men would do."

"No, but when you're injured, you're at your weakest, and sometimes that happens, especially if under a heavy drug regimen. So, the questions we need to be asking are, what are they hoping for? Is it who's in the clinic, or are they tracking everyone and what's happening to them? I don't know, but we'll have to figure it out to get to the bottom of it."

"Then, of course, there's the doctor."

"And then there's the doctor," Magnus repeated calmly.

"Sydney and Joy have been here for just about three weeks."

"Joy?" Ted asked. "Who is that?"

"The nurse," Jerry chipped in right away, and, when they looked at him, he flushed a bit.

"Right. Of course she's the other person in that area, isn't she?" Ted sounded grumpy.

"Yes, she's the only other regular employee in there."

"Interesting that we have women."

"Why?" Magnus asked, lifting his head and looking at Jerry.

"In this camp, men are easier."

"In this camp, men aren't easier, but it's easier when only men."

"Only men, yes," he repeated. "Apparently some marriages are already about to be in trouble." He gave half a smirk. "Because that's what camps with a mix of males and females will do to you."

The two men nodded and went silent.

"However, I don't think any of that necessarily pertains to what's going on here," Magnus stated, not happy with the conversation and where it went. "I requested copies of the files of all the accidents up until now. Do you have them for me?"

At that, Ted handed him a large folder. "This is for your eyes only," he declared, his voice clear and crisp, as he glared at Magnus. "I don't even think you should have it at all. We keep in touch with the related Russian, US, and German leaders as well. These reports are surface-level only, until we clear the individuals in question."

"If I had it all digitally, it wouldn't be an issue," Magnus noted.

Ted seemed to think about it and then nodded. "In a

way, that might not be a bad idea. If you want to, you can take photos or read through them and let me know when you have all that you need. Then we'll dispose of them, so there aren't any copies left. I don't want anybody getting their hands on this report"—he pointed—"and then you can work digitally from there."

"That's a better idea," Magnus approved. When he stood, they frowned at him. "Part of the problem with working in secret is I can't be away too long. I have to get back, before my role becomes suspicious."

"So where are you going now?"

"Part of my training up here is working with the dogs, so I'm heading out there to look after them."

"Looking after them? How much looking after them is there?" Jerry laughed.

"You'd be surprised." And, with that, he took his paper copies and walked to the door.

"What about the papers?" Ted asked. "I don't want them leaving here."

Magnus checked his watch. "I've got twenty minutes."

"You better read fast then," Jerry noted, with a hard laugh, "because those don't go anywhere."

Magnus nodded, sat down, and, completely blocking out the men, he went through each of the files. When he was done, he looked up. "Email me the digitals, and then you can dispose of these."

He handed off the paper copies to Ted, then got up and walked to the door, turning to look back at the two of them. "I'll check in later." And, with that, he was gone, ignoring the look of shock on their faces.

If there's one thing Magnus had learned, it was to assimilate information fast, sort through it, and extrapolate the important parts even faster, then carry on. He didn't care if they believed him or not. He'd read what he needed to read, and what it really meant was that absolutely nothing was going on, and that just pissed him off. He'd barely made it out to the dogs when his phone buzzed, and the files landed in his inbox.

He grinned. So that little display of reading ability meant something. Although he wasn't sure what it meant. These guys could be just playing him. He wasn't even sure the files were complete, and that pissed him off too. He'd been brought on board, whether they liked it or not. And, while that was a good thing, he needed cooperation from everybody, not just some of them.

He also needed to make sure that Ted and Jerry fully understood that Magnus's role was silent; otherwise everything would be in jeopardy.

He went inside the kennel area. He had work to do.

WHEN THEY FINALLY got around to leaving the scientists' quarters, Mountain was surprised at the joy he felt when he saw the Arctic Cat outside. They'd been working on the generators for hours, and, although he would be fine to ski back, a ride would be much nicer in these cold temperatures. Up here the long winter season's temps averaged -30ºF, with the short summer temps about 40°F.

He'd been out every damn day, blizzard or no blizzard, looking for signs of where his brother had ended up, working on a massive grid daily if at all possible. Seeing the Cat and knowing he would have a warm and easy trip back this time, … it was hard not to smile. "Did it come for us?" he asked quietly.

"It's ours. We're taking it back as part of our training." Salmo shrugged. "They used it earlier this week for something," he noted quietly.

Mountain nodded. As they got into the cab, and he started up the machine, he drove carefully, knowing that the snow and ice conditions were challenging. It was damn easy to get lost in the whiteout conditions, and the shades of white made it hard to see depressions on the surface. And, of course, crevasses could open up without warning.

As he drove, he asked Salmo, "Totally different camaraderie in there, isn't it?"

"Sure," he agreed quietly. "But that's very typical, isn't it? They don't have an ax to grind. They're all there to do research, and what is there? Six of them, eight maybe?"

"Maybe, although I understood one was ill and wasn't present," Mountain added, contemplating the numbers. "I think we only saw four."

"Sure, we only saw four, but that doesn't mean another half dozen or more are somewhere else," he added, that tone of his still cryptic.

Mountain nodded. "Nice to see that level of camaraderie," he repeated, not sure why he was belaboring the point, but it was something he wanted to see more of in life. And he wasn't seeing it at the camp.

Salmo added, "I think people are happy to be friends and to back each other up, as long as everything's going well, but once things aren't going well? … That's a whole different story."

"Interesting," Mountain murmured. "Always makes me wonder what brings people to training such as this."

"What brought you here?" Salmo asked, looking at him

with a smile.

"Orders," he replied succinctly.

"Right," Salmo muttered, and the smile fell off his face.

Mountain frowned, then asked, "That makes a difference, doesn't it?"

"Makes all the difference because it's really not a choice, and that sucks because, in these situations, you want to be here because it's where you want to be. It's pretty tough living in an isolated camp for any length of time."

"That's the thing though. It's not supposed to be for any length of time," Mountain corrected, looking at him. "It's supposed to be a short-term thing, just twelve weeks."

"Yeah, well," Salmo muttered, "let me know, when you are through, how that worked out for you."

Surprised, Mountain tried to get more out of Salmo, but he wasn't talking. Finally, fully intending to pry, Mountain continued. "I gather you're not here by choice."

"No, I'm not, but that's okay. While I'm here, I'll make the best of it. When I go home, I'll make the best of that too."

It was hard to argue with that sentiment.

They came around the shed, slowly parking outside where the dogs were kept, and Salmo started to swear, pointing. "What the hell is going on here?"

They both got out of the vehicle and bolted toward all the people around the kitchen area of the camp, only to find everything under control. There had definitely been a fire. It was out, but the charred remains stood as a testament to something ugly having gone on in their absence.

As Mountain stared around at the scene, he heard somebody barking out orders behind him. Mountain turned to see the colonel ahead of him.

At that, the colonel barked at him, "Where the hell were you?"

"On a scheduled visit at the scientists' center, fixing their generator," he reported calmly. "We snowshoed over, then drove the Cat home."

Mountain knew the colonel by reputation only, and, more often than not, his bark really was worse than his bite. At that, the colonel nodded. "Damn good thing, so at least you are out of this."

"Out of what?" he asked. "What happened here?"

"Kitchen fire." The colonel lowered his voice and still growled, like gravel being crushed. "Yeah, maybe you should find out whether this was arson or something else."

Mountain stared at him. "Kitchen fires do happen," he noted cautiously.

"Yep, they do. Maybe it was the same here," the colonel conceded, "but an awful lot of things are going on that shouldn't be happening at all."

"I won't argue with that. I have seen things that shouldn't be happening."

"Yeah, well, you'll tell me about them later tonight," he stated, as he turned. "After dinner I want a full report." And, with that, he stalked off.

Mountain winced, then got about the business of asking questions, knowing that he would be pissing people off because he had to ask the same ones over and over again. By the time dinner rolled around, he had a report ready to take up to the brass. Mountain gathered his notes and headed to the colonel's quarters, where he knocked on the door.

The colonel ordered him to come in. As soon as he turned and saw who entered, he dropped the papers that he had been reading and barked, "Well?"

Mountain nodded. "No signs of anything untoward with the fire," he noted patiently. "No starter fluid or any accelerant was used, but, given that it was the kitchen, full of all kinds of fire hazards, it doesn't really need a whole lot of help to start a fire. It just got out of control."

He nodded. "What about Chef?" He used the nickname Mountain had heard everyone use. The man's name was Elijah, but Chef had stuck.

"Chef is fine. He left the kitchen for a few minutes to grab a shower because he'd been there since before breakfast, and he left the stove on for the others."

"I'd guess that's the last shower he'll get while he's here," the colonel snapped, glaring at him. "Who was in the kitchen at the time?"

"His second in command was there, but seems they have a staffing problem. Anyway, a fight broke out in the common area, which drew all the attention, and, when they returned to the kitchen, the flames had taken off."

"Nobody noticed it right away?"

"They did notice it fairly quickly, and that's why the damage isn't more severe," Mountain confirmed, with a nod. "The kitchen will still function. Repairs are underway to get things fully back up and running again, but I hear they are serving a cold dinner tonight."

The colonel sighed and nodded, with an unpleasant facial expression. "Do you ever think that sometimes missions should be shut down?"

"Sometimes, yes," Mountain agreed. "I'm not sure that this has escalated to that stage yet though."

"Yeah, the *yet* part is what I don't like," he barked at him. "Something is sick here. I don't know what it is, but we need to find out. Yesterday."

DAY 3, EARLY MORNING

When Sydney woke the next morning, she felt an uncanny sense of wrongness. She bolted up, quickly dressed, and raced to her clinic. Just as she got there, the door slammed open, and somebody barreled out at top speed. She yelled after him, as she chased him down the hallway, but he booked it outside, and she knew better than to go out there.

As she turned around, Magnus stared at her. He was bare-chested, just in his PJ bottoms, a bit of sleeplessness in his eyes. "What happened?"

"He came running out of my clinic," she cried out in frustration.

Magnus took off and disappeared outside after the culprit, leaving her open-mouthed at his rash actions. Shrugging, she headed back to her clinic, hoping that Joy was there because Sydney had left everything wide open. Only she saw no sign of her nurse.

With that, Sydney decided she would no longer be sleeping in her close quarters but staying in the clinic, whether she had patients there or not. She quickly checked the time and noted it was just 7:00 a.m. Most of the others would be in the dining area, getting breakfast or at least coffee.

She checked up on the two male burn patients in her clinic. They were both sound asleep. Whoever had come in either didn't know patients would be here or hadn't had a chance to do anything.

Checking on the medicine cabinet, she confirmed it was still locked up. Feeling a whole lot better, she glanced around to ensure everything else was okay.

When Magnus strode in ten minutes later, carrying coffee for two, she immediately snatched one and cried out, "Thank God for that." She looked up at him—the last she'd seen him, he was chasing her intruder half naked, only now he was fully dressed. She shook her head and chastised herself for being so out of it. "Any luck?"

He shook his head. "No, unfortunately," he replied grumpily. "I've got two other men out looking. If your intruder doesn't show up soon …" Magnus didn't say anything to follow up.

She winced. "Sounds as if a storm is out there again too?"

"Yeah, it's pretty much been bad weather since I arrived," he noted quietly. "Not exactly conducive to escaping though."

"Unless he knew of somewhere and had a plan."

"The real question is, … how would he have gotten in?"

"We don't lock up any of the external doors to the base," she explained. "I mean, they're secured for the wind, but we're not trying to lock people in or out. This is not that type of facility, and, if people run into trouble, they need to know that they can come in here and take shelter." She frowned. "So, in a way, it's just an open public place."

"Did you get a description of him?"

She shrugged. "I can give you what I remember, but it isn't a whole lot." She quickly went through what she recalled, realizing it sounded lame. "I'm sorry. That's not much. It just seems stupid, but he was dressed all in black. He wore not full winter gear but outdoor gear, for sure. He was moving pretty fast for someone geared so heavily," she added, thinking back. "But then everybody here is fit and in shape, so no handicap to point out."

Magnus nodded in agreement. "Right, and everybody here is decent at subterfuge too," he admitted quietly. She winced. "Did you do a check this morning?"

She stared at him, not understanding at first, then it clicked. She quickly put down her coffee. She got up and pulled the device from her top drawer and quickly checked her clinic. To her dismay, almost immediately it started buzzing. She swore, as she looked over at him. He got up and followed her around, as they pinpointed where the latest bug was. He quickly removed it from the light where it was affixed and quickly dismantled it. Neither of her patients woke up; then, their pain medication was intense.

He held it up, his face grim, as he looked at her. "What are the chances that this is what your intruder was doing this morning?"

She shook her head. "I'm not betting on that," she muttered. "I just don't understand what they think will happen here, when I don't have anything to do with it."

"To do with what?" he asked, looking at her quietly.

"With what's going on, particularly after the colonel talked to me yesterday." She gave a quick shrug. "That was beyond bizarre."

"I won't say it wasn't a surprise," he replied cautiously, "but the brass? … They're people, just like the rest of us."

"Sure they are," she replied, with spirit. "Yet it seems somebody is trying to set me up, is thinking I'm involved, or is convinced that some top secret information is being talked about around here that they're hoping to get from me, but I don't know anything about that." She raised her hands in disgust. "My superiors are expecting a full report today too. Do I tell them about this?" She waved her hand at the bug. "This will raise the roof, if they think their team is in any danger."

He frowned. "No suggestion on that but your position is one of respect and has a little more expectation of privacy, so, if people talk to you and want that privacy, … they would do that here."

"Maybe." She stared at him. "However, it's not as if anybody here will talk to me about crimes. I'm the doctor. I'm, … you know, fixing coughs and scrapes and burns now."

"How badly were they hurt?" he asked, turning to look at the two men asleep on the two hospital beds.

She nodded grimly. "One's got a good-size burn on his arm. He's shipping out as soon as I can arrange it. So, right now, I'm just managing his and the second man's pain. Not a whole lot of treatment that anybody can do for burns here. I'm definitely not equipped for it and trying could do far more harm than good." She glanced back where the one patient was in a drugged stupor. "I'm hoping to get them both out today."

"That would be good," Magnus agreed, with a nod. "It would also mean that they could get supplies in."

She nodded. "That also would be good."

"Are you leaving with them?"

She turned and frowned at him. "It's always an option I have, but no." She shook her head. "I am the only doctor, so to leave would mean the people here would have no one. I'm not sure how quickly I could be replaced."

"Yet there's a nurse?" he confirmed questioningly.

"Sure, but she's not a doctor. So, if some emergency operation or major issues popped up, … she's not qualified for that."

"What kind of emergency operation are you thinking?"

She looked at him, shrugged, and explained, "The last time I was in a similar situation, I had to do an emergency appendectomy." He winced at that, and she nodded. "That's the thing. You don't know what will happen from one minute to the next. I can take X-Rays, splint broken bones, and quite a bit more," she added, with spirit. "Plus, I signed on for the duration."

"Which was what?"

"Twelve weeks, and then they would rotate me out with another doctor. If they can get one in."

"And you've done how many weeks so far?"

"Two and a half. No, just over three, I guess." Looking at the desk calendar, she nodded. "Almost three. You lose track of time in here."

"So just under nine more to go."

She nodded. "Nine more to go. Unless they shut down early. Or …" She stared up at the light. "If they feel they need to extend it. I just don't have a clue why anything I'm doing is of interest to somebody else."

"I don't either, but you need to be extra careful."

She nodded. "I don't go anywhere but the dining room and my quarters from here, and, from now on, I'll probably sleep here too." He winced at that, and she shrugged. "I have patients in here, and somebody was in here without my permission today. Joy was supposed to be here from midnight to seven." Sydney was starting to get angry, and that meant the shock was wearing off. "So, as far as I'm concerned, that's a done deal."

Her voice was firm enough, but, at the same time, she was lost in her own thoughts. "It's not that I always lock this door, but I do lock the drug cabinets, and they were not touched today. What does that say about the intruder?"

"You're sure?"

She nodded, and then she frowned. "I haven't done a full inventory, but nothing in the front was disturbed. It's hard to grab bottles from the back without the front ones falling down."

"It's an interesting choice of time too," Magnus noted.

"I was thinking about that because almost everybody would be having coffee, and my own habit is to always go straight to the dining area, grab a coffee, enjoy a cup, and then bring a second one back here," she replied in a quick analysis. "So, after three weeks, I've already established a routine, and I think … somebody probably isn't happy that I broke my routine."

"So that begs the question, why did you break it?"

She stared at him and gave half a smile. "Instincts." She chuckled, shaking her head. "I woke up with this feeling that something was wrong. I threw on my clothes and raced here. Maybe they heard me coming. I'm only next door."

"Did you say anything on the way over?"

She pondered that and then muttered, "I might have. I have a tendency to talk to myself. I might very well have said something."

"Something that would have tipped him off?" Magnus asked. "Were you loud?"

"Maybe," she whispered.

With that, Magnus nodded. "You keep an eye on yourself." And he disappeared.

Only ten minutes later Mountain stopped in. He looked at her and frowned. She smiled up at him, and again the thought crossed her mind that he was nothing short of huge. "I'm fine. You can talk to Magnus. He'll tell you all about it."

He shrugged. "Don't need to talk to Magnus. It's obvious something's going on, between the kitchen fire and now I hear about a break-in here. I'm here to talk to them." He pointed to the men still in a stupor from the medications they were on. "I've already talked to the rest of the kitchen staff."

"I thought Magnus was looking into it."

"He is, but so am I." And he gave her a wolfish smile. She frowned in confusion, and he nodded. "Don't worry about it."

"How can I not?" she asked, looking at him intently. "I mean, we have what? Four or five countries represented here, all working together. How is that *not* something I have to be worried about?"

He studied her face. "Anything in particular that you're worried about?"

"A third bug."

Mountain's eyebrows shot up.

"Magnus took the bug with him. I haven't had anything to do with anybody outside of the clinic's patients. So this intruder, could it possibly have to do with me?"

"And you've only been here for a few weeks."

She nodded. "Yes, and I've already earned myself a name for being standoffish apparently," she added, with an eye roll.

"Who told you that?"

"My nurse, Joy. Since women are in short supply, it's a

case of taking my pick, if I want it."

"You don't want it?"

"Hell no, I don't want it, particularly in my position here. No way. I'm here for what? … Nine more weeks? I think I can do without that drama."

He smiled. "It's the nature of relationships. … In a situation such as this, it's often a hardship for the rest of the crew to abstain."

"Exactly. I've seen it before. Some people have left partners, families, kids at home, and a budding romance isn't something they want in their face. Then there are those who are very lonely and maybe don't have as much luck getting partners."

He nodded. "Yet it's easier here."

"Is it?" she asked, looking at him sideways. "Maybe. It's still not for me."

"Do you have …" Mountain hesitated, frowned, and added, "Look. I know you can't talk about what's going on with the patients in the clinic and who comes in to see you."

She nodded. "Good, I'm glad you won't ask me about that then."

"But it would be nice if I could ask about some things."

"Yeah, I'm sure it would." She beamed at him. "Nothing criminal, let me tell you that."

He sighed. "Unless spouses are involved."

"I don't think adultery is criminal in the western world," she noted, with an eye roll. "It's pretty shitty, but, hey, I'm not here to be a moralist."

He laughed. "I've seen quite a bit of activity on that side already," he admitted, "and I just got here."

"Stick around," she noted, with humor. "You never hear the half of it, and who knows? … You might get lucky."

"Getting lucky isn't why I'm here," Mountain replied softly. "However, if you do notice anything odd, such as relationships shifting too fast or something"—he gave her a reassuring smile—"let me know, will you?" When she frowned, he nodded. "I wouldn't ask, except it's important."

"It's always important," she stated shortly. "But between the colonel, Magnus, you, … and the rest, I don't know who can be trusted and what is real."

He nodded. "Anybody you trust who could give you that verification?"

"I would have said you," she admitted, looking at him. "But, when you're here on the spot, that doesn't help."

"No, it sure doesn't." He smiled. "Anyone you can contact directly?"

"Tesla and her husband, Mason," she replied, with a clipped tone. "Maybe I'll talk to him."

"Good idea," he replied cheerfully.

She groaned. "That just means he's somebody who would support you unequivocally."

"Not only support me but he might know a little more than you expect."

And, with that, he was gone, leaving her staring behind him.

MOUNTAIN WAITED, WHILE the colonel studied him. So far the meeting hadn't gone well. Still, Mountain had a job to do, and, in order to do it, he needed data. "I would like copies of the reports on all the accidents and injuries up until now."

The colonel narrowed his gaze at him. "We already have

an investigation going on into all that." He was never friendly but was now downright unpleasant in the wake of the events of the day. "Are you thinking it's connected to the kitchen fire? To this third missing person, the Russian?"

Mountain frowned; the colonel wasn't usually so simplified in his questions. "How is it that we can overlook such a possibility?" he asked quietly.

The colonel tapped the desk for a long moment and then replied, "I'll let them know that you're being assigned to the investigative team."

His eyebrows shot up at that. "That might make me very unpopular."

At that, the colonel glared at him. "So do you want answers or don't you?"

"I want answers, but I want them on the down low. Leave Ted and Jerry to be the team, tell them about me, but let me work in the shadows. You know as well as I do, it's the only way to get to the real answers."

The colonel continued to glare at him for a long moment. "You've taken a lot on yourself, son."

Mountain didn't say anything, just waited.

Eventually the colonel nodded. "Fine. But just for a couple days, until we see how this goes. They should have answers soon."

"Good enough," Mountain agreed. "And you'll get me the reports?"

He nodded. "I'll okay it, but they won't like it."

Mountain smiled. "Of course they won't like it. They'll feel as if somebody is walking on their turf."

"Well, you are," the colonel replied, cracking a smile.

"I'll be quiet. They can have any credit. I really don't give a crap. I just wanted to see what the hell's going on here."

And maybe that honesty, more than anything, made the colonel nod and say, "Agreed. I'll set it up." And, with that, he turned and motioned at the door. "Now get the hell out of here."

With a smile, Mountain turned and left.

AS TESLA HANDED Mason his phone, she had a smirk on her face. "Seems to be a voice from the past."

He looked at her, smiled, then gently rubbed her round pregnant belly. "A lot of voices from the past are in our world, love."

"It's a woman," she stated in a teasing tone.

He frowned and answered the call. "Hello?"

"Mason?" asked the hesitant female on the other end.

"Yes, it's Mason," he replied. "Who's this?" There was silence, and he heard the phone breaking up around her, as if a terrible transmission.

Finally she got through. "It's Sydney."

"Sydney," he repeated, frowning, racking his brain, and then he lit up. "Syd?"

"Yeah," she replied, a note of relief in her voice. "Syd."

"What the hell? Where are you? What are you up to?"

"Three weeks ago I shipped into your Arctic Ice Training Program."

For a moment his mind completely blanked, as he thought about the woman he knew up in that nightmare. "Oh, good God," he whispered.

"Yeah," she noted in a dry tone. "Can't say I'm too impressed. I thought it would be excellent training for me and would be a good one for the résumé, but it seems something's rotten in paradise."

"Oh my God." He closed his eyelids. "How bad is it right now?"

"It's, … it's livable," she said quietly. "I'm not exactly sure what I'm supposed to say about how bad it is, but enough subterfuge is going on around here that I was hoping for some clarity and that somebody could vouch for a couple names for me."

He smiled, knowing what was coming. "I'm pretty sure I can." He chuckled. "Maybe you should tell me what those names are first."

"Magnus and Mountain," she said, with a ringing tone. "Now Mountain, I've known before. I was quite surprised to see him here, and I think he was probably surprised to see me. I don't know Magnus, yet he's been a huge help. I'm just not sure I can trust him."

"Do you want to tell me what it is that he's done for you?"

When she explained about the listening devices in her medical clinic, Mason felt something inside him freeze. "Somebody hid listening devices in your clinic?" he asked in horror.

"Yeah," she murmured, "we've just found a third one."

"Jesus," he murmured. "I hadn't realized things were that bad."

"You might want to check it out," she suggested.

Mason groaned. "I mean, no doubt about it. Someone is up to something there. We do have an investigative team in place, led by the US military." He paused.

Syd cleared her throat. "My understanding is that somebody from the Russian team will be joining the US investigators—as one of the most recent men to go missing was Russian, and one of the suspicious deaths was a Russian as well," she shared, "but I could be wrong about that."

"No, you're not far off on that. So what is it you want to know about Magnus and Mountain?" he asked cautiously.

She hesitated. "Please just tell me that they're the good guys."

He chuckled. "That I can tell you for certain," he declared, with a forceful tone. "They are definitely both on the side of right."

"I'm here to be sole doctor on hand for the twelve-week program," she noted quietly. "They asked me to fill in when they were short a doctor up here. They had somebody else. I don't recall the name. Dr. Feldrum or something similar to that." Her voice was hesitant. "I think that's the name, but he backed out at the last minute. They were responsible for bringing in the medics, so they felt they should get somebody quickly, and they asked if I would do it. I was more than happy to, until I got here and realized some serious problems are going on. But, when Magnus appeared and seemed to be a little too helpful, I started questioning the soundness of my instincts."

"Your instincts are sound." He chuckled. "I sent Magnus up there myself."

"Thank God for that because I wasn't sure if I should even be talking to him."

Mason heard her sigh of relief. "You can talk freely with him and Mountain, and, if you need to say anything directly to me," he added quietly, "then you can do that too."

"Yeah, well, I also have to remember who my boss is," she murmured.

"Have they asked you to check in at all, for a report?"

"I am to submit one soon. Up to now the reporting has been minor. You know, as a medic, I'm often overlooked in things such as that. But I report weekly."

He pondered that and realized she was quite right. "I won't make that mistake," he said quietly. "I want to ensure that you're safe though."

"Oh, I'm safe enough, although I wanted to know what the intruder wanted and whether he was the person responsible for the other two listening devices or not. However, after the kitchen fire, which we still don't know if that was an accident or—"

"What fire? I didn't hear about a kitchen fire."

"That was yesterday. I've got two burn victims here, waiting for an airlift out." She quickly gave him the details she knew.

Meanwhile, he looked over at Tesla, who stared at him, frowning. He pulled her gently beside him, as he spoke to Syd. "I do trust these two men. I'll get an update from them on the kitchen fire. You can report to them and to your bosses. We'll do everything we can to fix whatever is going on there, but we have to figure it out first." He hesitated, then added, "Are you sure you don't want to leave?"

"No, I'm not leaving," she said immediately, "and don't ask me again. I agreed to twelve weeks. Three are done, and I'll do my remaining nine."

"That's fine, but you really need to watch your back."

She laughed. "I'll watch my back, but who will watch everybody else's?" And, with that, she hung up.

"Do you need to go up?" Tesla asked.

He shook his head. "Not at the moment, no. That would show our hand way too quickly."

"Do you think you're that well-known?" she asked in a

teasing voice.

He winced. "Maybe not, and I'll give you that. Yet, at the same time, I'd be a little more concerned about somebody else showing their hand, and that's not something I want to deal with prematurely."

"No, I really don't either," she murmured, wrapping her arms around him. "As we know, things can go to hell really fast."

"They can. They sure can." He hugged her gently, whispering against her hair, "I need to make a few phone calls. Give me a couple minutes."

She nodded. "I'll be here when you get back." As he rose to walk out, she grabbed his arm. "Look. If you have to go up there, you go. I understand."

He smiled. "I know you do, and I appreciate that, but I'll do everything I can to stay right here."

"I'm not even close to my due date, so that's not an issue. We've got months and months yet."

He laughed. "Yeah, you said that last time, and, as I recall, he came very quickly. Although you're right. He was full-term."

"That was just good luck on my part, but that doesn't mean this one will cooperate," she added, with a laughing groan. When Mason frowned at her, she nodded. "Hey, every birth is different, so no guarantee that this baby will come superfast either."

"I hope for your sake it is because last time was incredibly difficult to watch and to not be able to help."

She burst out laughing. "Glad to hear your opinion of Mother Nature's job."

"Yeah, well, I've got a lot of opinions when it comes to her. The bottom line is, I don't want you to suffer any more than you have to."

"It's not suffering. I'm fine," she said gently. "Now go make your calls."

And, with that, he quickly left the room.

DAY 4, EARLY MORNING

SYDNEY OPENED HER eyes, staring around the tiny room. Her gaze narrowed. She was alone, and since the two burned men had been flown out, she had stayed in her own quarters. Not that she hadn't had qualms about that decision. The consideration of a good night's sleep over an empty and locked up medical clinic had won over. But something felt wrong. Again.

Only she couldn't explain it. She checked her watch—4:00 a.m. She got up and couldn't help but think it was creeping hour, the time when things went bump in the night, things that she didn't really want to think about. She dressed quietly in the dark, then opened her door silently and stepped out into the hallway. There was not a sound, no voices, no movement, nothing.

And yet, that sense of wrongness was still strong. She moved quietly down a few feet to her clinic door, opened it and stepped in, closing it behind her. There was a hush around her, not of silence but a hush of something off. She hated it and spun around to turn on the lights, then did a quick examination. Everything appeared to be completely fine, and that just made her feel worse.

She shut off the lights and stayed in the room, lying down on one of the hospital beds, pulling the blanket up over her, even as she questioned the wisdom of her actions here. It was one thing to be here when it was a safe and genial environment, but this was another thing, in the midst of whatever the hell was happening. She had heard rumors that changes in personnel wouldn't happen until everything was sorted out, just in case people disappeared into the woodwork.

She agreed with that strategy, but an awful lot more was going on here than personnel issues. It was easy to blame the current personnel, but that didn't make it real. Nearby was a scientist community, plus a local community, and definitely others who preferred to live out in the wilds. Not that she was knocking anybody for that, but it was hard to pinpoint the malicious events to just the people here at this compound. They made very good sitting ducks, and that in itself was worrisome.

When her phone buzzed gently with a text, she was unsurprised to see it was Magnus, asking if she was all right. She stared down at her phone, wondering how to answer that, but it's almost as if he knew because her phone buzzed again, with another message.

Come on. Talk to me.

She winced and sent back a message. **I'm okay. I'm in the clinic now. Something woke me, but I don't know what.**

He immediately wrote back. **I'm on my way.**.

She hated to say she was grateful, but dammit, she was. She didn't like what was happening, and that scared her even more. She waited, sitting up on the bed, for Magnus to show up. When she heard gentle footsteps outside, she smiled with relief and raced to the clinic door. As she opened the door, she heard a shout in the hallway and footsteps running. The shadow in front of her took off. She tried to see who and what, but they were already gone.

Magnus stepped in front of her and shot her a warning. "Get inside and lock the door. I'll be back in a minute." With that, he bolted off after whoever had been trying to enter the clinic.

She didn't know what the hell was going on, or why, but she went to her drug cabinet, making another check to ensure she hadn't missed anything the first time around. Inside the locked clinic, she perused the cabinet, frowning. She was pretty sure she had more of a couple of these medications. She went and pulled up the inventory and printed it off, so she had it to compare her count with, then slowly went through it.

When Magnus got back, he rapped on the door and called out.

She opened the door for him and stepped back for him to come inside. "I suppose he's gone."

He nodded. "He went outside into the cold."

"Was he dressed for it?" He looked at her curiously. She shrugged. "I mean, he was dressed all in black, such as before, but I didn't notice how much he had on in the way of actual gear, you know? How long would he last out there?"

"Good point, plus I have no way of knowing how much tundra survival experience he's got either. If he has some hideaway, then I'm sure he's fine. And let's face it. This wasn't the first time, right?"

She shrugged. "It's not the first time I've had somebody break in the clinic, and it's not the first time that we've missed them, so I guess not." She sighed loudly. "I should have stayed here over night, but I was so exhausted, I just wanted a good night's sleep." She walked to the cabinet. "I'm taking another look at the medication inventory, and I'm beginning to wonder if somebody did get in here." But then, with relief, she found that some of the containers had just been pushed back.

She quickly did another count while he ran the bug detector again. When he was done and smiled at her as he put it away, she sat back and looked at him. "False alarm. The items in the cabinet were shifted around a bit. I don't know if that was accidental or what. I'll have to ask Joy when she comes in. Nothing is missing, but it looks as if somebody may have gone for a reach-and-grab, but everything got pushed back instead of his hand closing around them."

Magnus nodded slowly. "Which means that something disturbed him. Yet the cabinet was locked, correct?" He looked at her with a raised eyebrow.

She nodded. "Nobody was inside when I got here, but something woke me. I just don't know what."

He nodded. "Good enough." He looked around, deep in thought. "We need a guard here."

"Not enough people for that, plus that'll just let everyone know we've got a problem—including our intruder."

"True, and again, given the relatively small numbers here, I can't guarantee that a guard will be completely impartial either."

"I was going to say that, but I didn't want to be rude," she admitted quietly. "It already feels as if I'm doing everybody a disservice by bringing it up in the first place."

"Yeah, everybody except for the guilty ones," he pointed out.

She winced. "How do we know who is behind it and who isn't? I guess there aren't any cameras outside, or are there?"

He smiled and shook his head. "No, not with the weather we're going through."

"And will it always be this weather? One of the hardest things is not just stepping outside and getting some fresh air."

"You certainly can, but you have to prepare for it." He shrugged. "The temperatures out there right now are minus fifty and then some, depending on the current weather, on the time of day, how much wind is involved."

She winced and nodded. "So maybe I'll just wait for another day."

He laughed. "Or wait for another lifetime by the looks of the blizzard outside."

"I hadn't expected these temperatures. I mean, I get it. These temperatures are expected, but I hadn't really understood."

"That is not on you," he stated quietly. "Not understanding the level and the types of cold with the wind chill factor is completely normal, though you should have been thoroughly briefed on it."

"And people go out there and do maneuvers? Seems dangerous."

"Absolutely." He chuckled. "You do know that's the whole point of this operation, right? But also complete groups of people live up here just fine. Obviously it's a starker lifestyle, and it doesn't offer a lot of the amenities of the average western civilization, but that doesn't mean they don't enjoy it just as much."

"Not to mention, for many of them, it's home."

"Exactly," he agreed, with a smile, "and there's no place quite like home."

"I never really understood that." Shivering, she sat at her

desk. "So now what?" she asked, looking around. "I guess I'll sleep in here tonight."

"You went back to your quarters last night?" he asked curiously.

She nodded. "I did because the patients had been flown out, but I won't tonight."

He nodded. "Probably not a bad idea," he replied absentmindedly. "Of course it won't take them long to realize that's where you are."

She winced. "Is that supposed to scare me?"

"No, not scare you," he stated, "but it is definitely something we need to be aware of. You especially."

"What am I supposed to do about it?"

"You? Nothing," he answered cheerfully. "However, as for me, I'll be staying here too."

She frowned at him, then immediately shook her head. "No way." Then she started to laugh. "Can you imagine what a ruckus that would cause? There would be an awful lot of raised eyebrows and no shortage of comments."

"I don't really care what the comments would be," he declared coolly. "I'm not letting anything happen to you. Remember? We've already had men go missing, some strange accidents and injuries, not to mention two dead."

"I know," she admitted quietly. "I wondered about the missing men, … if they were …" She stopped, as if not sure on how to say what was on her mind.

He looked at her with a serious expression. "What?"

"It's stupid." She shook her head again.

"No question or statement is stupid, especially right now, so if you've got something to ask or to offer, let's hear it."

She hesitated. "I wondered if they had another camp

somewhere. I mean, considering I have people coming in and out in the middle of the night, potentially stealing drugs, think about it. … Is there any chance that they're not missing at all?"

He looked at her, then sat down on the nurse's chair. "You know what? I hadn't considered that, but it's a good point," he muttered, as he stared off in the distance.

"If they were equipped, which everybody here is," she pointed out, "then it's quite possible that they are playing games."

"Oh, definitely some games are going on, I just don't know who, as in what nationality. What eludes me is the motive. Why even do this?"

"We also have to consider that, although people come and go, we've had just enough turnover here recently that it's quite possible somebody has come in that normally wouldn't be allowed here." He looked at her curiously. She shrugged. "Do we do identification checks on everybody here?"

He nodded.

"But do we do a deep check, or is there a chance that somebody knocked somebody out as soon as they arrived, and they're out dying in the cold somewhere? Meanwhile these guys have taken their place?" As he looked at her, his lips twitched. She narrowed her gaze at him. "Don't you dare laugh."

"I'm not laughing," he corrected calmly. "But, for a doctor, your mind works in a weird and wondrous way."

"No." She waved her hand dismissively. "I've just seen the shit that humans can do to each other, and I don't like it one bit."

At that, he stopped, studied her. "By the way, have you ever worked on any of the dogs up here?"

She frowned, shook her head. "No, I thought they had a permanent vet here. Is that not correct?"

"Oh, now that's a thought," he murmured. "I hadn't considered that Joe—the guy out there, who's looking after them—might be a vet."

"That's my understanding. These dogs are highly trained, and they are very expensive."

"Have you seen them?" he asked, looking at her sideways.

"Only on the first couple days. The weather was nice, the sun was out, it was warmer, and I got out several times and thoroughly enjoyed my visit with them." She smiled. "They're incredibly friendly."

"They are, and they absolutely love this weather. … And, not only that, they're just naturally happy animals in the cold."

"It was obvious that they are well looked after too."

"Good," he said quietly. "That's not another avenue I want to consider."

She stared at him and swallowed hard. "We, as a society, have a lot to work on, and I definitely have seen an awful lot of the worst that people can do to each other, but I'm not here dealing with serial killers and victims of domestic violence. At least I hope I'm not. I'm here dealing with accidents from training sessions and … friendly fire." She rolled her eyes at the term, but she had managed to get it out. "But any injuries to animals, particularly if they're deliberate"—she now had a touch of flint in her voice—"that I will not tolerate."

He nodded. "What I need to know is why is this clinic being targeted?"

"The only thing here is drugs, and, as we well know, that attracts all kinds of people."

DAY 4, LUNCH

MAGNUS AGREED, AND he kept that in mind as he stayed busy doing his own training, making it look as if he had absolutely nothing to do with the chaos going on around them, and that in itself was hard. He had to keep focused on what he was supposed to be doing and stay disconnected because just so much was happening at once. He crossed paths with Mountain on the way to the dining room and never got the "found him alive" signal. Missing for at least six days now. Each day made it harder to hope that Teegan was alive. How difficult this must be for Mountain to compartmentalize.

Magnus sighed, getting back on track. Since the clinic was a target, now Magnus would be protecting Sydney as much as he could, the gossip would flow. There would be even more talk.

Talk was dangerous. Talk had people looking at each other with suspicion, and, once you headed down that pathway, it got uglier and uglier. As he stood in line for lunch, he glanced around to see if he knew anybody to sit with. Yet he probably needed to sit with the general population and several of the other guys he may or may not have known.

As he went to sit down, Joy, the nurse, came over and smiled at him, giving him a teasing look. "Hey, I thought you'd be sitting with the doc," she joked.

He glanced at her, managing a look of feigned surprise, then shook his head. "Wasn't planning on it," he replied lightly. "Why?"

"Oh, nothing," she said in that same offhand insider-joke way that small places would so easily pick up on. "Just figured something was between you two."

He laughed. "Not that I'd say no, but believe me. The invitation hasn't been extended."

"Yeah, she's pretty stubborn that way."

Joy got into line, and that was the end of the conversation, but Magnus wasn't terribly comfortable with Joy's gossipy busybody attitude. He needed to mention it to the doctor down the road, just in case the nurse came back with another off-handed comment.

Yet, in close quarters such as this, it happened. People teased and joked; they had nothing else to do with their time, and of course relationships blossomed and failed very, very quickly. Usually they lasted a short time while people were here, but, once their time here was over, so was the relationship.

Just all about having a good time, not a long-term relationship or anything. Still, it wasn't his style. He quickly finished his meal, and, as he headed out of the dining area, one of the guys called him over. Magnus walked over, smiled at the rest of the men, realizing it was a mixed bunch, and they were all sitting here, enjoying dinner. Magnus laughed and socialized with them for a good twenty minutes, anything to make it appear this was his normal pattern. Then, as soon as he could escape, without making it obvious, he got up and headed out.

Even as he walked out, somebody called out and asked if

he was going to visit the doc.

He smiled. "I'm always up for visits with the doctor." He waggled his eyebrows. "Yet, so far, it's not doing me any good."

At that, there were catcalls, as people cheered him for striking out. Realizing what a strong male atmosphere was in place here, Magnus headed down to the clinic, even though he was determined not to. When he opened the door, he asked, "Hey. You okay?"

She looked up from the notes she was writing and frowned at him. "I'm okay. Just lots of paperwork right now. All these incidents and break-ins have to be documented."

He nodded. "Just wanted to let you know that apparently everybody has their eyes on us."

"Oh, Lord, as if we're having a relationship?"

He nodded. "Yeah, they were teasing me in the cafeteria."

She sighed. "To be expected."

"Anyway, in case anybody says anything to you, I made it sound like I struck out."

She looked up at him, amusement crinkling the corner of her eyes. "I'm not quite sure I recall an attempt, but thanks for the heads-up."

Awkward, and not sure what he was supposed to say to that, he just looked around and asked mildly, "Any other problems?"

She shook her head. "No, but then I haven't left the clinic either."

"Anybody come in?" he questioned.

She nodded. "Two, both fairly minor though."

"What were they?"

She hesitated, and he held up his hand. "Sorry, I get it.

It's confidential and all that. I guess nothing that could be construed as odd, weird, unusual, or something to be worried about?"

She shook her head. "No, I wouldn't say so."

He nodded. "Fine, I'll go with that then."

She laughed. "I mean it. … Thanks for not pushing."

He shrugged. "You have a job to do too. I wouldn't want to put that in jeopardy." And, with that, he quickly disappeared.

He headed toward his own quarters, waiting for the next training session to be called. His room was small, tightly managed, because it was so hard to keep it all heated; the cost for the fuel and the generators must be insane. He wandered around his room, as small as it was, before throwing himself onto his bed and staring up at the ceiling, as he tried to figure out what the hell was going on.

Deciding that staying here wouldn't be an answer, he got up and geared up. As he went outside, one of the men standing at the doorway to the change room called out to him. "Hey, you're going out alone? You know that's not smart."

"I was going to see the dogs. Missing mine at home, you know?"

The other man considered it and shrugged. "Sure, I guess. It's just not the smartest idea in these temperatures. Although, with the weather keeping folks at the base, more are inclined to go visit the dogs and at least step outside of the compound for a bit."

"Do these temperatures ever change?" he asked the guy.

He shrugged. "It's been how long? A week now maybe? I've seen the storms here last two weeks, but eventually the sun breaks through, and it completely changes the atmosphere. In the meantime though"—he motioned back toward the main building on base—"things can get a little hairy."

Magnus nodded. "I noticed."

"Any problems?" he asked, looking at him with a frown. "Because those kinds of problems need to get nipped in the bud fast."

"No, I don't think so. Just guys being guys."

At that, the other man, much older, rolled his eyes. "They should only send happily married men or older men up here in these circumstances. The minute you mix women and men, young men," he clarified, "you just run into trouble."

"I don't think older men are immune to the same issues," Magnus said with a smile, then shrugged. "But I get your meaning."

"I've been married for thirty-plus years and can't say I would ever want to mess that up with a mistake up here."

"Good for you." Magnus smiled. "Not too many people make it that long."

"No, but my missus, she's, … she's one hell of a woman," he noted. "I wouldn't want to be telling her that I done anything stupid up here."

"Would she forgive you?" he asked curiously.

He stared at Magnus. "You know what? … I don't know. I would think so, but I'm not sure I would allow that myself. I'd be harder on myself than she would be."

"Yeah, I hear you there. Anyway, if I don't come back in a couple hours …"

"Hours?" he asked.

"Yeah, good point, *hmm*." He looked down at his watch and considered it. "Make it an hour. I just want to get out and cuddle a puppy."

The older man laughed. "Better a puppy in this situation than what's in there." And he looked back toward the main hall, still teeming with all the men, and he chuckled again.

And, with that, all geared up, Magnus opened the exterior door. Immediately he snapped onto the safety line, while freezing cold wind blasted him, sharp bits of hard ice hitting him in the face, and gale-force winds made it almost impossible to move. But bending into the wind, grasping the rope line, he quickly, or at least as fast as he could, traversed to where the dogs were.

Once he got inside, he opened the second door and let himself into the main kennel area. Toby raced for him, just beating out another dozen dogs coming to greet Magnus.

Joe looked up at him. "What the hell are you doing out here in this blizzard?" he muttered. "You know that even the dogs are smart enough to be inside right now." And, with that, he pointed at several dogs, curled up on bedding straw.

"I guess the hay's good for them here, *huh*?"

"It's an easy bedding," he muttered. "Besides, it keeps them warm."

"I'm glad to hear that." He hesitated, then added quietly, "I need to ask you a few questions."

Joe's gaze narrowed, as he looked at him. "Yeah? I heard rumors about you."

"I guess that isn't any surprise, but I'm a little concerned about the dogs."

At that, Joe stiffened. "What are you talking about? You don't like the way I handle them?" he snapped, then turned to glare at him.

"No, no, not at all. They're in great shape." He was quick to reassure him. "I'm just worried that somebody may try to injure some of them."

"Nope, not happening," he declared vehemently, "not happening on my watch. I sure as hell wouldn't let it. They're my responsibility, but, more than that, I love these animals. They're a huge joy to be around."

"I agree with you totally," Magnus concurred. "I'm not complaining. Just seeing all the injuries happening in the main base, plus the accidents and the missing men on training sessions," he said a bit apologetically, "I'm concerned that the dogs might be targeted too."

"It hasn't happened yet." Joe continued to stare at Magnus, and Joe did calm somewhat, seeing where Magnus was coming from. He frowned. "Are you getting any inclination that it might happen?"

Magnus hesitated, shook his head. "I don't know. Is somebody quietly whittling down the human numbers? In which case, dogs are man's best friend and incredibly protective. So, what is it that we need to be careful of here?"

Joe slowly nodded. "I understand what you're saying, but I sure as hell don't like it." He glanced around, frowning. "But now that you've mentioned this, I'll look at everybody who comes in here in a different light."

Magnus nodded. "That's all I'm asking you to do. Just keep your wits about you."

"I'll have to look at you very suspiciously from now on too, you know? The teams are assigned to my unit on a daily basis. Some for sledding, some for training, and others for care. Now I'll watch them all like a hawk."

"You do that." Magnus chuckled. "I don't have a problem with it and wouldn't hold it against you a bit. I just want to keep these animals safe."

"And yet you're the one who just brought up that lovely little thought."

"Maybe. Not by choice, believe me. It's by necessity right now."

"And that scares me even more." Joe got up, walked over, and bent down to scratch the head of a dog curled up into a tight ball. "These dogs, … they are my family, and I won't take kindly to anything happening to them."

"Good, then keep them as safe as you know how," Magnus snapped, his voice harsh. "Because whatever the hell's going on here? … I don't understand it. So far, the brass are suspicious but don't really believe it's a dangerous position to be in."

"Oh, they probably believe it." Joe snorted. "They just don't want to acknowledge it."

At that, Magnus nodded slowly. "I guess maybe you've seen this a time or two."

He shrugged. "I've been in similar camps multiple times. Lots of good things to come out of it, such as a lot of great friendships, but also a lot of rivalries and hard feelings sometimes. As long as it doesn't interfere with my dogs, I really don't care what happens up there." He nodded toward the facility. "But the minute my dogs get affected, that's a different story. I'll get any asshole shipped out of here if they treat my dogs wrong. Don't you worry about that."

Magnus studied Joe's expression and believed it. "I'm glad to hear that, but I'm still leaving you with a warning. I'm not sure what the hell's going on, but, if it filters out here and comes your way, be ready." And, with that, he left.

DAY 4, DINNER

SYDNEY WAITED AS long as she could, leaving just enough time to get dinner before the line shut down. When she walked in, the dining room was full of people, huddling over their food. Still, people came and went, and, despite the traffic, there was silence as she walked in, confirming what she'd been afraid of.

Conversations relating to her and Magnus had been magnified out of curiosity. She walked forward to the counter, where she requested a small portion because she wasn't very hungry, and yet she knew she needed to eat. One thing about cold and survival, you had to maintain a certain amount of food just to stay square with everything going on in your world.

She took it over to an empty table and sat down. Almost immediately some degree of conversation continued around her. She ate quietly, sitting completely alone at her table, wondering who would be the first to break the tension. When one of the Russians walked over and sat down beside her, she looked over at him and didn't smile, didn't say anything.

He just waited, a big smirk on his face.

"Can I help you with something?"

"Yeah," he said, "I just thought I'd have a, you know, private one-on-one with the doctor."

"Then you can see me in my clinic tomorrow," she stated, her tone calm and cool. She'd seen this before a time or two.

He continued to smirk. "How about tonight?"

"How about not," she replied, her tone getting sharp.

He shrugged. "You're alone, and we heard you already turned somebody down, so I figure you're on the lookout for something better."

"And, when I find him, I'll let you know." Her tone was fast and sharp.

The others heard the rebuke and immediately laughed at him. He took it hard and glared at her. "You aren't so fucking high and mighty," he spat, as he got up. "I'd watch your back."

She stood up immediately and was right in his face. "Is that a threat?"

Silence hit the room all around her. She faced it head-on, as she glared at the man who had just threatened her.

He stood tall, towering way the hell over her. "I don't need to threaten anybody." His tone was nothing but a threat, as he got right in her face and snapped, "And no need to take anything by force either. Women come to me all over the place."

"Good, so your job now is to leave this one alone," she declared, her voice hard and clear. "Sounds as if you'll do just fine, as someone will find their way to you."

He sniffed, then turned and strode off.

She turned and looked at the rest of the room and said in a calm and determined tone, "And that goes for the rest of you." With that, she sat down quietly and finished her meal.

There wasn't a sound until she got up and carried her dishes to the kitchen, where Chef looked at her with a commiserating expression, while the others just winced in her direction. She gave them her dishes, thanked them for dinner, then turned and walked out. Almost as soon as the door clicked behind her, she heard the buzz of conversation begin.

As soon as she got out into the hall, she headed toward her clinic, but she knew it wasn't over. The Russian disliked a public refusal, and he sure as hell didn't like her comment. That was fine; she would deal with him as she had to. If that meant getting him shipped out of here, she'd get that done too. As she approached her clinic, she found the damn door open. Swearing, she raced inside to find her Russian suitor lying on a hospital bed, looking at her in a taunting move.

"I've been waiting for you, Doc."

"That's nice," she said, with some venom. "Just in case you're under any misapprehension about what that bed is used for"—she pulled out a large hypodermic needle and tapped the end of it—"I don't have a problem giving you something to keep that thing down."

He looked at his erection, pushing up the sheet in front of her, and got angry. He hopped out of bed and moved quickly to her, his hands out.

She stepped back, just as he got close, opening up the door, and spun around to land a good kick to his backside. "Keep on going, buddy, and don't bother coming back." Carried by his own momentum, it took him a moment to get turned around.

With fury and rage taking over his face, he turned to step back into the clinic, when he was literally picked up by the scruff of his neck and tossed down the hallway. By now, several people were watching.

She stepped out into the hallway, looked at all of them,

furious. "If this is how you treat your doctor, I highly suggest you all go home before you need my services. I don't fix injuries that I've inflicted in self-defense."

And, with that, she looked at Magnus, who had tossed the Russian hulk down the hallway, nodded an acknowledgment, then went back inside her clinic and closed the door behind her.

MAGNUS STOOD IN front of the colonel, narrating the events as he knew them. As soon as he was dismissed, he stepped out with gratitude, only to find Mountain waiting for him, glaring. Magnus shrugged. "Wasn't anything else to do," he muttered in a low tone.

Mountain nodded. "It's distracting."

At that, Magnus froze, looked over at the hulk of a man, "I wonder if that part's on purpose."

Mountain raised an eyebrow slowly and then nodded. "A good thing to keep in mind."

"That may very well be what it is, but we still can't leave her alone," he pointed out. "She's had several attacks in the clinic."

"So I've heard," he muttered. "I'm going in to talk to the colonel now."

"Will that do any good?" he asked, with a tilt of his head. "Although pressure should be applied stateside."

"Regardless, our amorous Russian friend is not sticking around."

"Good. I'm sure that will help the doc sleep better at night."

"Absolutely. But remember. The rest of the Russian's

team is still here—well, except for their missing man—so you'll have to keep an eye on them too."

With that, Magnus nodded and quickly walked down the hallway toward his room, bypassing it, and continuing to the dining area, where he grabbed up a cup of coffee. He looked around casually, checking to see what reaction he would get from everybody else, but they all seemed to be ignoring him. Yet he knew that they were watching quietly from a distance. The kitchen staff just smiled and asked if he needed anything to eat.

He shook his head. "I can wait. I'm just grabbing up a cup of coffee."

"Yeah, anything to keep from sitting out there, *huh*?"

"As far as I'm concerned"—he offered a hard smile—"anything I did, he deserved."

There wasn't a comment until he turned to see two of the Russian team standing up and glaring at him. He looked over at them, smiled, and asked politely, "You got a problem, gentlemen?"

One stepped forward with precision, but the other grabbed him. "No, we don't have a problem, but we've sure got our eye on you."

"That's fine." He nodded. "I've got an eye on you guys too, particularly if you're of the same bent as your out-of-line buddy," he added, and this time his voice was hard. "We don't take kindly to doctors being harassed and sexually assaulted in this place."

At that, both men stiffened, and the rest of the audience went silent around them, as they watched the happenings. "What's the matter? You didn't know about it? Didn't you get reprimanded? Maybe you're itching to get shipped out yourselves."

One of them snarled. "We sure as hell don't deserve it."

"Then you'll just leave her alone." Then he hardened his tone and added, "Plus every other woman in this base."

"Women are free game, as long as they say yes."

"Just make sure that *yes* is not when they're drunk, high, unconscious, or terrified," he snapped, glaring at them, crossing his arms as he stared at them.

The two men stood there for a long moment, then turned and walked out.

Magnus slowly relaxed, looking around to see if anybody else would challenge him. When it appeared that everybody was ignoring him, he nodded and sat down with his coffee.

One of the Swiss members came over, sat down, and reached out a hand. "I'm Johan," he said cheerfully. "Glad to see that."

Magnus shook his hand. "Nice to meet you. I'm Magnus."

"It's nice to see somebody stand up for women."

"Everybody should stand up for women."

"Agreed, but it can be a touchy subject because an awful lot of women want to be treated as equals."

"As they should be, but they still shouldn't have to take this bullshit," he said in disgust. "The doctor's here for a reason, to serve, just the same as the rest of us. She doesn't need that crap."

"Besides, you're sweet on her, aren't you?" he asked, with a grin.

"I respect her, put it that way. I also realize she's in trouble here, and that is something I will not condone," he snapped, his tone harsh, as he studied the man in front of him, wondering what brought Johan over.

Johan held up his hand peaceably. "I just want you to

know that I'm not part of any of that and that I respect what you did there."

"You're part of the Swiss team?"

"I am, but I'm only here for another day or so."

"I didn't think anybody was leaving."

"I'm taking an early discharge to get out. I don't know what's going on, but I'm leaving on the next plane."

Since that was news to him, Magnus nodded. "Interesting. What kind of mess is happening around here anyway?"

"Maybe it's nothing. I don't even know all the details myself."

"Still you're leaving?"

"I am," he confirmed, with a smile. "Then I have another excuse anyway. I was only supposed to be here for two weeks, and, since I've completed that, I'm done."

"Good enough."

Magnus stayed and talked with Johan for a few more minutes, waiting to see if anybody else would jump up and cause trouble, but it looked as if everybody had calmed down, at least for now. Card games were going on at one side, and a chessboard was out in another corner, as people found ways to occupy their time. Soon after Johan left, Magnus got up, refilled his coffee cup, and headed out.

The storm outside had been raging for at least a week now, and tempers were short, since nobody could do what they came to do, but it was all part and parcel of being here. It wouldn't be so bad except for this element of fear that seemed to permeate the place.

Magnus wasn't even sure how or why, but it was there, a subtle reminder that all was not well. Then again, it was understandable in a way. The minute any serious accidents started to happen, people lost all confidence in the security, safety, and well-being of everyone here, and that was, in itself, a problem.

As long as they could hang on tight, the training would continue, but it felt as if the other shoe would drop soon enough. Magnus headed toward the medical clinic, and, when he got there, the door was open, and he heard voices. A woman was inside, talking to Syd. With a nod in her direction, he quickly left and headed to his room.

Twenty minutes later he sent her a text, asking if she was okay. The response came back, just one word.

Yes.

He needed to confirm her plans, so he texted her. **Where are you sleeping tonight?**

She responded right away. **In the clinic.**

He frowned at that, not sure that he liked it one bit, but he understood her reasoning for it. She felt incredibly responsible, and that was good. Yet, at the same time, it also sucked. It sucked on so many different levels that he didn't even know what to do about it. He pondered it for a long moment and then got up and headed there.

DAY 4, EVENING

LATER THAT EVENING, when Magnus knocked on Sydney's door, he got no answer. He checked his watch and saw it was ten o'clock. He quickly sent her a text, asking if she was up.

When there was no answer, he pondered opening the door and going in. She kept it locked, but, at the same time, she hadn't said good night. Neither had he asked her to let him know when she went to bed. As he stood here, wondering what he should do, another door opened down in the hallway. He looked up to see one of the Russians coming toward him, smirking.

"What's the matter? You going to try again?" he asked in a raucous tone.

"Just making sure she's okay and one of you guys didn't come after her."

At that, the smile fell off the other man's face, replaced by a glare. "We don't need to force anybody. Women *like* us—unlike you, I guess," he taunted, again with a smirk.

Magnus just nodded, leaned against the wall, and waited while the guy passed. Something was so easy to dislike about him, and that wasn't fair. There are enough people in this world one could dislike without it being an issue, and it was easy to just hold his nationality against him. Yet this was a peacekeeping mission, and everybody was supposed to be doing their best to get along, but Magnus would likely be the one brought to task for it. He shrugged and knocked on the door with a crisp rap. When still no response came, he got worried. He checked the door, but it was locked.

His instincts had him pulling out his tools and quickly popping the lock, and, as he stepped inside, he called out, "Syd? Are you here?"

When no answer came, he turned and looked around, then popped on the lights. Sydney was on the floor, collapsed, her head wound bleeding all over her clinic.

As he dropped to her side, she moaned, and he whispered, "It's okay. Take it easy. Take it easy."

She opened her eyes briefly and then closed them against the light. "Good God, my head feels as if it's split."

"What happened?"

"I left the clinic to grab my stuff from my room and to come right back. I returned to the clinic, and, just when I turned around to lock up again, somebody struck me on the back of my head," she whispered. "Help me up."

"No way," he argued firmly. "Head injury. You need to remember that and don't move quickly. I'll move you to the bed."

He picked her up and carried her gently to the closest hospital bed and stretched her out, then quickly sent Mountain a text. Mountain joined them a few minutes later, staring worriedly down at Sydney.

She smiled. "My fault, it was stupid."

"Yeah, how's that?" he snapped.

"I guess somebody got in here without me knowing."

"Did you lock it when you went to your room to gather a few things?"

She shook her head. "No, I didn't, and I guess that was

the stupid part, wasn't it?"

He didn't say anything. He walked over to her desk, pulled out the bug finder, and did a quick scan, but nothing was found.

"I'll set up a surveillance camera in here," Magnus announced, and not an inch would he give on this issue.

Her eyes widened, and she squeaked in shock and pain. "I don't know about that. This is a medical clinic."

"Yeah? Well, in that case, they'd better not come here looking for something that's completely illegal or to do something equally illegal, should they?"

She winced. "I don't really have any right to stop you, I guess," she said slowly, as if trying to think her way through the legalities of it.

"No, … you sure don't, not after you've been attacked, and you've had several break-ins. Plus we've had too much theft in here as it is." He looked at Mountain, standing at her side, and then back at her. "When you get a minute, if you're capable and you can get up"—he motioned at the cabinet—"we need to check the inventory."

"Or you can contact Joy," Sydney suggested, "and have her do it."

"Actually we'd rather not," Mountain said in a cool voice.

She looked at him in shock. "You're not suspicious of her, are you?"

"We're suspicious of everybody at this point," he noted quietly. "Something that you need to be aware of."

She groaned, and, with an ice pack that she had Magnus find for her, she slowly sat up. Then, with his support, they walked her over to the medicine cabinet, where she studied it.

"It looks the same," she muttered, "but I have to do an inventory check. The lock doesn't seem to be jimmied though."

"I'm not sure that lock needs to be jimmied anymore, what with the number of times people have been in here. There's a good chance somebody has copied the keys already or can pick the lock in seconds."

"Which is how I got into the clinic to check on you," Magnus pointed out.

She winced. "That's great."

Just then a commotion came, as the clinic door burst open and in came the colonel. He glared at Sydney. She glared right back. "Thanks for the support," she muttered under her breath. "Nice to know that you're there for me."

"What the hell happened?" He looked over at Mountain. "Answers now."

"Yes, she was attacked in the clinic," Mountain stated, glaring at him. "Remember how I mentioned she needed security?"

The colonel stared at him in shock, then turned to Sydney. "What do you mean you were attacked?"

She explained, but he kept shaking his head, as if not able to understand a word. Through it all, he stood there, his hands on his hips, staring at her, as if trying to sort it out.

After the umpteenth time that he shook his head, Magnus lost his temper. "Sir, obviously something's going on here that needs to be sorted out at the moment, but she's clearly in danger."

"Chances are she was in danger, but she's not anymore," the colonel said in a clipped tone.

He stared at him in shock. "Why would you say that?"

"Because he's already knocked her out, so, if he wanted

something, he would have taken it already. He didn't kill her but clearly had his chance."

"How do you know what he did or didn't do? She hasn't had a chance to check over the inventory yet," he snapped.

"The lock hasn't been jimmied. I can even see that from here."

"Yeah, but it wasn't jimmied the previous times either," she noted, her voice quiet.

He turned and shot her with a laser-eyed look. "You're with the British team, aren't you?" Even as he watched, she raised one eyebrow and slowly nodded. He harrumphed. "I'll be talking to them."

And, with that, he quickly turned and walked out.

She looked over at the other two men, and she asked, "Did I just get blamed for this?"

Magnus winced at her tone, then snorted. "Yeah, in a way you did. Not to worry though. That's not how it will end up."

"You think?" she quipped. "Because, if somebody here isn't doing his job, … it's the colonel."

"Please don't tell him that," Magnus said, with half a smile. "Because we're much better off with somebody like him than somebody who won't let us operate in the dark."

"What does operating in the dark do for us right now?" she asked, with a slight groan, as she eased herself back onto her bed. "I am now staying here in this room full-time, protecting these drugs, which apparently may or may not be the target of some people's needs, though I don't understand why if that's the point. If they need something, they can come to me. If they don't need the drugs, then why would they even be after them? I mean, they could sell them, but it's not as if a market is up here. The group of scientists nearby would have their own medications," she added in a confused tone. "So none of this makes any sense."

"It's the drugs that concern me," Magnus said, walking closer to look at her head wound, "because you're right. You don't keep enough here to sell any big quantity of drugs, and if somebody was after it for personal use, would you give it to them?"

She winced. "By law I would have to report them if it was recreational drugs and would only prescribe something such as that if they were experiencing dangerous withdrawals or needed it to maintain safety and stability. This situation is a little different than most, with people together in close quarters under adverse conditions. Someone in that situation could really turn the whole place upside down. Yeah, I guess they wouldn't want me to know because it's not ideal to get outed from the military as a junkie. If that were to get out, … you know that it wouldn't look so good with your boss."

"I get it. And this being an international effort, it would reflect badly on whatever country it was as well."

"Right. What about the Russians?" she asked.

"That is another issue altogether," Mountain said quietly. "It looks as if the two of them will be staying. The one who accosted you has been disciplined, but he's requesting a chance to stay and to complete his training, saying he was drunk, and it won't happen again."

She looked over at him in disbelief. "You know he wasn't drunk, right?"

"I know that, but it's also a loss of face in a big way for him, so going home would have quite the repercussions."

"And why should I care about that?"

"You shouldn't," Mountain noted, "but I do, and I'm

also concerned about what he will do from here, so …" He looked over at Magnus, who just nodded.

"Yep," Magnus confirmed, "that's my job now."

"What's your job?" she asked, her voice getting faint. He walked over and placed a hand on her forehead. Her lips quirked. "I don't have a fever."

"No, but you might have a concussion."

"No, I don't," she firmly protested. "However, I do need to get some sleep, knowing that, when I wake up, I won't be in the middle of this damn chaos again."

"Go to sleep then. I'll stay here and stand watch."

"Not needed. Just lock the door on the way out." Then she groaned. "Of course that won't make much difference, will it?"

"I've ordered new locks for you," Mountain said. "We'll take care of that immediately."

And, with that, he disappeared.

DAY 4, ALMOST MIDNIGHT

SYDNEY WASN'T AWARE of falling asleep, but, when she woke up a little later, she felt a whole lot better. She shifted up on her arm and looked around, and sure enough there was Magnus, sitting at her desk, working on a laptop. "Is that your laptop?" she asked, hoping it was.

He nodded. "Of course. Don't worry. I would never cross those lines."

"I'm glad to hear that," she muttered, as she slowly shifted vertical. "Has anybody been here?"

"Just Mountain. He changed out your lock, and we have new keys for you. You are not to give them to anybody, including Joy."

"Great, that's encouraging, as well as awkward."

"It also keeps her from being a suspect."

"Oh. Good point. In that case it's a good thing, isn't it?"

"It is, but Joy may not see it that way."

In fact, when Joy walked in not very much later, she cried out, coming right to her side. "I heard you were attacked."

Sydney gave her a flat look. "Yeah, and who told you that?"

Joy flushed. "One of the guys," she muttered, turning to look at Magnus, who stared at her with an intensity that quite obviously made her uncomfortable.

"Are you okay?" Joy asked, looking Sydney over.

Sydney smiled and nodded. "Yeah, I'll just stay here for tonight."

"I'll stand watch," Joy offered. "If you've got a head injury—"

"No, you won't," Magnus interrupted. "I'm staying."

Joy sneered at him. "And I suppose you're a doctor too, are you?"

"No, I'm not, but I've had a ton of medical training and medic experience in the field, so no thanks to the offer. The doc is staying exactly where she is, and I'll be standing watch."

At that, Joy hesitated, then looked over at Sydney. "You know that there are already enough rumors that the two of you are involved."

"And the rumors are wrong," she gently replied, "but the Russian attacked me earlier, and Magnus hauled him off me and made sure he didn't come back after me, although somebody else did. Magnus wants to confirm that it's not the same guy and that it doesn't happen again."

"Ah." Joy nodded in sudden understanding. "That does make more sense." She still shot Magnus a look. "Just as long as he doesn't have designs on you."

"Doesn't matter if I do or not," he said in exasperation. "Sydney's an adult and can make her own decisions."

"Not if she's injured and hurt," Joy shot back.

He slowly stood, towering above her. "What did you just imply?"

Joy swallowed and glared at him. "She's my friend, and I want to make sure she's safe."

His eyebrows shot up. "Damn good thing you explained that because otherwise we'd be having a different conversation right now."

She put her hands on her hips and glared at him. "You don't scare me."

"Stop it, both of you," Sydney snapped at them. "I don't know what the hell there is about this camp that gets tempers short, but that's enough. I'm fine, and he's staying to stand guard. I already okayed it, Joy, so go get a good night's sleep. You need to be rested."

Joy walked to the door. "You can call me anytime, if you need me."

"I won't need you, but thanks for the offer. I really appreciate it."

With that, Joy went out, slamming the door hard. Sydney winced and groaned at the noise, even as Magnus bit off an expletive as he raced to the door.

"Don't worry about it," Sydney muttered.

As it was, when he opened the door, Joy stood there, her hand over her mouth, staring at him in horror.

"Yeah, just think how Sydney feels right now."

"I'm sorry. I'm sorry," she cried out. "I have a temper, and it tends to get the better of me."

"I noticed," he bit off, "but, if you ever pull another childish, thoughtless, selfish stunt like that again, where it hurts her, believe me. … You'll answer to me."

She stared at him intently, then nodded. "Just make sure you look after her. I don't know what the hell's going on in this place right now, but I feel something really ugly is brewing."

"Let me know if you hear anything more than what you *feel* out there," he stated, his voice hard as he studied her.

She nodded. "I wish I did," she muttered. "Right now, I'm wishing I'd never even come to this hellhole."

"It's meant to be a hell of an experience, a once-in-a-lifetime learning experience," he offered quietly. "An awful lot of beauty is out there."

"I haven't been out enough to get a chance to look. I've been here three weeks, but it took time to get settled, and then this ugly weather moved in, and that's been it for me."

"There are flights in and out, if you need to go home."

She shrugged and looked around. "Maybe. Just something is very depressing about this energy right now, and it's definitely shifted since I've been here. At first it was fun-loving and happy, but now it's …" She shrugged. "I don't know. I don't even know what to call it." With that, she turned and walked away.

Having heard the conversation from her bed, Sydney called out to him. "Now do you want to get in and lock up, please?"

He stepped inside and pulled the door closed, locking the two of them in.

She stared up at him as she added, "You might as well sleep on the other hospital bed. I'll change the bedding out in the morning."

"Do you keep two hospital beds ready all the time?"

She nodded. "If two beds are here, then two beds are ready," she muttered. "Sometimes I only need one. Other times nobody does anything but sit on them. … Honestly, just having them ready, … in a way, it ensures you don't have to use them."

"Hey, I am not arguing with that," he noted quietly. "I just wondered how steady the traffic was in here."

"Not steady and oftentimes it's just females." He looked over at her with a question on his face, and she shrugged. "They still have periods and other problems, all kinds of issues that men don't have to deal with on a regular basis, and they're still my patients. Apart from that, it's minor cuts, injuries, flu, upper respiratory infections, that sort of thing."

"Of course." He nodded. "An awful lot to be said for staying home, where things are nice and easy."

"Yeah, well, easy never really was my style," she muttered.

He laughed. "Why am I not surprised?"

She gave him half a grin. "I sure hope you guys get to the bottom of this."

"Me too," he muttered quietly at her side, as she yawned. "Get some sleep," he murmured, looking at her in concern.

"Stop giving me orders," she replied, equally good-natured.

"I will, just as soon as you start listening."

"Ah," she replied. "I've never been so good at that either."

He groaned. "You don't have to be difficult about it."

"I'm not being difficult. You are here, aren't you?" And, with that, she rolled over and pulled the blankets up over her shoulder. "I'll talk to you in the morning."

MAGNUS WASN'T SURE what instinct had him coming earlier to the medical clinic to say good night to Sydney, but he'd long since learned to listen to that nudge. He had a connection with Sydney that he hadn't expected to find in the Arctic, and it's not as if they even had a chance to explore their relationship, not with all the crap going on right now. He didn't understand why somebody would break in to the clinic—unless they were after the drugs, but that meant somebody had been shipped up here with a serious drug habit. Someone who hadn't had a chance to get sober and either hadn't been tested or somehow found a way around the testing.

That was also suspicious as hell. Either way, not a whole lot of choice but to stand-guard and watch. He quickly sent Mason an update, knowing he would need to stay on top of all this. Magnus also asked if anybody else was coming in to give them a hand. Mason's response came right away. A simple yes, but he didn't elaborate.

Magnus groaned at that because yes meant nothing, yet all kinds of things.

He slept fitfully through the night, hearing the wind whistling outside, damn grateful he was inside and not caught out in that storm. He thought about the missing men, realizing that the chances of their even being alive at this point were pretty slim, knowing that that included Mountain's brother.

But Magnus always knew that sometimes truth was stranger than fiction, and he had to hope that those guys out there still had options; anything else was too harsh to consider. That was not the way he would choose to go, if he ever had that choice.

DAY 5, EARLY MORNING

THE NEXT MORNING Magnus woke to the sound of steady even breathing at his side. He looked over to the other bed, where Sydney had tucked under the blankets, breathing steadily, her color good. As he shifted to get up and to head to the bathroom, she opened her eyes and looked at him groggily. He smiled. "It's early yet. Go back to sleep."

"No, I'm awake." She yawned. "I don't think I'll get back to sleep again."

"In that case, I'll pick up some coffee on my way back," he muttered.

He let himself out and quickly locked the door, checking the hallway. No sign of anybody. He used the facilities, grabbed his gear, had a quick shower, then headed to the dining area, where he poured two coffees and brought them back to the clinic.

He didn't care who watched at this point in time and was pretty sure that the news would be all over the base that she'd been attacked. That wouldn't go over well with most people here; that was for sure. He didn't see a sign of anybody all the way back.

He had to put down the coffee in order to unlock the door, so he did, quickly unlocked the door, and pushed it open. Picking up the coffee, he stepped in.

Sydney was sitting up in the bed, looking at him, and then smiled. "I really didn't expect room service, you know?"

"That's all right," he hip-checked the door closed behind him.

"Anybody say anything?"

"No, but I didn't see anybody."

"Not even in the dining area?"

He shook his head. "The staff were working in the background, and nobody was around. I got in and out without encountering anyone."

"Good," she replied. "I'm not really looking forward to getting the third degree from everybody."

"Nobody should do that."

"No, maybe not, but you also know what most people are like."

He nodded, then sat down. "I know we asked you last night, but I'll ask you again."

She held up a hand. "I didn't see my attacker," she repeated firmly. "I didn't hear anything either. I opened the door, came in, then turned around to lock up, and *boom*."

"Right. So he was here waiting for you then?"

"Yes, although presumably, if you've changed the locks, that can't happen again."

"Not in theory," he stated, holding up the keys and handing them over to her. "You're once again safely inside a locked door, but you're still on a base where a multitude of people are very adept at picking locks."

She stared at him grimly and then nodded. "Nice reminder, thanks."

"I don't want to be the bearer of bad news," he noted quietly, "but I won't tell you that all is okay, when obviously it isn't. We don't know who did this, but we'll find out today."

"Sure you will." She sent half a look in his direction. "And I suppose you'll look at the Russian first."

"I really don't think it was him," Magnus offered, lost in his thoughts. "Unless you think he could have been the one you saw running away that morning."

She pondered it and then shook her head. "No, I don't think so. He's too big. I highly doubt we have two different people breaking into my clinic."

"But, in that Russian guy's case, … I think he was after you, not so much after what you're protecting here."

"Nice thought," she said, half under her breath.

He smiled at her. "I understand that you don't want to consider that, but we won't be allowed to forget it regardless. And we must be prepared for any possibility."

"Right. I can't believe they're allowing him to stay," she muttered.

"I know, and that will hit a lot of us raw, … so you don't need to worry about him. He will be under watch himself on a regular basis, so not to worry. Whether he goes or stays, … that is on the colonel."

Just then an alarm rang out through the base. He burst to his feet, frowning.

"What is that?" she asked, as she put down her coffee, struggling to her feet.

"It's an emergency. Stay here," he barked, "and lock yourself in."

And, with that, he bolted out the door.

DAY 5, MIDMORNING

AGAIN SYDNEY STARED at the door, wondering what the hell was going on. She felt better, had remade the beds, and was up and moving around, when a knock came on the door. Joy announced herself to Sydney. She walked over, unlocked the door, and opened it, letting Joy in. She looked at Joy and asked, "What's going on with the alarm?"

Joy's face was a mix of macabre interest and horror. "That Russian, the one who attacked you, he was murdered overnight. They found him dead in his bed."

Sydney stared at her nurse in shock. "What?"

Joy nodded. "Yes, that's what the alarm was about. Somebody had just found him."

"Good God." Sydney turned to look around her clinic. "What the hell is going on here?"

"I don't know, but there's talk of dismantling it."

"And yet a lot of time and effort went into creating this place," she said, with a wave of her hand. "So it would be far better to figure out what's going on and continue. Just packing it up is not the best solution."

"Maybe, unless, … you know, we can't continue because of it."

Sydney knew what Joy was trying to say, even though she seemed incredibly distracted. Sydney added, "Everyone will be asked if they have an alibi for last night."

Joy stumbled and looked at her in shock. "Not me," she squeaked.

"They'll have to check out everyone because how else will they find out who was where? That way they can narrow down who could have been available to kill this poor man."

"*Poor man*? He's the one who was pushing himself on you."

"Yes, he did. He wanted something from me that I wasn't prepared to give him, but it's not as if he beat me up or anything. He used poor judgment. Let's put it that way."

She stared at her. "You really don't hold it against him?"

"No, of course not," she muttered, sitting in her chair and massaging her temples slowly.

"How are you feeling?"

"I'm okay—a little groggy still."

"I'm surprised they don't ship you out."

She opened her eyes to stare at Joy. "Why would you say that?"

Joy frowned at her. "I mean, … you are a part of this whole thing."

"Part of what?" she asked in exasperation. "One crew member got a little too amorous, but how does that make me part of anything?"

Joy's jaw opened, then closed, as she shrugged. "I don't know. I just figured that you were likely to be shipped out, as he was."

"And yet he wasn't being shipped out," she said quietly. "After the investigation they all decided that he would have a second chance, so he was allowed to stay."

Joy exploded with shock.

Sydney sighed. "Come on, Joy. You've got to remember that this place isn't here to cause trouble. The whole purpose of this facility is to create an environment of peace, where all these countries and their teams can get along. And sending the Russian back early to Russia wouldn't work out so well for him."

"I think somebody forgot to tell the Russians that," Joy replied waspishly.

"Maybe. At the same time, it's also important that we stick together and not turn on each other, as if we're on some mission to kill off everybody," she muttered.

Joy laughed. "I forgot what a softy you were."

"Am I a softy?" she asked, looking at her nurse.

"Yeah. I mean this guy jumps you, and, while you could insist on him being shipped out—or insist on being shipped out yourself—here you are defending him. As for me, I can't see why anybody would want to stay here beyond a couple weeks. I mean, … hell, it was fun for the first week, but I'm so over this weather." She moaned. "I just want to go outside. I'm getting stir-crazy."

"I think that's part of the problem overall," Sydney stated in a firm tone. "Everybody needs to get out and to get some fresh air, but it's not as if the weather has been very conducive. This blizzard is a problem, and we've all become rats in a maze at the moment."

Joy stared at her and swallowed. "Yeah, but you know, those rats in a maze, … over time all they do is turn on each other, until only one is left." And, with that, she turned and walked out of the clinic, leaving Sydney to stare after her in shock.

MAGNUS WALKED INTO the meeting with the investigators

and sat down. They immediately looked at him and asked, "What the hell's going on?"

He told them about what happened last night, and they were not only shocked but disgusted at the behavior of the Russian.

"But, if you're looking to see if I had anything to do with the Russian's demise, I stayed with the doc and stood watch over her all night."

"Of course you did. Can you prove that?"

"Unless you've got cameras in every one of the hallways," he said lightly, not wanting to bring up the camera in the clinic if he didn't have to, "how could I possibly confirm it?"

"What about the doc? Did she sleep all night?"

"As far as I know, yes," he said, with a firm tone. "We woke up, me first, and I got up and had a shower, went and got coffee for the both of us, and, when I returned to the clinic, she was awake. I was checking to see how she was doing, when the sirens went off."

Ted nodded. "It's a bit of a shitshow right now." He shook his head. "I mean, there are a lot of rumors, but nobody's really talking. I have to tell you though. You were number one on the list of suspects. You still are."

"Which is exactly why I'm here telling you that I didn't have anything to do with it." Magnus stayed calm; inside he wanted to roar about them wasting time. "As far as I was aware, last night there was a good chance he would get shipped out or put on watch, which resolved my problem totally."

"Are you in a relationship with the doc?"

"Not sexually, if that's what you mean. If we weren't here, I might pursue it," he said cheerfully. "She's a fascinating woman. I just met her—five days ago—when I arrived."

The men studied him intently and then sighed. Ted and Jerry looked at each other and then back at him, asking, "So who else would want to take out the Russian?"

"His teammates," Magnus replied immediately. "For them, … to go home early would be to go home in disgrace, which is no small thing, considering where they are from."

"No, of course not," Ted agreed. "Their punishment would be pretty extreme, I'd imagine."

Magnus nodded. "Complete failure in that sense, but I can't say for sure that it was them. I don't know where they were all night."

"According to them, they were both sleeping in their room for the whole night."

"So, they alibied each other?"

Immediately Ted nodded. "Yeah, and that's what they'll say about you and the doc."

"Of course." Magnus gave a half nod. Another thought occurred to him. "I get that everybody here is on a peacekeeping joint-training program, *blah-blah-blah*." He waved his hand. "But what are the chances that somebody might have done this, all of it—the accidents, missing personnel, injuries, break-ins, all of it—just to cause trouble between our countries?"

"You mean, once this Russian guy proved to be an asshole, they took advantage of that fact because it seemed maybe you would go after him?" Ted asked.

"That's what I'm wondering," Magnus agreed. "I don't know any other reason, and I don't know what his relationship was like with his team. I don't know anything about it really," he admitted, with another wave of his hand. "But when you think about it, that is a pretty strong motive."

"It's not a very good one though," Ted noted quietly.

"No, and, when you put it together with the rest of the events going on here, I guess it doesn't really line up. But, since the first two deaths were ruled 'accidental,' this is the first actual murder we have had so far, isn't it?"

Ted nodded. "Yes, it is—but only because we don't know what happened to the three missing men."

DAY 5, LUNCHTIME

FOR THE REST of the day, Sydney rested quietly in the clinic. Several people came, mostly to see how she was. She was surprised and pleased to see that almost all were concerned about her, having heard the news of the attack on her, and several asked if she knew anything about who her attacker was. She kept her answers fairly noncommittal, letting everybody know that she didn't have any clue. The last thing she wanted was the attacker thinking she could identify him.

Gossip, and especially that kind of gossip, had a tendency to morph into some other message entirely, especially depending on who was passing around the news. So Sydney definitely didn't want to get into it any more than necessary. It was hard enough to get through the day, since her head had already started pounding again around noon.

She made sure she stayed well hydrated, and, by the time 1:00 p.m. came around, she looked over at Joy and asked, "Any chance you can handle the clinic while I take a nap?"

Joy nodded. "Absolutely." She pointed to the files in her hand. "This is moving at a pretty slow pace anyway." Frowning a bit, she looked carefully at her boss. "You're looking a little peaked."

"It goes along with the head right now." She reached up, wincing as she patted the goose-egg-size bump on the back of her head.

"Not a problem. You go get some rest. I've got this, and, if we need to get you, we will." She shrugged. "In the meantime, I'll hold down the fort." Hesitating, she looked at the beds and asked, "Did you want to go back to your quarters or just nap here?"

Sydney hesitated. "I'm tempted to just lie down here and crash. At least then, if anybody comes in, they'll see me here. If they need something, either they can get it from you or they can come back later, when I'm awake. That's an optimal solution, I guess."

And, with that, she walked over to the bed she had slept in before, pulled back the single sheet that covered the bed, and stretched out. Within minutes she was sound asleep. She woke to hushed voices. Without taking a peek or shifting, she listened to the conversation. Magnus had stopped in to check up on her.

She smiled and murmured, "I'm awake."

Magnus walked closer and gently stroked her cheek. "Hey. How're you feeling?"

She looked up at him and smiled. "Better, I think. I was feeling a little rough earlier and thought maybe a nap would help."

"And did it?" he asked, his gaze questioning.

She tilted her head. "I think so." She slowly shifted upright, pleasantly surprised when her head didn't pound and the room didn't spin. "Actually that seems to have done the trick." She yawned, then got up and did a few simple stretches. "Everything okay here?" She looked over at Joy, who nodded.

"Honestly, nobody even stopped by." She smiled. "It's almost as if they knew."

"Maybe," Sydney replied, with a concerned tone. She looked at Magnus and asked with a searching gaze, "Is everything okay elsewhere?" She tried to keep her tone even, but, at the same time, tried to get him to understand what she was asking.

He nodded and responded in a low tone, "The investigators are working on it. We already have one team in place, which is aggravating, because if they were investigating, how did this happen in the first place?"

"That's what I don't understand," Joy replied to what Magnus had implied. "I mean, it makes all the other accidents look even more suspicious."

"It does at that," Sydney admitted, looking over at her nurse, since she'd heard Magnus. "It's a matter of just staying safe."

"Staying safe and maybe not staying alone." She pointedly looked over at Magnus.

"Maybe. And maybe if Magnus had been here, it wouldn't have happened. There's always that consideration."

Joy nodded.

Sydney sighed and added, "It's hard to know just what it means."

Joy stood. "Now that you're up, I'll go grab my lunch." She stopped, turned back to her, and asked, "You want me to pick up something for you?"

She frowned. "I'm sure our foodstuffs are pretty low, and I don't know what they're serving, but something fresh—like a salad—sounds good."

Joy laughed. "In your dreams. I think it's stew or spaghetti."

"Right." Sydney winced. "I'll wait for dinner."

"I'll see if there's any yogurt for you."

"That would be good."

With that, Joy took off, happy to do something at least.

Sydney looked over at Magnus. "Any news?"

He shook his head. "No, none. I've been cleared, but be aware that the investigators will come and talk to you."

"*Great*," she muttered. "More questions."

"Of course."

"And you're on the official investigation team?"

"I'm unofficially on the official team," he corrected and burst out laughing at the look on her face. "Crazy, right?"

"But I'm not supposed to know, and they won't want me to know, right?" she clarified.

"Exactly. However, if you do say anything, don't feel bad about it. No need to push it. I'll just explain it to them."

"Okay, you are—" Her words were left unsaid because a knock came at the door.

Magnus opened it to see Ted there, letting him in. "Hey, I was just checking up on the doc," Magnus noted. He quickly introduced the two of them. "Doc, meet Ted."

She looked up to see an older man, with what seemed to be years of service, though she didn't know what exactly. Army maybe, it was hard to say. A bit of everything was represented here. She smiled. "I understand you're handling the investigation of the murder."

"Actually I'm handling the investigation into all of it," he noted calmly.

She nodded. "I presume that means the attack on me."

"Absolutely," he confirmed in an even tone, as he walked closer and eyed her critically. "How are you feeling?"

"If you'd asked me that before I had a nap, I would have said *pretty cruddy*. However, after the nap, I'm starting to feel a whole lot better."

At that, Magnus stepped up. "I'll see you in a little bit, Ted. You can talk to the doc on your own." And, with that, Magnus quickly disappeared.

Ted looked over at her and smiled. "He seems to have taken quite an interest in you."

"And it's appreciated," she noted quietly. "After one man attacks you, it's nice to know that others out there are true gentlemen, who are up for defending you," she murmured.

Ted nodded, his face serious. "Maybe you could tell me what happened between you and the Russian."

She went over the events from the cafeteria and then what happened in the clinic.

"And the time from when you left the cafeteria and came here?"

She shrugged. "Maybe ten minutes at most. I went to the washroom. And, when I returned to the clinic, the door was open, and he was already inside."

"I understood that you've already had problems with the locks?"

She nodded. "I'll tell you right now that the locks have been changed."

He looked at her, turning to check out the door.

"Mountain arranged for me to get a new lock. He already installed it, from what I've been told."

"Good," Ted replied succinctly. "That should never be something of an issue here."

"No, it shouldn't be," she agreed. "But, once drugs went missing, it seemed the inventory in my cabinet was disturbed a couple more times, as if someone were searching for something and couldn't find it or whatever," she explained, looking at him pointedly. "I also don't know if you've heard, but listening devices have been found here as well."

He frowned and nodded. "I had heard that. I don't suppose you have them, do you?"

"No, I sure don't. You can ask Mountain about it."

"That I will." He frowned, as he looked around the clinic. "So what kind of drugs were stolen?"

She nodded. "Painkillers mostly, and some heavier narcotics."

"And you have no idea who's responsible for that?"

"No, I don't," she murmured quietly, easing back, keeping the movement steady and slow, so it wasn't too jarring for her head. She may have been subtle, but he noticed. "You seem to be moving a little too … carefully."

She gave half a smile. "I still have a good-size lump on my noggin," she shared, with a harsher tone than intended. "So, if you need to see it to prove to yourself that I got hit over the head, please feel free to do so."

He hesitated and then nodded. "Would you mind?"

"Nope, not at all."

She leaned forward, so he could see the back of her head.

He whistled. "Okay, that is a good-size lump."

"Yes, it is, and, if I was at home, I would be staying in bed for a few days," she added. "But that won't work out here."

"No other doctor is here, is there?" he asked, looking at his notes.

"Nope. One nurse, though she's quite capable of handling most of the regular stuff, but nothing too advanced," she murmured.

"Right. That's Joy Hanson, right?"

"Joy Willow?" she replied curiously, looking at him.

He looked down at his notes and nodded. "Right." He

then wrote down *Willow*.

She wasn't sure if the last name meant anything or if it was just another paperwork gaff she didn't need. "Anyway, you can check with her. It might be her married name changed to her single name after a divorce or something."

"Right. I understood that she was single."

"I think she's single at the moment and recovering from a divorce. Hence a little bit more socially active than I would necessarily care to see in our base."

His gaze narrowed, as he considered her words and then nodded. "Camps such as this do seem to bring that out though, don't they?"

"Absolutely they do." Sydney gave a light laugh. "And believe me. I do get plenty of requests for condoms and birth control." His eyebrows shot up at that, and she smiled. "When there's nothing else to do …" She let her voice trail off.

He laughed. "I guess that is to be expected, which is partly the reason you were accosted, I suppose."

"Exactly." She gave a careful nod of her head. "On the other hand, that poor man didn't deserve whatever happened to him," she added. "I don't even know how he was killed. At least, not the details."

"Yet I assumed you examined the body?"

"I haven't had a chance to, though I would like to, particularly since we have no other doctor here."

"I would like you to, if you're okay to do so."

"Absolutely. I expected him to be brought here actually."

"He's been taken to the coolers. And, if nothing else, … we'll store him outside."

She got to her feet. "Let me take a look and see what I can sort out."

He walked her down to the kitchen area. When they got there, he led the way through to the back. Of course the freezers were more or less the half-outdoor type, with some run on generators to keep food cool and not frozen solid.

As she walked into the cooler, she noted that the door was steel and double size. "It seems so strange to be paying money for a freezer, when outside you have Mother Nature's brutal work at the ready."

"Maybe that's why. This one at least is one we can adjust to control the temperature."

She nodded, then walked over to a body wrapped in a sheet. She knelt at his side, pulled back the covering, then turned and looked at Ted. "Can you give me a hand?"

Together they uncovered him, and dispassionately she surveyed the Russian she'd had such an unfortunate meeting with earlier. She studied his features and nodded. "Takes a lot to strangle somebody."

"Is that what happened?" Ted asked.

She pointed to the ligature marks on his throat that were even now showing up nicely; then she peeled back an eyelid to see the petechiae in his eyes. "Strangled," she repeated, "and he's a big man." She checked immediately for a head wound, then nodded and found the lump in the back. "Struck from behind, knocked out—potentially knocked out or at least stunned for the moment, so they could get one up on him—then strangled."

She examined the marks on his neck. "This was done with a fairly fine string of some kind. Not wire because it didn't cut through. Maybe rope, maybe a fine cloth. I don't, … I don't know," she murmured. "Our base is full of potential weapons."

Ted nodded. "And no shortage of highly skilled people

to use them."

"True. It was suggested that something happened to rile up the relationships between the countries, damaging the program," she shared quietly. "I'd hate to think that's what this was about, though I also hate to think it had anything to do with his behavior toward me."

"You mean, such as a gentleman taking offense?"

She looked over at him. "Which would immediately make you think of Magnus, I suppose."

He laughed. "Lots of things made me think of Magnus," he admitted. "But I won't jump to conclusions just because he's more of a gentleman than the others."

"Glad to hear that." She gave him a half smile. "I really need Magnus to be one of the good guys." After hearing silence beside her, she looked over at Ted. An odd look crossed his face. "What?" She looked at him intently. "What did I say?"

"I just, … until we know more, it's probably best you don't depend too much on anyone."

"Meaning Magnus?" she asked quietly.

He nodded. "If you know what I mean." His tone was almost apologetic.

"Oh, I know what you mean," she declared. "Though that's hardly fair, when he's the only person who's risen to my defense." Then she stopped, winced, and corrected herself. "No, not the only one. A steady stream of people came through my door today, all very concerned about my welfare. And, of course, Mountain has been looking after me as well."

"You certainly managed to pick up a couple big players here," he murmured, looking at her.

She shrugged. "Maybe so, but I also know Mason."

His eyes rolled at that. "I get it." He chuckled. "Something about Mason just tends to bring out the good guys."

"I think he collects good guys," she stated, with a smile. "At least I'm hoping so."

He laughed. "Me too."

After some more discussion and examination of the body, plus more questioning, Ted brought her back to the clinic, and he took his leave. She had given him a list of the medications that had been stolen, and, as the door closed behind her, she sat on the bed, resting her throbbing head on her hands.

"Thank God that's over."

EVERYWHERE MAGNUS WENT, there were murmurs. Nobody overtly said anything, not saying anything for that matter, with smiles all around. However, that sense of being watched was too strong and ever-present. He shrugged it off because they didn't know he was one of the good guys, and that was just fine. If they didn't know, maybe they would treat Sydney decently, and that's what his concern was right now, since somebody was out to get her.

And that wasn't cool.

As he walked through to pick up his dinner, he looked at the selection, and Chef bent to whisper something to him.

"Did you want to take the doctor something?"

Magnus looked up and shrugged. "Last time I talked to her, she was doing fine and expected to come in herself."

He frowned and asked, "Is she really okay?"

"I believe so." He turned around and asked, "Why? Does the rumor mill say otherwise?"

Chef nodded. "People are saying she's quite badly hurt."

"No, not at all." Magnus smiled. "I can put that one to rest." He pulled out his phone and quickly called her. When she answered at the second bell, he suggested, "It would be a really good idea if you could come down for dinner. Some people are passing around rumors that you're badly hurt."

"Oh my," she said, with a heavy sigh. "I'll be there in five."

"I'll hold your spot," he replied, and, with that, he smiled at the chef and nodded. "She'll be here soon."

Chef looked relieved. "She's a sweetheart. I'm glad she's not badly hurt."

"She is healing, indeed," he agreed. "She's always treated you well, I presume."

He nodded. "Friendly, always puts up her dishes, doesn't treat us as if we're servants, more like coworkers, you know?" Chef laughed. "Something that people tend to forget when they're in a camp such as this. So many think and act as if 'That's your job,' and as if they think we are beneath them somehow. They can't even bus their own tables to save us a few steps during the meal rush." He shook his head. "And sure, it is our job, but some people have a way of making you feel better about it than others."

By the time Magnus got to the end of the food line and was reviewing his dessert options, he heard noises behind him, and then a cheer broke out. He turned to see Sydney walking into the dining area. She smiled at all the attention and lifted a hand. "See? I'm fine, guys. I'm totally okay."

At that, several people called out.

"Hey, we weren't so sure."

"All we heard were rumors today."

"We never saw you."

"I'm fine," she repeated, with a smile, "but I am hungry."

"Oh, that's a good sign." Chef motioned her to the front of the line. "Come on over here. I'll make you a plate."

He served her a solid amount of food, which she frowned at. He declared in a clear and firm voice, "You need to eat in order to heal."

"Oh, I won't argue with you there," she replied, with a laugh. "But this? … It is a lot of food."

"If you don't need it all, that's fine," Magnus noted beside her. "I'll eat the extra."

She rolled her eyes. "You can't possibly." And she motioned at his plate. "That's a pretty huge serving you've got there yourself."

"Don't worry. I've got this."

As they sat down and started eating, she looked around to see who was watching and noted basically everyone was. She looked over at him and rolled her eyes. "Seriously?"

He nodded. "Yeah, seriously."

She shrugged. "I'm just fine, and I don't know why anybody would think otherwise."

"I think Joy may have suggested you got more seriously hurt than you did."

Sydney stopped, put down her fork, and stared at him.

He shrugged. "I don't know for sure. … I'm just letting you know that I'm hearing some things."

She sighed. "Great, so I'll have to talk to her now, will I?"

He laughed. "We have to talk to people anyway, so you might as well talk to her and make sure all is well."

"*Great*," she muttered. When she finished, she looked at her empty plate.

"See? Look at that." Chef pointed, coming to check on her, before beaming. "You polished that off in no time. That is a good sign that you're on the road to recovery."

She smiled at him. "Thank you," she muttered. "I'm definitely on the mend." And, with that, she looked over at Magnus and asked, "Any chance the weather has broken?"

He winced and shook his head vehemently. "No, and it's not likely to let up for another couple days."

She groaned. "All I want is a bit of fresh air."

Chef laughed. "If that's the case, come on to the back." He had a grin on his face. "We've got a door that opens just a little bit." He shrugged. "We use it for smoking."

She raised her eyebrows at him but followed him eagerly through to the other end of the kitchen. Magnus was behind her, obviously planning on following her to the end. They opened the door. She noted the wind blowing the snow around on the ground, and the blast of cold air that hit her was a shock. Yet, at the same time, such a sense of freshness came with it that she stood here for several long moments, just deep breathing.

When she stepped back inside, she looked over at Chef, with a smile. "Thank you, I really needed that."

He nodded. "Sometimes you just gotta do what you gotta do. And, in a place such as this, that's even more important. Now"—he motioned her back to the kitchen—"go get a good night's sleep, and I'll see you in the morning."

And, with that, he ushered them out of the kitchen. The rest of the kitchen had already been packed up for the night, with the staff dismissed. Surprised, she looked at Magnus. "I didn't expect everybody to leave so quickly."

"They've implemented curfews."

"Curfews?" she repeated, looking at him.

"Yep."

"But why? Nobody can go anywhere."

"Nope, but, as long as everyone is in their room and not roaming the hallways, … the brass doesn't have to worry about where they are."

"Ah." That made it clear enough for her. "I guess I'm heading back to my clinic then, aren't I?"

He nodded. "And I'm taking you there."

"Okay. Any particular reason?" she asked cautiously.

"Yeah, because they haven't figured out who killed the Russian, not to mention who bashed you over the head," he added quietly. "And, until that point in time, I'll be sticking close, so you might as well get used to it."

She winced. "You're killing my reputation. You know that, right?"

He shrugged. "Your reputation will survive. My job is to make sure that you survive with it."

DAY 6, EARLY MORNING

SYDNEY WOKE BUT stayed in the bed, pulling the covers up around her. Even from within the clinic, she heard the winds and the storm outside that raged incessantly. She checked her watch—six in the morning. The other clinic bed creaked, and a voice in the darkness whispered, "Are you all right?"

She smiled, knowing it was Magnus. "I am." Then she groaned. "Apparently my bladder is not."

He chuckled. "Yeah, that's usually the one thing you can't argue with, when it comes to getting out of bed."

"I don't want to get up though," she whispered, curling up into a tighter ball. "It sounds horrific out there."

"The wind's been blasting all night," he murmured. "I feel sorry for anybody caught out in it."

"But would anybody be?" she questioned.

He hesitated and then added, "I hope not."

She shifted, rolling over carefully, so she could look at him, delighted that her head wasn't bothering her. "Do you think any of the missing men are out there? I mean, still alive?"

"It's possible. I don't want to say it's plausible, but I just know that stranger things have happened. And remember. All of the men here are very good at winter survival. However, something must have happened to them, putting them in a helpless situation, perhaps stranded without any tools or equipment," Magnus suggested. "I wouldn't think they'd have done it by choice. If it were by choice, they'd have gear. If not, then chances are, … they aren't anywhere close to as well protected as someone should be out there."

She lay here for a few quiet moments, processing what he'd just shared. "Do you think somebody has been kidnapping these people?" she asked, trying to keep the fear from her voice. "I can't imagine what it would be like for anybody stranded out there, knowing this would be the end of them."

"We all die sometime," he admitted quietly. "And, no, that isn't how I would want to go myself, but, as death goes, it's fairly peaceful."

He was right. Hard to contemplate but true. Going to sleep was what ended up happening out there, and you just didn't wake up again. "Has anybody checked with the scientists at the center? Have they been contacted and notified that we're missing people?"

"Oh yes," he murmured. "That's the standard protocol. Plus the village of locals has been contacted as well."

"I'm sure they love that. What is that, two times, three times already?" She shuddered against the thought. "I mean, they must think you guys don't know how to do anything right."

"It has occurred to me," he replied in a dry tone. "I'm sure they're all wondering whether we're safe to be left alone."

"But they haven't had any problems, right?"

"Not that I know of. I was heading up there myself today."

"Oh, I'd go with you but …" Then she laughed. "It would mean going out in that."

"As long as we have our team, supplies, and fuel, we'll be fine."

"Right. It does seem a bit colder this morning. At least inside."

"Yes, it is. They're lowering the base's temperature control in order to extend the fuel usage because the storm will continue for another few days."

"I hadn't realized how much the weather affected me," she murmured, snuggling deeper into the blankets and trying to ignore her bladder. "Until I came here and acknowledged firsthand what this perpetual cold can do to you."

"Again, if you're inside, where you're safe and sound, it's not too bad. You stay in, and you go out for little bits at a time, and life isn't so rough—as long as you have a stocked temporary setup, where you're safe inside for a few days. At least all the locals are safe in theirs."

"I guess they have to keep generators going too, don't they?"

"We can't get dry firewood up here, but they have other means, and they stay very warm inside their housing."

"I guess."

"And don't forget. These really bad storms aren't around all the time. This one? … This just happens to be a bad series of them."

"I remember the sunlight when we first got here. It was stunning out there."

"It still is"—he laughed—"but, at the moment, Mother Nature is exerting herself."

"Sometimes she's just a bitch, isn't she? And always dominant, even when we tend to forget that. Often mankind tends to think that we have her tamed, but we haven't. So, when she does shit here and there, it's just to remind us that she's still the boss." She grinned at that.

"How's that bladder doing?"

"It's pretty rough," she admitted.

"Come on then. Maybe if we make a trip to the bathroom, you can go back to sleep again."

"I don't think so," she muttered. "It's after six."

"It is, but you still don't have to get up for a little bit."

"I do now," she noted, throwing back the covers and sitting up, shivering at the instant cold. She grabbed the big heavy pullover she often kept close by. "I'll be back in a few minutes."

But he threw off his covers and stood too. "I'm coming with you." She frowned at him, and he shrugged. "I might as well use the facilities too."

She chuckled. "That's the thing, isn't it? When you have the opportunity to use it, then you don't have to worry about it anymore."

"Exactly."

As they headed down the hallway, she walked with her arms wrapped tightly around herself, moving as quickly as she could. When they came to what they were using for latrines here, she stepped into one, while he went into the other. She was done very quickly. When she stepped out, she wasn't surprised to see him standing there, waiting for her. She also acknowledged the fact that she felt a significant sense of relief upon seeing him. "What did you do wrong in a past life that resulted in your being on babysitting duty?" she joked.

He grinned. "Whatever it was, I won't say it was wrong. From where I stand, it seems pretty-damn right."

"So, this is light duty for you, is it not?"

"Doesn't matter whether it is or it isn't. I have no objection at all to looking after you."

"I have to admit that I appreciate it more than I would have expected," she murmured. "I don't know quite what's going on, but, until we figure it out, it's nice to know that somebody has my back."

"And we'll be there, until this is completely resolved." He chuckled. "And we would have been, … even if you hadn't contacted Mason." When she shot him a sideways glance, he nodded. "Yep, I heard about it."

"Of course you did." She gave him an eye roll. Defensive, but unapologetic, she continued. "I don't know what your deal is here, but you seem to be fairly well connected."

"So do you, as it turns out." He glanced over at her, one eyebrow raised.

She shrugged. "You know, after years of being out in the world, doing various projects similar to this, it puts you into contact with a huge range of people, as you well know."

"And well-connected people too apparently."

"Maybe." She smirked.

As they made their way back to the clinic, she hopped back up onto the bed and stared at the blankets. "I should probably just go get some coffee and stay up."

"I can go if you want."

As he stood there in front of her, he was fully dressed. "I don't know how you can get dressed so fast."

"I never got undressed," he admitted, with a wry look. "It makes things much faster on the other side."

She rolled her eyes at that and laid back down, pulling a blanket over her. "Then, in that case, you can absolutely go get coffee."

With that, he walked to the door and asked, "You want me to take the keys and lock up behind me?"

She frowned at that and replied, "No, it's probably okay. I should open up anyway, just in case. Although I'll give you the spare set for safe keeping."

With that done, he walked to the door. "I'll be back in a few minutes."

Not wanting to be still in bed when somebody might need her, she got up, turned on the one single light that she had, and walked around the small space, making sure everything was ready for the day. So far, every treatment had been fairly minor, other than the more serious injuries plus the kitchen burns of the two already airlifted out, which those were much more than minor. However, now that they had a body in the freezer and a murderer loose among them, she knew that nothing would be the same again.

Hearing sounds at the door, she called out, "Just a sec and I'll give you a hand." She walked over and pulled open the door, and walked into a hard fist.

COMING BACK WITH two hot coffees that he'd overfilled, Magnus came to the door and nudged it gently with his leg, hoping that she'd hear him. Realizing that she'd probably gone back to sleep, he put the coffee on the floor and reached for the keys he'd brought along, just in case. The door wasn't locked.

Swearing, he popped it open, walked in with the coffees and froze, when he saw that the room was empty. He dropped the coffees on the desk and spun around, calling out to her, but there was nothing. He raced to the bathroom, calling out for her, and again heard nothing. He immediately pulled out his phone and heard crackling sounds, which meant that the storm was killing all communication.

He raced toward Mountain's bunk and found Mountain standing outside, talking with somebody. At the look on his face, Mountain dismissed the other man. "What's going on?"

"She's gone," Magnus snapped urgently, and he quickly explained.

With that, sirens went off. People stumbled from bed, as they tried to figure out what was happening now.

Magnus frowned at Mountain. "Maybe she just went to get food?" he suggested hopefully.

Mountain shook his head. "You and I both know that's not what's happening but definitely go check it out."

With that, Magnus raced to the cafeteria, where the staff was trying to get breakfast prepared. However, with the alarm ringing out, Chef looked up and asked, "What's going on?"

"Have you seen the doctor?" he asked urgently.

Surprised, Chef shook his head. "No, not since last night. Last I saw her, she was with you."

"I was, and I was with her up until a few minutes ago, when I came for coffee," he replied urgently. "I left her in her room, locked up, but, when I came back, she was gone."

Chef stared in shock. "Jesus Christ." Lowering his voice, he looked around. With a hoarse whisper, he asked, "What the hell's going on here?"

"I don't know," Magnus admitted, "but this? … This can't happen."

He headed to the main exit and the double doors that they used to come and go. He quickly dressed in his outdoor gear and headed out, while Mountain searched inside the base. Hooking on a safety line, Magnus checked for prints, and definitely prints were out here, but he couldn't tell whose they were for the blowing snow. But there was some more recent ones.

He raced over to the dog shed and called out, “Joe.”

The owner shook himself awake, looked up at Magnus, and glared at him. “What time is it?” he groused.

“It’s six thirty a.m., quarter to seven now. Listen. The doc is missing.”

At that, Joe scrambled to his feet and stared at him. “What the hell?” he cried out. “When? How the hell did that happen?”

“She went missing from inside the base in the last half hour. They’re doing a full search, and I came out here to confirm that none of the dogs are missing and that you haven’t seen anybody.”

“I haven’t seen anybody, and you just woke me up,” he replied, with a flick of his hand. “But the dogs would have woken me if anybody had come in.”

“Can you check, please to make sure all the dogs are here?”

Without even arguing, Joe got up, started counting the dogs, then turned and headed outside to see how many might be out in the storm. Several snow-covered bundles stood up when he called out, then shook themselves off and came running.

Magnus couldn’t quite understand why the dogs would want to be out there in a storm, but they seemed to be perfectly at home, even in these harsh circumstances.

Joe came back in, swearing heavily. “I’m missing two dogs.” That frantic note in his voice Magnus understood all too well.

“What about gear? Are there any sleds missing? Anything out of place?”

"I'm checking, give me a second," he muttered.

"And only two dogs? That's not enough but for one person to use with a sled, is it?"

"Not generally, no. Unless they're taking skis and just using the dogs for direction. Yet she would be a dead weight."

"I know. I know," Magnus growled.

Together they raced to the blocked-off section, where all the sleds and the outdoor equipment were stored, and saw the footprints outside.

"Jesus Christ, somebody's gone out in this storm," Joe muttered.

"They've gone out, but, considering the small racing sled"—Magnus pointed at the tracks in front of them—"whoever that is, … he's not alone."

Joe nodded. "I'll harness up two sleds. You coming?"

"I'm coming," he stated, "but we also need a full recovery team."

"The doc fucking better not be dead," Joe roared in a fit. "How the hell did someone take my dogs without my permission?" He swore, as he added, "I still don't know how it happened."

"My next questions would be, who feeds them, and would the dogs take food from anybody else?"

"A couple of them would. Dogs are very food motivated, which is why I have a strict rule about nobody being allowed to feed them."

"And, if somebody did feed them, maybe they drugged them?" he asked Joe, turning to face him.

"Maybe. I don't, … I don't want to say no. They're still animals."

"Right. Chances are somebody has been catering to

them and has managed to build up some trust with a couple sled dogs and is using them for some purpose in this mess."

"My dogs have a hell of a good sense of direction, even in this storm." He worked in a frenzy to get a team of dogs attached to two sleds. "They're not like you and me. They don't need lights. They don't need a compass. So, if this kidnapper was heading someplace in particular, and maybe the dogs know where that was, then the kidnapper would take the dogs."

"How would the dogs know where the kidnappers were going though?" Magnus asked, even as Joe set up the harnesses and locked in six dogs.

"That's the question. The only way they would know is if the kidnapper had some way to direct them to a certain place or if it's a site the dogs know well. Often, when we go out, we take a certain trail, and we often head to the village."

"Exactly. Let's go to the village," Magnus said immediately. "If they wanted to keep her alive, the village would make the most sense."

"But why keep her alive?"

Magnus frowned at Joe. "Why take her out of here at all? If they wanted to kill her, they could have done it here, just like the Russian."

Grim-faced, Joe nodded. "Let's go." And, with that, they opened up the doors to the shed and mushed the dogs straight through, right into the storm.

MOUNTAIN SNAPPED OUT orders, even as the colonel listened but didn't interfere. As soon as the room cleared, with everybody doing a full-on search of every corner of the compound, Mountain turned toward the colonel. "Two dogs are missing."

The colonel's face thinned, and he nodded. "So that's what you're thinking then."

"It's not what I'm thinking, as much as what we know so far."

"What I don't know is the why? Why her?"

"The only reason would be for her skills," he stated, looking at the colonel curiously. "Or revenge."

"But why wouldn't somebody just leave her dead here for that?"

"I don't know. We're missing an awful lot of information that we need answers to." He looked around at the military complex. "For anybody kidnapping her, the timing had to be pretty-damn tight."

The colonel just nodded.

"They must have known Magnus went to get coffee and knew what the window of time was in order to immediately pick her up and take her out, before anybody had a chance to argue. They must have had an escape plan in place—or even had it already set up earlier, so that coming and getting her was secondary."

The colonel paced around the small space. "If they had wanted to kill her, they could have just done it on the spot. That would have been easiest by far, so why take her, unless—as you said—they needed her skills."

"She's been losing drugs too …"

"You're thinking somebody close by is injured or sick and needed help?" he asked cautiously.

"I don't know what to think. All I know is we have a missing doc, and, right now, that's on me."

"No, it's not on you," the colonel snapped. "It's on all of

us. This is … We should have shut down this training camp. At least put it on lockdown, and that's on me."

"You and I both know the brass won't shut down the training and disband everyone because they don't want whoever is here and is behind this disappearing in the wind."

"Yeah, well, the brass has also been reducing our supplies and our fly-ins because of the storm, so we're running on empty for a lot of this, and that's not cool either," he muttered.

Mountain turned and stared up and down the building, as every room and closet was searched high and low. Even a quick inventory of supplies and every available hiding space on the camp was investigated. When the results came through, Mountain already knew the answer. He looked around at the worried faces and nodded.

"She's not here," Mountain confirmed for the colonel. "The only thing I can tell you is that we also have two sled dogs missing. And two teams have already headed out searching, but in this storm …"

Everybody nodded grimly.

"It also means," one of the men snapped, his voice loud and harsh, "that we don't have a doctor here in case anything happens to one of us. Maybe that's part of the reason for all this."

"Maybe," Mountain agreed, "but there's got to be a reason for setting that up too. So far we haven't got answers to any of our questions."

That pissed him off the most, the fact that they had nothing.

"It seems a ghost is coming and going," one of the British team said quietly. "We need to set up cameras."

"That we would, but we're also running very low on

power, and everything's glitching out on our communications, computers, and laptops. Nothing's working well. The storm is killing all of it," Mountain shared, keeping his voice calm. "That doesn't mean we're not trying, but it does mean that we are hampered by the weather." He motioned to the colonel. "I need to talk to you. In private."

And, with that, the two men stepped into the medical clinic.

Mountain spoke first. "I did check the cameras, particularly the one here in the clinic, and we don't have much. Unfortunately they're not working well because of the storm outside."

"Right. It's not exactly something we had thought to set up ahead of time, and it's not something we would normally do in an international operation anyway." The colonel growled deep in his throat. "I need a working phone. I think we need more help up here."

DAY 6, MIDMORNING

THE FIRST THING that struck Sydney was the cold, and it literally struck her. It seemed as if ice, snow, and something cold kept flicking onto her cheek and off again. She struggled to reach up and brush it off, covering what was very tender skin at this point, only she couldn't move her arms or her hands. She shifted, horrified to find she was completely constricted.

She twisted her face, trying to hide it from the cold searing into her skin. Numbness started to take hold. Body movement was so important in order to stay warm, but, numb as she was, she would be in the worst shape possible. She cried out, "Where am I? What's happening?"

Her body involuntarily shifted all over the place. As she bounced and moved swiftly, she noted that the cold was mostly coming from the wind and that the rest of her was bundled up in some fur. She tried to snuggle in deeper and get that exposed cheek covered up. She managed to do it somewhat, when somebody—whoever was here with her—seemed to understand the problem and pulled a fur covering over her face.

One problem aside, she assessed the next. There was no light, no nothing. She was glad enough to know that she could breathe, and, for that, she was grateful. The fur now covered up the icy feel on her face and would also filter the cold air, so she could breathe easier. She was tied to a sled, and probably dogs were mushing her through this cold.

For whatever reason, she had been kidnapped. She waited the longest time, until suddenly the sled slowed, and she thought she heard other voices. She was taken, still bundled up in these furs, into some building because almost immediately the cold fell away, and the noise increased.

Her ropes were untied, and she was picked up—still in this bundled-up blanket—and carried over somebody's shoulder. She tried to cry out, but nobody cared. Of course they didn't. Did they even know who she was, or was she just a random victim? When she was dropped none-too-gently onto a softer surface than she expected, the blanket was roughly snatched up from her, and she shivered as the cold hit her. She wrapped her arms around herself.

Of course she hadn't come out prepared for winter travel, and the blankets she had been wrapped up in, although great, had now been removed. She stared up at the stranger's face and cried out, "Who are you, and what do you want with me?"

He didn't say anything but pointed. She turned to find a man stretched out in a makeshift bed. She recognized him as one of the missing men from the military base, from photos of each shared all over the base.

She immediately bolted to her feet and dropped down at the man's side. She glared over at the man who had kidnapped her. "Why is he here? He should be back at the camp."

He just shrugged and didn't say anything. She checked for vitals and found a weak pulse. By the looks of it, her patient was dealing with hypothermia, and his breathing was quite shallow. She checked him for injuries, but there didn't appear to be any. She sat back and stared down at him, then checked his pupils, wondering if this was drug related. She couldn't remember how long this guy had been missing, but she thought it had to be several days by now. She thought his name was Terrance. She looked back at the man who had brought her here. "Did you kidnap him too?"

He stared at her, his eyes almost pure black, when a voice from the far side interrupted. "No, he was found outside."

Sydney spun around to the person who spoke English.

A young woman smiled at Sydney.

Seeing the amiable expression on her face, Sydney asked, "Do you know where he was found? And what condition was he in when he was found?"

The young woman motioned at the men in front of her. "Just as he appears to be now, as you can see. We've been trying to keep him alive."

In exasperation, Sydney said, "I need him back at the camp, not here. Instead of bringing me here, you should have brought this man to us."

"He was conscious at first."

At that, Sydney stilled, looked at her, and asked, with some urgency, "And?"

"He said he couldn't go back. Declared it too dangerous for him to return. So we kept him here."

Sydney shook her head. "The problem is, he's hypothermic, and the cold is too much for him. I can't be sure what exactly is happening without some of my tools." Yet his body temperature, although cool, wasn't the danger she had been expecting.

She wondered, as she leaned over him, wishing she had a way to check for diabetes. That shouldn't have happened overnight, of course, but it was possible that he was a diabetic and that somehow he had gotten caught out here without his medication. She glanced back at the other woman. "Why didn't you ask the clinic for help?"

"For the same reason we didn't take him back there," she said calmly. "Your ways are not our ways, and we don't want to deal with those men, if we don't have to."

"And yet when this man is dying you kidnap me?" she asked.

The other woman shrugged. "We took a vote, and that is what was decided."

She blinked at that and turned back to her patient. He was warm enough, but it seemed as if he were almost in a drug-induced coma. "Did you give him something? Any drugs or medications, herbs, or anything?"

The other woman shook her head. "They tried several things, but they can't get him to wake up. He fell asleep, and he's been out the whole time."

Sydney nodded. "The problem is, it could be any number of things, and I don't have any way to find out while I'm here," she declared in frustration, glaring at her. "All you're doing is causing everybody in the military camp to panic right now. This man's been drugged, for all I can see."

The young woman shrugged. "You can say what you want, but my family will do as they see fit."

Sydney sat back. "Can you at least send word that I'm okay, so that they don't come in here with weapons?"

"How would they find us?" she asked curiously.

"They have dogs, and they will track me here." She looked back toward where the base was. "You went there to kidnap me."

"They came to get help for him."

Sydney nodded. "I get that. Believe me. I really do. I appreciate the fact that you're trying to help this person, but you also have to understand that, by taking me, … the military won't be very happy with that."

"It doesn't matter if they're happy." She gave a small smile. "And believe me. I can talk to these men until I'm blue in the face, but it won't make a difference to them."

"Right, got it. Anyway, I need my patient back at the base, preferably airlifted out, because I'm not sure what's going on with him," she muttered, as she stared down at the young man.

His pulse was there, just not as strong as she would like it. His color was borderline, but it was the laxness of his face that worried her. "I mean, it could be anything from a stroke to a medication reaction to a diabetic coma," she noted quietly. "When did you find him?" she asked, looking over at the other woman.

"Yesterday morning."

"Yesterday morning?" she cried out. "Where?"

"Out in a snow cave."

"Was he alone?" She stood and looked down at him. "If he was alone, and he was in a winter cave, any number of things could have befallen him out there. But he was awake, and he said he couldn't go back, is that correct?"

The young woman nodded.

"Okay. I'm not exactly sure what I'm supposed to do with this at the moment," she muttered to herself. "I need to get him back to the clinic. I can run some tests on him there at least. I can check his blood sugars and even test his blood to see if he's been drugged."

"Who would drug him?" asked the other woman, her expression worried.

"It's possible that he was alone in the cave for a long time and that maybe somebody left him there to die. However, maybe he wasn't alone originally," she said, thinking hard and fast. "Did you see tracks around the snow cave? Anything to indicate that he wasn't alone there? Anything?"

She nodded. "There were a lot of tracks," she admitted. "All of them coming from the base. All older."

"Snowshoe tracks, dog tracks?"

"Both."

Sydney thought about that and nodded. "A lot of military training is being done out here."

The other woman just nodded.

"I suppose now you want me to fix this, without having any way to know what's going on."

The young woman nodded. "That's exactly what they want."

"And they won't let me take him back?"

The young woman turned to talk to the people behind her. A loud argument ensued, exchanging heated words back and forth.

Sydney bent down again and checked her patient's pulse again, but she had absolutely no clues. Without any wounds, without anything else to go on, she needed to start testing, yet how was she supposed to do that here? She checked for movement, found no stiffness, all his joints moved, his hands curled. His eyelids opened, but there was no reaction; the pupils just stayed wide. That bothered her the most. Drugs possibly, stroke possibly, aneurysm, coma definitely.

She looked over at the young woman. "I know you're keeping him warm here, but he could remain unconscious and slowly die. I presume he hasn't had any food or water since you've had him here."

The young woman looked at her and then shook her head.

"Exactly. I need to get him back to my clinic, so I can set up an IV and get liquids into him," she snapped, standing up again.

She turned and glared at the people behind her. The room had filled. She wasn't even sure exactly what this room was, and she didn't have time enough to care. She started snapping out orders. "I need him back at the clinic, so I can give him liquids. Otherwise he will die."

An argument raged around her, over her, through her, as everybody else decided the fate of the young man in front of them. She hated it, but, at the same time, … she needed their cooperation. They had saved him; they had brought her here specifically so she could help him, but she needed to be back at her clinic in order to do so.

She also needed to get word out that she was alive and well, before all hell broke loose. She knew perfectly well how Magnus would take this, and it wasn't his fault. But then again, given that she hadn't been asked if she wanted to come and hadn't been given a choice was really frustrating because now Magnus would know how she had been treated, and that would cause even more problems.

Finally the young woman stood in front of the crowd and started yelling.

The elders fell quiet, as they stared at her. She turned and looked back at Syd. "They say it's not safe."

"It might not be safe, but he will die here. That much I can say with absolute certainty. You have to know that."

She needed the young woman to go to bat for this man. She wasn't certain that his name was Terrance. She bent and checked his pockets but found no ID, nothing. She didn't know if anybody had taken something off him or if this was literally the way they had found him.

Considering that he may never be seen again, it was quite possible that whoever he had been with had determined to leave no identification on purpose. It infuriated her, but she didn't know what she was supposed to do here, as she waited while the young woman struggled to get somebody to come on board with what Sydney needed.

Finally, after a muttering of discontent, one of the men nodded. In a guttural English, he said, "I will take you."

She looked up at him gratefully. "Thank you. Thank you very much." She bent down, checked on her patient, and again murmured, "We need to go soon. Like yesterday, so please hurry."

He nodded, and, with that, the whole group turned and bundled up the patient and secured him on the same sled she had come in on.

She looked back at the young woman. "Thank you for this."

The woman shrugged. "I don't know that you should thank me." She raised one eyebrow. "They don't trust you."

"Maybe they don't trust me, but I haven't done anything wrong."

"Maybe not you but people from there," she said, clearly indicating the direction of the military training center, "aren't trustworthy, as far as they're concerned."

She winced. "I'm sorry to hear that. I understand, but I do need to help him, and I can't do that here."

"I told them that in the first place," she admitted, with a sigh. "Yet it's always hard because they don't understand everything that you're saying."

"Of course but I do appreciate everything that you're doing."

"I don't even know what I'm doing," she muttered, but she got up and led Sydney over to a pile. "You'll need clothes."

"Yes, I'd appreciate that," she muttered. "I'm freezing."

And, with that, she was given a big parka, gloves, and a hood that came down over her face. "You'll have to ride on a different sled."

She nodded. "That's fine. I just need him back. Let's go now." She was led out to a second sled and winced. A whole team sat there, waiting. "I gather you really don't trust what's going on here, do you?"

"No, they don't, and that will be the problem."

"Good enough. Let me go back. I'll explain what they did, and they won't be in trouble. But I do need to get the patient back quickly."

And, with that, she was quickly loaded up onto one of the sleds, and they took off. She was on a different sled from the injured man, but, as she headed back toward the base, she kept going through everything that might have gone wrong. She needed to check him for needle marks, for one thing. She also wondered if he could have ingested something.

The problem was, she could do what she needed to do in order to stabilize him, but then he needed to go to a hospital with the proper facilities to really treat him, but they were probably hours out. With that, she dropped her head, buried it deep into her arms, and waited.

It would be a while before she had any answers, and, right now, all she had was more and more questions.

WHEN A SHOUT went out, Magnus turned to where somebody pointed and saw up ahead several dog teams coming toward them. He turned the sled, urging the dogs to head that way, not believing his eyes. When he looked, an arm was lifted in greeting. Then he saw Sydney, sitting on a sled, all bundled up in a huge sealskin parka.

She called out, "We're heading back to the camp. We have one of the missing men, who is injured."

He stared at her in shock, but then immediately nodded and turned his team around, heading back toward the camp, following on their heels. His mind was filled with questions, but he knew it would be a little bit before they got any answers.

All he could think was, *Thank God that she was safe*, still wondering who the hell had come in after her. The unknown group moved quickly, efficiently, as a unified unit. These people were capable and comfortable out here.

As soon as they got back to the base, she stepped off the sled, talked to the people behind her, as they unloaded the patient and carried him inside, Magnus presumed to her clinic.

As he approached her outside, she looked at him and said, "You can't get angry." He just glared at her, and she nodded. "If you want cooperation from these people, you cannot get angry." She turned to the men, explained who Magnus was, and thanked the men for finding the missing person.

They just nodded and glared at Magnus.

She told Magnus, "The man is Terrance. One of our missing men."

Magnus nodded. “I know.”

“These guys found him in a snow cave. Tracks were all around, human and canine. From what they told me, he was conscious for a bit, and, in that time period, he told them that he couldn’t go back to the training center. He’s been unconscious ever since. Naturally they didn’t want to return him if he wasn’t safe, but I insisted because I don’t have any way to treat him back there. And, honest to God, I don’t have much I can really do here but stabilize him. I need to get him airlifted out as soon as possible.”

“Fine. … How did they get in the base?”

“They just walked in, and I guess they found me without too much trouble, but remember. We do have signs up to direct people to the clinic.”

“So, they all read and speak English.”

“They read and speak some English, but not as well as we would like them to, and better than they would like.” She smiled. “A young woman back at their village spoke English quite well.”

“Of course,” He shook his head in disbelief. He reached out a hand and thanked them for helping one of his friends. They seemed to relax a little more at that.

Then the men turned and looked at her, and she nodded.

“We will keep him safe,” she said, with assurance. “And you’re right. Something bad is going on here right now, but please understand that we are working on it.”

The men seemed to accept that, and, within minutes, they were gone again.

Soon Magnus and Sydney made it to her clinic. Magnus waited as Sydney attended her patient, Joy at Terrance’s side, staring at him in shock.

"Where the hell has he been?" she cried out. "How is he still alive?"

"He had been in a snow cave and was rescued by a group of locals from the nearby village," Sydney explained quietly. "That's why I was picked up, in an effort to get help for him."

At that, Joy stared at her. "Good God, you were kidnapped so you could help him?"

She nodded. "I know it sounds ridiculous, but yes. They don't trust anybody here because Terrance told them that it wasn't safe for him to return. However, their English isn't great, so I don't know what he might have truly said. They took it to believe Terrance was in danger here."

Joy kept shaking her head. "What the hell is going on in this godforsaken place?"

"Not sure, but we'll get to the bottom of it soon enough," Sydney muttered. And, with that, she got to work.

Magnus stood guard. No one was taking her from him again.

DAY 6, EARLY AFTERNOON

UNDER MOUNTAIN'S WATCHFUL eye, Sydney sat back from checking her patient for the hundredth time and still couldn't stop worrying. Terrance hadn't surfaced in any way yet. His vitals were stable but on the weak side. She wanted him flown out immediately. This definitely wasn't the place for him, but, once again, the weather was shutting down all flights.

When she heard the door open, she looked up to see Magnus walk in. She smiled at him.

"Hey." Magnus walked over and gave her a quick hug. "How are you feeling?"

"I'm fine. Tired and obviously a little more wary about what's going on here." She shrugged and looked from one of them to the other. "Yet I'm absolutely ecstatic that Terrance was found."

"How he was out there in a snow cave on his own is what we're still trying to figure out," Magnus said. "How did that happen, and why would he say that he wasn't safe? I gather he hasn't spoken since you brought him here."

She shook her head. "He's not talking. He's not even close to being awake, much less able to talk," she said quietly. "And I doubt he will be, at least while he's here. I'm doing the best I can, but no doubt he should be at a well-equipped facility, where they're better able to treat him."

"And yet this is where these hypothermic accidents happen."

"Absolutely." She gave Magnus an acknowledging look. "Which means, I'm doing what I can, but I'm sure this isn't a normal event. I'm waiting for the blood test results right now, but I have very limited testing options available."

"Right, and that just compounds the problem, doesn't it?"

"It absolutely does, not to mention the fact that I don't know anything about him. We have no medical records for him, at least nothing that says anything. I don't have a family history. I don't know if anything may have been latent that suddenly flared. Just no way to know at this point. As much as you want answers"—she smiled at the frustration on their faces—"I don't have any to give."

Mountain nodded. "That's pretty well what the stateside doctor said too."

"Of course I've been in touch with him constantly, and I'm doing everything I can." She shrugged. "But this isn't a situation where I can just turn around and pinpoint what happened because it doesn't work like that. Medical diagnoses are a series of trials and errors, investigations to find out what's the source of these symptoms."

Mountain growled in frustration, then turned and stormed off.

She smiled at Magnus. "I suppose you're on babysitting duty again."

"Hope I can do a better job this time," he said quietly, clearly feeling terrible about it.

She winced at that. "Stop. You can't be with me twenty-four/seven, you know? Besides you were only getting coffee."

"I should be with you around the clock, at the rate

things are going. Either me or Mountain." He gave her a half smile. "You never, … I mean … What exactly happened?"

She shrugged. "I opened the door, thinking it was you, struggling to get in with your hands full of coffees, and walked right into a fist."

He stared at her in shock.

She nodded, then reached up to show him the bruise on her cheek. "I woke up, tied on the sled, in the cold." She winced at the memory. "But they did treat me well, and I certainly don't have any objection to them seeking me out," she murmured. "But I gather he thought I would resist being taken to where he wanted me to go, so the easiest thing in his mind was to knock me out. And you have to admit that he was probably right." Magnus just glared at her, and she smiled. "And, yes, I know that's not what you want to hear."

"No, it sure isn't," he muttered, as he shook his head. "The whole thing is absolutely bizarre. We're still trying to figure out why Terrance was in that snow cave."

"Did you see it?" she asked curiously.

He nodded. "Yeah, as soon as Terrance was dropped off, I went out with the team to take a look, and your … your kidnappers," he noted, with an eye roll, "they took us directly there."

"Oh, good, that must have helped."

"Should have, but it didn't. His ID was in there, plus a couple coats and some winter gear to survive out there for a while, but no answers. No real explanation as to what he was doing and no indication as to how long he'd been there. There was nothing."

"Was there food? Any supplies?" she asked curiously.

"A little bit, yes. We're wondering if he wasn't coming back and forth, taking what he wanted from the base for the day and then disappearing again."

"Which either implies that he was willfully staying away from the base or was with somebody, who was keeping him away or was involved somehow," she guessed, with a thoughtful headshake. "What possible reason would there be for him staying underground like that? I mean, particularly when the weather turned so harsh."

"That's what we're still trying to figure out," he admitted quietly. "And there are no real answers, at least until he gets better."

"It's always that way, isn't it? I want answers, and I want them now. If he would just wake up, we might get some, before he leaves."

Magnus started to laugh. "Yeah, now you know how Mountain feels."

"I never know whether to speak about his missing brother or to just avoid the subject."

Magnus nodded. "Believe me. Mountain knows how you feel. It's written all over your face."

Sydney sighed. "And I'm not exactly sure how much of this involves Teegan. I forgot to ask the villagers whether they had found or had seen anybody else out there."

"Good point," he murmured. "Would they have told you?"

"I would think so, but I certainly don't know that for sure," she murmured. "I don't think they are a problem for us. They are irritated that we're out here and are getting people such as Terrance into trouble." She looked back at her patient. "I don't think they understand why we're here, what we're doing, how we could possibly lose somebody, or why he would be hiding from us."

"No, I definitely got the impression they're less than

impressed with our presence."

She chuckled. "Do you blame them?"

He grinned. "No, … I really don't. But, at the same time, it's hardly our fault."

"No, particularly if this was done willfully," she murmured. "Now, if Terrance wasn't out there on his own, that's a different story."

"Did you see any signs of his being held a captive?"

"I looked," she replied, immediately turning to her patient. "I checked for signs of restraints but didn't see any. There's not a mark on him, except a couple injection sites." She cast him a sideways glance at that.

"Right. I did hear about that. We don't know if they're recreational drugs or not, right?"

She shook her head. "I don't have any way to determine that here, short of those blood test results, which just look for a few suspect drugs. Of course, if he woke up, that would be a different story."

Magnus nodded grimly, as he looked around the room. "How's Joy handling it?"

"Honestly she's not. She's asking to get out on the first flight."

"I'm not surprised," he murmured. "If you were picked off while you were here, Joy probably thinks it could happen to anybody."

"And it could," Sydney admitted. "I'm certainly not any self-defense expert." She shrugged. "I have basic training, like all of us do, but, when it comes to fighting off somebody who's much bigger than I am …"

"He was much bigger, wasn't he?" he asked, staring off in the distance.

"I'd say an easy one hundred pounds on me, yes," she

murmured. "And, if he wanted to do something, he could do it."

"Any chance …" Then he hesitated.

"Any chance he's involved? I won't say no because I don't understand why this all happened in the first place. He didn't look to be somebody who was on drugs. The whole family looked to be fairly clean of that influence, but again …" She shrugged.

"Right. Again you don't know for sure."

"Of course not. You could talk to the young girl though. She was quite open about everything going on, as she knew it to be. I just can't confirm that she knows all that much, but she's very aware of what is happening there."

"Maybe I will then." He nodded. "We're going back to the village in a bit. We have a few things they could use, so we will take those supplies to their village as a thank-you."

"Oh, good." She smiled. "We definitely want to stay friendly." Suddenly she turned to look at him thoughtfully, "Did anybody check in on the scientists?"

"That's next on my list." He smiled. "I'll stop in there and let them know we found our missing man."

"*One* of your missing men. I'm sure you've made that distinction."

His face turned grim, as he nodded. "Oh, yes, we've definitely made that clear. What we don't know—and it would be very helpful—is if he went willingly. Or is somebody around here kidnapping our men and keeping them hostage out there for some reason? Although I don't have a clue what that reason could be."

Long after he was gone, once a security guard had been stationed outside her door, she stayed close to her patient, checking in with the military base in California, regarding his condition. Her boss from back home had questioned her about what went on. She'd told him as honestly as she could. He'd just muttered something about learning lessons and stupid assignments because he had disagreed with her coming in the first place.

She could barely even remember much about the place she'd been taken to, except that it was a hell of a lot warmer than this place. Maybe because it was small, so more body heat was gathered into the confined space. She didn't know, but they certainly understood how to live in these conditions better than she did, maybe better than anyone at the base did. The local villagers had had generations of adaptation.

Wearing a smile, Joy walked in and announced, "Just wanted to let you know I've asked for a transfer."

"Good enough." Sydney nodded. "Hopefully you can get out of here soon."

Wrapping her arms around her chest, Joy added, "This is just too weird."

"Too weird?"

"Yeah, too weird. It's one thing for somebody to disappear and to go missing, but to find them after they've been in a snow cave for quite a while? That, ... that's just too weird."

"Maybe he got snow-blinded and couldn't find his way back home again," Sydney pointed out. "What if he went out there to practice something he was struggling with, such as a phobia? Maybe he thought he could handle this on his own but got caught up in that snowstorm. You know perfectly well how easy it is to get turned around out there. People lose their sense of direction and get lost in conditions much better than this all the time."

Joy sat down on the chair, hard. "Oh my, I didn't even

think of that."

At that, Sydney nodded. "That's because you're letting fear do all the talking right now," she murmured. "And that's not always the best person to advise you."

"What, now fear's a person?" she quipped, with half a groan.

"If you find that fearful person inside you, it's the same as talking to a person when you try to talk them off the wall, isn't it?"

"I guess." Joy shrugged. "Can't say it's anything I was worried about."

"Good. In that case, don't do it now either, just relax. You've put in for the transfer to get out of here, so, with any luck, you'll be back in the States fairly quickly."

"Now you seem to feel that I'm making too much of it." She slumped into her chair.

Sydney stared at her in astonishment. "You can't know what I'm thinking, so why would you say that?"

She shrugged. "I don't know, maybe because of the way you just presented that fear theory."

"They did take me by force," she reminded Joy. "Believe me. My jaw's still feeling it."

Immediately Joy hopped up, walked over, and reached out to gently touch her jaw. "I am sorry about that. They were pretty rough."

"I don't even think *rough* was the intended part of it." She huffed. "I think they were just trying to be effective, so they could get out of the base fast, without being seen."

WHEN MAGNUS ARRIVED back at the settlement, he called

out for the young girl, named Shye. She stepped out and motioned for him to come in.

He stepped inside to find most of the same people he'd seen gathered here before, all frowning at him. He nodded, made his greeting as peaceably as he could, and said to her, "We have a few more questions."

She sighed and nodded. "I can try to answer them, but, as you can see, they're not happy."

At that, he turned and took another look. They all stared at him, and, to her credit, they didn't look terribly impressed.

"The doctor is working on Terrance right now, trying to get him stable," he shared, looking for a response that would appease them. "But I need to ask, have you ever seen anybody else out here?" he asked quietly.

She frowned at him. "Are you missing somebody else?"

He swallowed back a retort and replied amiably, "We think that Terrance might have been with somebody."

She turned to the others and asked them. Immediately they gave headshakes, but nobody spoke up.

"Did they see anybody a few weeks ago? Have they seen anybody at all out here?"

One of the men, obviously understanding English because he didn't wait for the translation, spoke up. "Yes."

Magnus turned to him. "When? Where?"

He shrugged. "Outside." Then he started speaking in his native language at a rapid rate, and Magnus turned to Shye.

Shye smiled. "It was two weeks ago, and he saw one man with a sled."

"That would make sense," he replied quietly. "We're all sledding."

"He wasn't with a group. He was alone, but only experienced people should be out here alone."

"And we aren't experienced, so he's right," Magnus said immediately. "Nobody should be out here alone, and nobody else really understands the workings of this place, such as you do."

She nodded. "Yet everybody thinks they do," she added quietly, "much to our disgust. There's always the possibility, … come spring, of finding bodies of the dead."

He stared at her. "Does it happen a lot?"

She shrugged. "It depends on how many people decide to come up here for a winter experience. Lots of times they come to us for assistance, for guidance, for directions, things such as that," she noted. "And we inevitably tell them to not go solo, but off they go anyway. It isn't all the time, but it's happened enough that now we just shrug and tell them that there's a good chance they'll die. They don't listen and go anyway."

"Then they die?" Magnus asked.

"Sometimes they do, yes. It's a curiosity for us."

He could understand that. Hell, he didn't understand why people didn't listen either. These villagers were the people who understood the environment they lived in up here. "Are you happy living here?"

She looked at him and shrugged. "It's home."

"Of course. I understand that. But it sounds as if you've been educated elsewhere."

She nodded. "I have been, in many other places, but I like it here."

He smiled. "Then you are truly blessed because you have found where you belong."

She gave him a beaming smile. "That is true—and another thing which most outsiders don't understand."

He visited with them for a little bit longer, trying to get them to see that he wasn't a bad guy and that he was here to ensure something such as this didn't happen again. However, even as he left, he wasn't sure they believed him. Shye walked him outside, seemingly unaffected by the cold. He smiled at her. "That's a big advantage to living here, isn't it?"

She tilted her head. "When we are here all our lives, we know better than to go out." Then she laughed. "Better than you apparently."

He nodded. "But I am still looking for other men," he admitted. "So, while it may seem foolish, I don't want anybody else caught out here."

She studied his face for a moment and then nodded. "I will tell the others that more men are out here."

"We lost two just in the past week—one was Terrance, whom you found—and another one about two weeks ago." She turned to look at him, as if she wanted to say something, then let it go. He nodded. "Believe me. We know."

And, with that, he strapped in the dogs, giving each a quick cuddle and a treat for their patience. Toby, the leader, was quickly becoming his favorite, then turned and headed out. Next stop was the scientist camp. If they were smart, they were all tucked inside. They weren't very far off Magnus's path, so, when he arrived there in good time, he entered and shouted out, "Anybody here?"

All around came a chorus of greetings. He looked up to see a circle of smiling faces. That was another symptom of being here; you got pretty tired of the same people over and over again. He smiled at a couple scientists he already knew. "Hey, I just wanted to give you guys an update." Then he filled them in on what had happened.

"They kidnapped your doctor?" one of the scientists

cried out.

He nodded. "She will be okay, but obviously she's a little shaken up by it."

"Yeah, you think?" one of the other women snapped, staring at him. "How did he get in?"

"We don't lock up at the base. Do you here?" he asked pointedly.

She flushed, looked around. "No, but maybe we will from now on."

Several of the men looked at her, then realized what she was saying and nodded. "Maybe. We hadn't considered it an issue."

"No, of course not," Magnus agreed quietly. "I don't think any of us did. But now it's a whole different ball game." And, with that, after visiting for a bit and warning them, he asked, "Have you seen anybody outside?"

Everybody gave a flat-out no, until one of the head scientists said, "Look at the conditions out there. Nobody's going anywhere. We have lots of lab work to do, so we're all comfortably tucked in here, and that's where we'll stay."

DAY 7, MORNING

SYDNEY WOKE THE next morning, got up, and checked on her patient, but there was no change. They couldn't get flights in or out last night, and now all she could do was sit here and hope that Terrance survived long enough to get out. When she heard an odd sound, Magnus sat up in the chair, looking at her.

"How is he?" he asked, his voice guttural.

"Alive," she stated. "That's about all I can say right now."

He nodded and then tilted his head. "I don't know if you hear it right now."

She stopped and listened. "I don't hear anything."

"Precisely. It sounds as if the storm's finally broken up."

She looked at him in delight.

"I'll go check and bring back some coffee." He stopped, handed her the key. "You know what to do."

She smiled, nodded, and, when he was gone, she quickly locked the door behind him and returned to her patient. If the storm was over, that meant she could pack up this guy and ship him out, but they needed enough of a break in the weather to get a plane in. Of course they needed more supplies as well. This many people went through a ton of food, even when being conservative.

She settled back down again, waiting for the coffee to

arrive. When a knock came on the door, followed by Magnus's voice, she wasn't at all surprised to find Mountain standing alongside Magnus, frowning at her. "Can we get a flight in today?" she asked.

"It looks like it, yes. We're waiting for Central to give us a report from their end."

"That would be wonderful," she beamed.

"How is he?" Mountain's gaze went to Terrance, still eerily lifeless on the bed.

"He's alive, but you know that I'm not equipped to treat him here," she murmured.

He nodded. "Nobody expected this to happen or for you to treat hypothermic patients up here."

"No, they sure didn't," she muttered. "But, if we can get him out, assuming this is a recoverable event for Terrance, he should have a chance."

At that, Magnus shot her a look.

She shrugged. "For all I know, something organic could be going on with him for a long time. There is no guarantee that what we see right now is a result of what happened to him here."

When they looked at her in surprise, she nodded. "The human body is wondrous, but, at some point in time, it does fail."

Mountain winced and nodded. "He's young, and he's fit though," he argued.

"And I've seen thirty-year-olds have heart attacks, and they were fit too," she said quietly, giving him a hard look. "Again, the human body is magical, but it's also a bitch."

"We're back to that … Mother Nature thing again."

She smiled. "If you want to look at it that way, yes."

"It's not that I want to," he muttered, "but it sure seems

to work that way."

Soon she was given a forty-minute warning that her patient was being picked up and to ready him for travel. After seeing him safely loaded, she breathed a heavy sigh of relief as she entered the base again, her lungs still recovering from the shock of the cold air. But the sky was bright blue, and that, along with her patient on his way to the hospital, made for a better morning. She looked up to catch Magnus watching her. She smiled. "Now at least he has a fighting chance."

He nodded slowly. "You're really relieved, aren't you?"

"Absolutely," she murmured. "I can stabilize him here, provide supportive care, and monitor for trouble, but I cannot bring a man back from the brink like that, not without more advanced equipment and diagnostics."

He nodded. "How about a late breakfast?"

She looked down at her watch and groaned. "I did miss breakfast, didn't I?"

"Yep, but they know, and I heard some food is left."

"Let's go take a look then." She felt immense relief inside. With any luck her patient would get to his destination quickly, and they could start running tests.

She downed her breakfast, not even sure what she was eating. She was giddy with relief that she'd had the chance to transport her patient. Thankfully the poor dead Russian's body was also airlifted stateside. Still it was a reset to her day. When she got back into her clinic, several people waited to see her.

They had probably been waiting until her patient was dealt with. She put on a bright smile and got to work. Magnus stood outside her door throughout part of the day. Occasionally she caught an odd look on his face as if he wondered at the steady stream of patients coming in to see her. He was the type to never see a doctor unless he was badly injured. And she'd met many like him but these circumstances changed the regular habits for many people and if nothing else, knowing that she was there willing to see and hear them made all the difference.

When she caught a break, he poked his head around the door, glanced at her, and asked, "Do you get five minutes to catch your breath now?"

"Maybe, if nobody else is out there." She brushed the hair off her face.

"Is it always like this?"

"No, not always, but sometimes, in situations of calamity, people come in because they're feeling uncertain. Not a whole lot that I can do for them, outside of providing some reassurance that they aren't dying and that whatever they're feeling right now will pass and that they're not alone."

He smiled and nodded. "I guess it's more stress than anything, right?"

"It can be," she agreed, "but not always. I can't tell them to just suck it up. In most cases, they do, but then for some there's that breaking point," she pointed out firmly, "and I'd rather see several in order to find that one case, before anybody gets there."

MAGNUS AGREED WHOLEHEARTEDLY, but he was still surprised. Only thirty or thirty-five people were here on base, though he needed to do a headcount now because several more had come in on this last flight. He wasn't even sure whether any more of the Shadow Recon team had flown in or not. He could desperately use a few more men around here, if only to help them keep an eye on the doc, with her penchant for getting into trouble.

Later at dinnertime, he looked around to see a few strange faces. And a few others appeared to be gone.

When he walked up to get food, Chef saw him and came around closer to Magnus, from the back of the counter. "Things can't be that bad, as I see new people have arrived."

He nodded. "And we got the injured man out. And you have your cooler back."

"Thank God for that." Chef shook his head at the reminder of the body in the cooler. "I talked to Terrance a couple times, and he seemed perfectly normal."

"Normal? As in not some crazy dude who would go out and try to stay in a snow cave during one of the worst blizzards possible, for fun?" Magnus quipped.

"Exactly. And that makes me sound like an idiot for saying something now."

"If he ever sounded off in any way, I really do need to hear about it."

Chef looked at him with a piercing gaze and then nodded. "I wondered if you were part of it."

"Part of what?"

He smiled. "I know you can't talk anyway."

"Good, so in that case, what did he have to say?"

"He always seemed to be a friendly guy, the kind who wanted to be bigger, better. He thought the winter here wasn't a big deal. I warned him about that attitude because it can get you in trouble real fast."

"It sure can," Magnus agreed. "So, do you think he would go out solo and stay in the snow cave on his own, just to prove that he could?"

"Oh, sure, he'd do it on a dare. He'd do it for five bucks.

He'd do it because it was fun. I don't think he'd stay out there though." He took a deep breath. "That's the difference."

"Ah, good point," Magnus muttered. "Very good point."

"He would have come home if he could have."

"So, what are the chances that he was involved with somebody else on this, and they took off and left him? Maybe he got ill and couldn't get himself home."

Chef nodded. "I've given some thought to something such as that, but you didn't hear it from me." And, with that, he headed into the back of the kitchen to continue his work.

But Chef had given Magnus something to think about, and, as he headed back to the clinic, he looked in on Sydney, sitting there doing paperwork.

She smiled. "There's a completely different atmosphere to the place right now."

"There is, but also new people came in, and I think just seeing new faces makes the ones here feel as if maybe there's no problem."

"That's a good thing then," she said, with a tentative smile.

He agreed, but, at the same time, it was also daft to bring in new people if there were any problems because that just meant having to sort out who was here and who wasn't. Better to stick with the same crew, so they had the exact same set of suspects. Now the suspect pool had widened, and, for all he knew, the guys who had been involved in this nightmare had gotten a flight to freedom.

DAY 7, DINNERTIME

WITH HER PATIENT safely airlifted earlier this morning, the rest of her day was a breeze, although busy. It felt as if a whole lot of pressure had been released from the base. People were more relaxed. Everything was easier, and dinnertime was full of laughter and jokes. She smiled as she walked in to see Chef looking at her.

He grinned. "Seems you got yourself a little bit of time off now, *huh*?"

"You wouldn't know it, if you'd seen my clinic today. Steady traffic all day." He looked at her with raised eyebrows. She shrugged. "It just goes with the whole atmosphere thing."

He nodded. "Don't take it personally, but I would have to be nearly dead to find me in your clinic."

She grinned. "You and a lot of other guys."

"So, shall I assume it's mostly just the women coming to see you?"

She laughed, shaking her head. "You could, but you'd be very wrong. It always amazes me that the antidoctor crowd just assumes that all men are that way as well, and it's just not so."

"Interesting," he murmured. "As long as I don't have to come in, it's all good."

In a matter of moments she had dinner on her tray.

When she turned around to find a place to sit, several people called out to offer her spots. Smiling, she replied, "While I appreciate all the invitations, I admit to being on the tired side."

She opted to choose a spot off on her own. Several catcalls rang out, calling her a spoilsport. She just lifted a hand in acknowledgment but didn't say anything, since it was all good-natured banter. This was a whole different story compared to how it had been with the rude Russian. When things went out of the realm of fun, then it became ugly and troublesome. As she sat down and started eating, she looked up to see a shadow looming over her. … Magnus.

He set his tray gently beside hers. "Don't even try telling me that you're fine and that I can go sit somewhere else," he stated, with a smile, "because it won't work."

"Okay, in that case, why bother." She continued to eat the meatloaf she was working on.

"How is it?"

"Quite good actually. I know we got some new supplies in, so that will give us some more interesting menu options over the next few days, but today we're still using up leftovers."

"I get that, I really do, but it will be nice to have something fresh." He pointed to the green salad in front of her.

"I grabbed that, desperately in need of some greens," she admitted.

"I didn't even notice a salad when I was up there."

"You ought to go get some because it won't last long, and that will be it, until the next shipment."

At that, he got up immediately, walked up and grabbed a bowl, before coming back.

She smiled. "I'm glad to see you're smart enough to listen to good advice."

"Of course. Plus I've been in similar situations before, but you tend to forget. Greens are an essential part of a good diet, only you may not realize it, until you go without."

"They are, indeed."

They sat together, enjoying a quiet peacefulness. When a few other people stopped by and sat down at their table, she just smiled and welcomed them. Pretty soon they had a good dozen sitting there. Magnus looked over at her and whispered, "You're pretty popular around here."

"Or maybe they're just happy I didn't die," she muttered.

Several of them wanted to hear the story firsthand, but she was adamant that she didn't want to rehash the details. "It was bad enough the first time around," she joked. Most of them were good with that, but a couple wanted a little more.

Finally Magnus just looked at them and said, "No."

Instantly an awkward silence surrounded the table.

She laughed. "Since being attacked under his watch, Magnus now considers himself my bodyguard. So you'll take that into consideration, won't you?"

Several of the others laughed, but two of the men looked at him and glared.

"And, yes, I'm totally okay with it," she added, with a firm smile in their direction.

They relaxed a bit, but one of the men sniggered. "You know, if that job had been posted, a lot of us would have signed up."

"Maybe so." She smiled gently. "But I'm good with it this way."

That was as much as she would give them, and it would

have been more than enough in any situation she'd encountered before, but she just wasn't sure that people were into listening right now.

Refusing to let the change in atmosphere get to her, after being so happy about the freedom she'd experienced earlier, she finished her meal and stood. "I'll take my coffee with me and see if I can get caught up on some paperwork." And, with that, she said her goodbyes. With a final wave, she made her escape. She wasn't at all surprised when Magnus came along behind her. "You didn't have to leave. It might do you some good to socialize with them a bit."

He rolled his eyes. "Are you kidding? Those guys are trying to figure out how I ended up on doctor duty," he replied, with a smile. "I wasn't about to hang around and be grilled with questions. Or the challenge behind them."

"Hey, they've been cooped up with nothing better to do. Remember?"

"I know, and I'm trying to take that into consideration, but even I have my limits."

She chuckled. "Yes, and I understand. But, by and large, break-ins and various attacks aside, I've found everybody here to be really friendly and open. Most of them speak excellent English, and some are learning to, while they're here. I even heard some lessons going on the other day."

He nodded. "I've heard a little bit of that as well. I know the Swiss team seems to do pretty well."

"And two Italians are here." She looked over at him. "Did you know that?'

He shook his head. "No, I didn't. Any intel on what nationalities recently arrived?"

"I haven't got the files yet. Hopefully I get them before anybody gets sick."

"Is anybody sick yet?"

"Nope, and I want to keep it that way. We really don't want something to run through this place now, though it's always a risk when new people come in."

"I know. The scientists said that they had that problem one year. A new guy came in, and his stomach bug symptoms started a couple days later. That just set off everybody, and it cycled through a couple times before it was over."

She shook her head. "Sounds as if it was pretty rough."

"I can't imagine."

She nodded. "Just think about everybody being sick. Everybody running for the toilet, or everybody running at the sight and smell of food." She chuckled.

"Yeah, that didn't sound like anything I want to be part of." He grinned.

As they unlocked the clinic door and walked in, she froze. "Not again," she groaned.

She pointed out the cabinet, and this time around it was smashed, with medications all over the floor.

HOLDING HER BACK, he quickly took photos, then sent them to Mason and Mountain. "Seems not everything is resolved."

"You know, for just a moment there, I'd forgotten about all the other headaches we're dealing with," she murmured.

"This is a good reminder." He pointed to the cabinets. "We can't ever forget."

She groaned, then nodded and walked over. Grabbing a pair of gloves, she started picking up big pieces of glass.

"Hang on a minute. Let me get a broom."

And together they cleaned up the mess. Then, with her inventory list in hand, she started an account on the medications. When she was finished, she frowned. "What the hell is going on here?" When Magnus raised an eyebrow, she added, "It doesn't seem anything's missing." When he stared at her with a frown, she nodded miserably.

"I don't know what to say," Magnus replied.

She frowned, as she looked down at the list in front of her. "But it might explain why there's such a mess."

He looked at her and understood what she meant. "You mean, they expected something to be here that wasn't?"

She nodded. "Exactly." She sighed. "And that's something that I'll have to settle myself."

He shook his head. "I don't know what you mean."

Just then Joy walked in, took one look, and gasped.

"Yeah," Sydney said, "not much fun right now."

"See? This is why I've asked to leave," Joy cried out, her eyes wide.

"Leaving is one thing, but creating a huge mess and now trying to get out of it by leaving is not such a good idea." Sydney stared at Joy. Magnus stared at Sydney.

Joy stared at her in shock, then her bottom lip started to tremble. Almost immediately Magnus's gaze went from one to the other and snapped, "You want to explain?"

"No, she doesn't," Joy cried out.

"And yet you know I have to," Sydney stared directly at her nurse.

It didn't take him long before Magnus understood. "Are you the one doing this?"

"No, of course not," Joy said in horror.

He waited, his mind shifting through options. "But you did tell somebody about the medication."

She bit her bottom lip, then nodded, and it all clicked for Magnus. She muttered, "I didn't realize this would happen."

"What do you mean?" Sydney asked, as she glared at her assistant. "You're a nurse. You know what it's like to manage medications in a place such as this. You know how dangerous it is, yet you were still telling people?"

"Just that there had been some break-ins and that some of the drugs were still here," she said, "although I presume they're not now."

"Oh, they're still here," Sydney said slowly, "because I moved them."

"You moved them?" Magnus asked, turning to look at her.

She nodded. "I had my suspicions." She kept her gaze on Joy.

Joy looked at her in shock. "No, no, no, no, no, I didn't break in and steal them."

"No, you didn't have to. You got somebody to do it for you. Somebody who is also vulnerable."

Joy stared back at Sydney, panic on her face. "Please, you can't say anything."

"I can," Magnus growled, his voice hard and angry. "What the hell have you been up to?"

She raised both hands, palms up. "I really like a guy, but he only wants me because of access."

"Of course." Magnus stared at her in disgust. "So you've been feeding him the idea that you could get what he was after, … so he would stay with you?"

She looked over at him, distraught. "You don't know what that's like."

"No, you're right," he said in disgust. "I don't. That is

not a normal healthy relationship."

Once again, her bottom lip bubbled up, and, in shock, he watched as Sydney gave the woman a hug.

"Now you need to tell us everything," Sydney murmured, "because there's been more than enough of this trouble. I need these drugs, and today we didn't have anything go missing, but that just means he will come back again. So you need to tell me exactly who it is," she stated.

"Was that why I wasn't allowed to go on that flight?" she practically screamed. "I asked to, and they told me that I could. But then they wouldn't let me on."

"You could have, yes." Sydney looked over at Magnus, then back to Joy. "However, I stopped it."

At that, Magnus looked at her with respect, while Joy looked at her, horrified.

Sydney nodded. "I've long suspected you, certainly after the last two attempts. What I didn't want was you getting off free as a bird, leaving me to never find out what this was all about. So, if you tell me that it's all about a guy, I will get seriously pissed."

At that, Joy broke down and started bawling.

DAY 7, AFTER DINNER

SYDNEY LOOKED OVER at Magnus. "I told Joy that we had a large amount of painkillers on hand," she said quietly. "I was suspecting that the information would filter out."

He nodded and studied the sobbing nurse. "She took one hell of a chance in this camp."

"Which is also why she was getting cold feet and desperate to get out," Sydney murmured. "On top of that, I'm pretty sure her boyfriend ditched her because the access was being denied."

At that, Joy sobbed even louder. "My God, what have I done?"

"Aiding and abetting in the distribution of drugs for starters," Magnus said. He picked up his phone and texted Mountain again. Within minutes, the door opened and slammed shut, with a little more force than necessary.

Sydney glared at Mountain for that, but the big man just glared right back. She shrugged. "Okay, I get it. You think I should have told you a little earlier."

"Yeah, it would have been nice."

"Maybe, but I had to be certain, and now I am." She motioned to her nurse in the room.

"She could have flown out today," Mountain stated. "What were you thinking, withholding that information?"

"She would have, but I stopped it. She needs to tell us all about it. Especially who her boyfriend is," she pointed out. "I wasn't prepared for my dispensary to be caught up in this mess, especially making it look as if I was involved somehow, because I'm not."

"Of course not."

"But you've surely had the thought," Sydney challenged Mountain.

Looking a bit abashed but understanding where she was coming from, Mountain turned to focus on the sobbing woman. "So now you'll give us a full accounting."

Joy nodded, still crying, but finally managed to calm down enough to explain. One of the men off the American team was sweet on her. The men winced, hating to hear that of course. When her boyfriend realized she had access to the medications, he told her about the pain in his back—not wanting anyone to know because it would prevent him from going on missions, and he'd be put on medical leave or disability or something. He wouldn't be able to do what he loved. To avoid all that, he needed the drugs.

"So I just, … I didn't think anything of it. I didn't think it was bad. That's what they're here for, right?"

At that, Sydney groaned silently. Was she really that behind with the goings-on in her own clinic? "The drugs are here, and yet they aren't, as you well know," she snapped, fire in her tone. "They're not here for you to hand out to these guys at will. He could have come to me, and I would have monitored his progress. Real addiction issues can be here, as you know too."

Joy nodded. "I think that's an issue for him," she muttered. "Because, no matter how much he got, he just kept demanding more and more."

"So you were giving them to him on the sly?"

She nodded, shamefaced. "I was, but I didn't really set off with that in mind," she whispered, rubbing her nose on her sleeves. "Somehow it just became what I did, and then he just wouldn't, … he wouldn't stop. It was never enough. Then things started happening at the clinic. I didn't know if he was involved. After you were kidnapped, I realized I was in something I couldn't get out of, and that's when I requested a transfer."

"So it really had nothing to do with the murders or anything else," Sydney stated, looking at her nurse closely. "You were running to save your skin."

"No, no, of course not." Then she gasped. "You don't think I had anything to do with that, do you?"

Joy appeared horrified, yet from the look on the men's faces, they weren't so sure about Joy, and honestly neither was Sydney. "The problem is, once you cross that line, it all becomes a slippery slope. We can't be sure where you stand, or if there's a line you won't cross." That was the sad truth. "And right now, having crossed this one, maybe this buddy of yours was found out by the Russian group. Maybe somebody bugged him about it, wanting more details. Maybe somebody wanted in on it. Maybe somebody wanted some drugs for themselves."

Sydney stared at the woman in front of her, not recognizing her. "I don't know what all you've done and how far you've gone in this," Sydney stated, with flint in her tone, "so, from my perspective, I can't trust anything you say."

At that, Mountain told Joy to grab her things because she was going with him. She started to scream in protest, but Sydney stepped forward, grabbed her by the shoulders, and declared in a very clear voice, "Stop it, unless you want to alert everybody in this compound to what you've done. Just go quietly, and he'll treat you with respect. But do not at any point in time think that you'll get any special deal now."

"I made a mistake."

"A pretty big one, as mistakes go. It's over, Joy. Your nursing career, military service, all of it. It's over. You would do well to accept that and to move on because, if you make a ruckus, there will be hell to pay."

HEAVY AT HEART, Magnus walked away from where Joy was being guarded, until the next flight out. She would go straight to the brass for questioning and for disciplinary action. Not his problem, but it was the look of defeat on Sydney's face that got to him. He walked into the dining area, only to be immediately waylaid by Ted, the head investigator, who asked in a harsh voice what the hell was going on.

With a glance around, noting they were attracting unwanted attention, Magnus replied, "Grab a coffee and let's have a private conversation."

Ted shot him a look but acknowledged that this wasn't the time or place and picked up a coffee for himself, and the two of them headed back to the small space Ted was using for an office. When they got in and sat down, Magnus quickly explained what had happened with Joy.

Ted stared at him in shock. "Seriously?"

He nodded. "Yes, seriously. But she still wouldn't tell us who she gave the drugs to. Just one of the American team."

At that, Ted's gaze narrowed. "I want to talk to her."

"That's fine. She's being held under guard in the supply

room."

He snorted at that. "A hell of a place to put somebody who has been stealing supplies." He gave half a nod to that point. "Very quickly, word about what happened will be all over the camp, so it's likely that whoever she had been providing with drugs will be revealed pretty soon."

"That a good thing though," Magnus said. "When you think about it, she's potentially in danger. I don't want anything to happen to her before she's shipped stateside."

Ted snorted. "Yeah, that's all she needs, right?"

"The brass won't go easy on her, when back in the States," Magnus replied quietly, "but that's not our problem. What we need to sort out is who she gave the drugs to and if they had anything to do with the other crimes."

"That would be nice to know." Ted looked up as Jerry walked in, frowning at them both.

"You want to clue me in on whatever is going on here?" he bit off.

Magnus nodded. "We weren't trying to keep you out. It's all just gone down, and I'm providing a time-sensitive report," he added calmly.

That seemed to appease Jerry somewhat, but he still scowled at Ted, as if they already had issues between them. Not that it was a good thing because, in a situation such as this, already way too much was going on. Magnus went back over the most recent intel, as Jerry stared at him in astonishment.

"She was giving drugs to her boyfriend?"

He nodded. "And the problem is, she won't tell us his name."

"Sure, but somebody in the compound knows who it is. It's not as if you can hide a relationship here," he snorted, looking over at Magnus. "Everybody's pretty sure you and the doctor are an item."

"The doctor and I are friends," he agreed, "and I'm certainly keeping an eye on her, but I wouldn't say we are an item."

"So, the Russian basically set that up?"

"Got his ass kicked for it too," Ted pointed out.

Magnus looked at him. "Do you really think that was the issue?"

Ted just shrugged. "It's not something that we can ignore, since it happened right afterward."

Magnus contemplated that and then agreed. "I certainly didn't kill him, but I can see how that could become an issue."

"And are you telling us there's nothing between you two?" Jerry pushed.

Ted looked at him and asked, "Is that relevant?"

Jerry shrugged. "I'm not sure if it is or not, but it seems as if everybody is involved in some subterfuge around here. So, yeah, all of this is relevant."

"Okay, well, we are not currently an 'item,' as you called it, though I do happen to really like her," he admitted, calmly staring at Ted, Magnus's gaze narrowing as he looked at the other man. "But I hardly think it's the time or place for something such as that right now. We both have jobs to do."

"I don't know. If it's a case of jealousy, and somebody is after her, anything you do makes you look suspicious." Ted tilted the corner of his lips in a sneer.

"Now hang on a minute." Jerry raised his hand. "That's not fair."

"Maybe not, but we can't ignore it either," Ted said in a

cool tone.

Not exactly sure where he was going with this, Magnus studied him and added, "And yet, if you're looking for somebody, that's a good way to do it, isn't it?"

"Meaning?"

"Meaning, you're looking for a scapegoat. I seem to be a good candidate, according to you."

"You didn't even try to be a bad one," he said in exasperation. "You glommed onto the doctor pretty-damn fast."

Of course Magnus had very specific reasons for that, but he wouldn't go into that with Ted. He didn't like his line of thought or that the doctor was about to be dragged into this more than was necessary.

"I think the doctor herself could be part of this"—Ted nodded—"but since you are obviously involved in the investigation, you can do your thing."

Disgusted, Magnus got up at that point, turned to look at Jerry. "I'll talk to you later." Then he walked out.

He heard the two men arguing behind him, but Magnus was just fed up enough that he didn't want to listen to any of it, so he headed to the dining area to get coffee and to see if anything could bolster Sydney's mood after what she just had to do with Joy.

As he walked to the buffet line, Chef looked up. "Hey, I was just making cinnamon buns for breakfast tomorrow, if you want one."

He nodded. "I wasn't expecting that, but I would definitely say yes, please."

As Chef brought the tray over, he lowered his voice. "An awful lot of rumors flying."

Grim, Magnus nodded and quietly replied, "The rumors are likely to get a whole lot worse in the next little bit."

"Did you catch somebody?"

"We caught somebody doing something. It's just not what we were looking for or what we expected."

At that, Chef groaned. "And that's a problem because it detracts from the real investigation. Yet, at the same time, you can't ignore it if it's a major violation."

He wasn't fishing, and that was a good thing because Magnus wasn't in any position to say anything. As he picked up two cinnamon buns and two coffees, he put them all on a tray. "I know this will probably cause more gossip, but I'm taking these back to the doc. She's had a pretty rough day."

Chef nodded. "I'm a little worried about her," he admitted. "It's complicated enough with men and women working together in these scenarios, but, when the women end up being targets, that's when it gets really ugly."

"I hear you." Magnus really liked the older man and was hoping that Elijah really was exactly as he seemed. "Listen. If you see anything troublesome, you know who to talk to." And, with that, he started to walk out.

As he suspected, even his tray caused sidelong looks and some smirks, but he ignored them and headed on to the medical clinic. There, he tapped the door with his foot and called out, "Sydney, it's me." When the door was unlocked, and she opened it to let him in, he was more than a little relieved.

She saw the look on his face and smiled. "Yes, I'm still here, and I'm fine."

"I'm sure glad to hear that. It will take a while for my stress levels to drop after the last time."

"I hear you," she murmured quietly. She took a look at the tray he carried with interest. "Food therapy?"

"Hey, why not? If you don't need it, I certainly do."

"I could eat," she admitted. "It's either that or let all that stomach acid roll around in my gut and create an ulcer."

He commiserated, knowing exactly what that felt like. "Grab a cup then, and we can relax for a bit."

As she picked up a cinnamon bun and inspected it, she asked gingerly, "What about Joy?"

"She's being held in the supply room."

She groaned. "Great, so of course everybody knows that by now."

"Not yet, but they will soon enough when somebody goes down there."

"They got her in there without anybody knowing?" she asked.

He shrugged. "No idea. Not my assignment, not my problem."

"Got it. Unfortunately though, when something such as this happens, it becomes a problem for us all, and that makes it tough. I still can't believe she was stealing the drugs."

"I can't believe she was thinking no harm was done," he declared in a caustic tone.

She winced. "Yeah, I'm with you there. It's obvious that not only do we need the medication for anybody here but that her boyfriend has a serious problem. If he didn't have an addiction problem himself, it's even worse if he's selling it—especially if he's selling it to somebody with a potential problem up here. Nobody is allowed recreational drugs or pharmaceuticals, nobody who hasn't passed inspection."

She took a sip of her coffee and added, "I have access to medical records for people who do have to take medication, so really there's no other excuse. They can come to me. On the other hand, it is nice to have an idea as to what's been going on, but I'm still curious as to why the dispensary was broken into, if she was delivering what he wanted."

"I was wondering about that myself." He looked over at the medicine cabinet. "What are the chances that she wasn't giving him enough, and, once he knew where it was and had her key—well, he made another key or knew how to pick the lock—nothing could stop him from coming to get whatever he wanted, particularly if she had started to say no."

"According to her, she was trying to cut him off, once she realized he had a problem."

"Too bad she didn't understand that all of this was a problem."

"Yep, you and me both," she muttered.

A knock came at the door, and it opened peremptorily. The colonel walked in, took one look at the two of them, and frowned. Magnus immediately frowned right back. The colonel barked, "I want a firsthand recount of what happened."

At that, she stood and gave him a simple explanation of what she knew.

His eyebrows shot up. Then he looked over at Magnus, who immediately agreed with her account.

Sydney added, "Currently Joy is under guard in the supply area."

He nodded. "Yes, I understand that one of our men has been put on guard duty," he said in a bitter tone. "She is American, is she not?"

At that, Magnus nodded. "Yes, she is part of the American team."

He swore. "Talk about giving our side a bad rep. So far, it was just the Russians who had gotten into trouble, and now we have a murdered one to deal with, so the inquiries are stacking up pretty fast. They want to send out a Russian envoy to investigate the death of their man—well, actually investigate three Russians, the first who died of now suspicious acts, the one who shortly thereafter went missing during some recent war games, and now the out-of-line Russian who was murdered," he grumbled. "I can't say that I blame them because, if that had been any of ours, we would do the same. The only good news is, with the weather turning again tonight, nobody is flying anywhere right now, and that includes her." He looked at Sydney. "Do you have anybody else here that you can call on to be your new nurse?"

She nodded. "One other is on my list as a potential replacement, and I have worked with her a couple times since I've been here—such as when Joy was off shift, sleeping, or whatever. A couple times Joy just wasn't available, and maybe now I know why."

The colonel nodded. "Let me know if you need any extra personnel in here. Nurses are like doctors. You don't need one until you need a one, and then you need ten of them."

She smiled. "Let's hope we don't need any, and, if and when anybody does need our attention, we have exactly what they need."

At that, he turned and looked back at her. "I wasn't in favor of a female doctor."

She didn't say anything, just nodded, not sure where this was going.

"Generally it's not a good idea," the colonel added.

Sydney frowned. "Generally it's not a good idea to denote the sex of a worker, no matter what. It doesn't matter that I'm female *and* the doctor," she added quietly, "just that I'm a doctor."

"And in these situations you can see why," he snapped,

his voice hard, as he waved a hand toward the general population areas.

She nodded. "And, if you want to bring in a male doctor to replace me, I won't stop you, but I can't say I appreciate the idea that you assume a male would be better."

He frowned at that. "It wouldn't be better, but we'd have less trouble."

"I don't think that's true." Magnus straightened immediately. "I think it's more important for everybody to know she's off-limits, and that should stop it."

The colonel contemplated that, then his assessing gaze turned to Magnus. "Presumably she is off-limits."

He grinned. "Oh, I would think so, but it's certainly not something the two of us have discussed."

"Maybe it's time, and then we'll send out an informal alert," he said, cracking a smile for the first time at Sydney, and, with that, he was gone.

DAY 7, EVENING

"DID YOU AND the colonel just discuss me being off-limits because of you, as in you had first dibs?" Sydney asked in astonishment.

Magnus winced. "It was crude, and it was very wrong of us, but, given the circumstances, it did appear to be a potential answer."

She just blinked at him.

"Unless you don't want anybody to get the wrong impression."

"They already have the wrong impression," she said, almost absentmindedly, as if processing what had just happened still stunned her. "I hadn't considered that I would be treated in such a way."

"And you are fully welcome to lodge a complaint," he said formally. "However, considering the circumstances we're in, it did seem to be a good idea in order to ensure nobody would try and come after you again."

"Oh, I don't have a problem with nobody coming back after me again. The offhand way the two of you just discussed it is my problem, as if I weren't even in the room. And the presence of women on the team wouldn't matter at all if the men could keep it in their pants."

"Ouch. Point taken. Honestly all the colonel was doing was making the same comment many others have made."

At that, she put down her cup, turned, and looked at him in astonishment. "What the hell? … People are talking about us? Like that?"

"Yes, talking about us, watching us, whispering, and then some." His lips quirked. "Hence my suggestion."

"In that case, I guess it just makes sense that we allow them to continue in that mistaken belief." She glared at the relief on his face.

"Thank you." A half grin appeared on Magnus's face. "I can't say it's doing my ego much good to hear you analyze it quite that way, but … I'll live."

She smirked. "I don't think your ego needs any stroking. I'm a job. You're doing your best to keep me safe, and you've been doing that since the beginning. Believe me. *Being the little woman who needs the big man's help*, I appreciate it."

When he winced, she realized that wasn't quite what he was after either. She stared at him and added, "You know, if it were under different circumstances …"

He immediately pinned her with that gaze. "Yes?" he asked, waggling his eyebrows. "Different circumstances, meaning what?"

"If we were working under normal circumstances, and not out here in this frozen hellhole," she began, followed by a wave of her hand, "I might consider putting this relationship to the test." Then she laughed. "I mean, I never expected to find someone here that I like and certainly not someone that I really like—even though I am mad at you right now."

He beamed. "That is damn faint praise, but I'll take it," he replied immediately, "because I really like you too. It would be better to go home—either your country or mine, and figure this out in a more normal setting, go on a couple dates, and see if this has legs." He cranked up his smile. "So, in the meantime, we need to keep you safe."

"And you too," she added pointedly. "The last thing we want is anybody else dying, whether that's one of you guys or me. So let's try to keep everybody alive from here on in. How's that?"

"Sounds good to me," he agreed, with a smile. He got up and walked to the door. "Which also means that, regardless of what everybody thinks or believes, I will be sticking very close."

"Even now?" she asked quietly.

He nodded. "Especially now. We're still not sure who Joy's boyfriend is. I know that people have gone to interview her, but whether she spits out a name, I don't know. We'll have to interview everybody here as to who might have seen her with someone."

"*Great,*" she muttered. "That seems to be more stress for everybody."

"Exactly," he agreed, "and not something any of us want at all."

DAY 8, MORNING

WHEN SYDNEY WOKE the next morning, she felt a sense of sadness but also a sense of relief. At least part of this mess had been solved. The fact that Joy wasn't willing to talk about the person she had given the drugs to was very disconcerting. Sydney wanted to talk to her again and see if that would make a difference. However, if Joy hadn't done so in the first place, giving her a chance to think about it wouldn't likely make a difference. Sydney rolled over to see Magnus, sitting at her desk, working on his laptop. She sat up and frowned at him.

He looked up and smiled at her. "No need to be grumpy."

"I just keep forgetting that you're here."

"Ouch," he said in mock humor.

She grinned. "Of course, if you were delivering coffee on a regular basis, you'd be hard to forget."

He rolled his eyes. "Right, I'll have to hustle to keep my job here, is that it?"

"Nope, not at all." She chuckled. "Yet, at the same time, coffee would not be a bad thing."

"I'm on my way." He hopped to his feet. "At least this way you'll get a few minutes to wake up on your own."

"I need to make a trip to the latrine anyway."

He immediately sat down. "I'll wait."

"What? No armed escort?"

"Oh, believe me. I'm thinking about it." He looked up at her, frowning.

"But there haven't been any problems overnight, right?" she asked cautiously.

"Not that I know of. It appears all is well, at least so far."

"That's not as reassuring as it could be." She winced. "Somehow that makes it sound even worse."

"I know. I know," he said, with a wave of his hand. "But we would have been notified if something had gone on."

Knowing at least that much was correct, she hopped out of her bed, stood, stretched, and then grabbed her bag. She didn't want to shower right now. She wasn't even sure they had hot water available at this point, since it was heavily rationed when it was generated. However, she wouldn't be long in the latrine.

After she returned to the clinic, he looked up and smiled at her brightly. "Good, we didn't lose you in the meantime."

She rolled her eyes. "I was counting on not getting lost or beaten up again," she murmured.

"Believe me. That would suit me just fine too." He grinned. "But, if you want to stay here, I'll go grab coffee."

She nodded and settled back on her bed, as she contemplated the day ahead, wondering how much resistance she would face about talking to Joy again. When he returned with coffee, she asked him point-blank.

He looked at her and shrugged. "I don't see any reason why not. Maybe she'll talk to you, maybe not."

"That's what I'm wondering." She took a sip of her coffee, thinking of her options. "I doubt she'll tell us something useful, but we can always hope. I presume interviews are on track for today."

"They are, though some were started last night. Plus the colonel set up an interview system where everybody will be questioned, with certain people allowed to listen in on the proceedings."

"Right. Hopefully I don't have to deal with that. Except that I'll have a steady stream of people through here from the stress of it all." He frowned at her. She smiled and nodded. "Events such as this set off all kinds of unaddressed fears that people have ignored for the most part, until the stress ramps up, making true issues hard to ignore."

He didn't say anything, just nodded, and, as the day went on, her words came true, as she ended up with a steady stream of people coming through her clinic before noon.

To afford her patients some privacy, Magnus stepped out of the clinic and into the hallway, as needed. When he returned, he commented, "Every time I check here, it's busy."

"I know, but I did warn you."

"And I didn't believe you, so shame on me."

She laughed. "You'll learn."

He grinned. "I like the sound of that."

She flushed, rolled her eyes at him.

"Your request to talk to Joy has been approved, but you can't talk to her alone."

"Of course not." She sighed. "I mean, after all, I might be an accomplice, right?"

He winced and nodded. "Let's just say it's much better for you not to be alone with her, just in case."

"That's fine, but who will be with me?"

"I will. I'll record it." She stared at him in shock, and he shrugged. "Again, I believe it's to your benefit."

"Fine, I just wanted to talk to her, to see how she was.

We became friends over the last few weeks, and obviously I didn't know her all that well, but, at the same time, I wasn't really expecting all this …" She stopped. "It doesn't matter."

"It does matter because this is a friend of yours, who has now contaminated your clinic."

She winced at that. "Not exactly how I want to think of this."

"Maybe not, but you can bet that other people are."

"God," she whispered. "That's definitely not anything I want as a blight on my record."

"Exactly, so we'll go right after a late breakfast? Or before we eat?" he asked, with a raised eyebrow, as he looked at his watch.

She nodded. "Has she eaten?"

"Sure, we won't starve Joy to death."

DAY 8, LATE MORNING

SIDNEY DIDN'T SAY anything, and, by the time she was escorted to the kitchen, nearby where the supply area was located, Chef took one look at her and beamed. "Hey, how are you feeling?"

"I'm doing okay," she answered, with a smile. "Thanks for asking."

"Hey, in these places, you got to have each other's back," he muttered. He motioned at the room behind them as they walked past. "Unlike that one."

"Has she said anything to you at all?" Sydney asked him.

"Nope, I don't talk to her. She's got a guard full-time, and frankly I don't interact with him either. It's just better that I keep my nose clean and mind my own business in these situations. I mean, otherwise my tendency will be to offer her coffee and all kinds of stuff. What she has done is terrible, but, man, … she looks pretty rough."

"I get it," Sydney murmured. "Can't say I had a great night and morning myself."

He nodded in commiseration. "And what she does in your clinic throws you under the bus too."

She winced at that, but what could she say? Chef was just reiterating what everybody else would be saying too. When she walked into the back room, the guard stood and looked at her, then over to Magnus. They discussed something for a few minutes, while Sydney studied Joy, who was curled up, facing the wall, ignoring everything going on around her.

"Joy?" she asked in a low voice. Joy's shoulders jolted, so she wasn't sleeping. Joy was trying to block out the world. Sydney sat down on the bed beside her. "I came to talk to you."

"Go away," she snapped.

"I was hoping that, before things got any worse, you would prefer to talk to me than to some of the other people likely to be back and forth on a regular basis."

"They already are," Joy uttered in a muffled voice. She turned to look up at Sydney, her face puffy, red, covered with tear tracks. "I didn't even think about it." Joy was almost on the verge of tears again. "What's wrong with me that I didn't even think about it?"

"Because you wanted something bad enough that you could justify doing the wrong thing to make it happen," Sydney answered softly.

Joy sniffled, wiped her face on her sleeve, and sat up to lean against the short wall. "And yet it was wrong. So wrong. Just look what I have done to my life. This is all I ever wanted. All I wanted was to be a nurse, and I signed up to serve my country." She sniffled. "And then somehow along the line, I suddenly fell in love and instantly became an idiot."

At that, it was all Sydney could do to not wince and agree, since so many women did the same thing. She didn't want Joy to feel as if she were alone. However, at the same time, Sydney couldn't condone her nurse's actions in any way.

Joy looked at her. "Are you in trouble over this?"

She shrugged. "I don't know yet. I'm still here, but they don't seem too happy with me either. After all, it was my dispensary, my staff," she said quietly. "It was my responsibility, *is* my responsibility. So does it reflect badly on me? Yes, absolutely it does."

Joy sniffled several times. "I'm sorry," she pleaded, and the tears broke free again. "I didn't mean to make your life hell too. I was just trying to keep him happy."

"And yet you couldn't keep him happy, could you?"

She shook her head. "No, not at the end. He was getting …" She shrugged. "Demanding."

"Drugs are like that, as you well know."

"Yeah, they sure are. Suddenly you don't even know who they are anymore. The drugs are their priority over anything and anyone else."

"And that's part of the problem right now," she murmured. "Apparently you're not being very cooperative when it comes to telling people who you gave the drugs to."

She gave her a haunted look. "No, I'm not."

"And why is that?" she asked curiously.

She lowered her voice and whispered, "Because I'm afraid of him. I mean, you say I'm under guard, but he leaves all the time. He goes to the washroom and leaves all the damn time to get coffee and food. If anybody wanted to do me harm, particularly considering all that is going on around this place right now," she noted, "I have no doubt that he would make it happen."

Sydney stared at her for a moment. "That's worrying."

"Yeah, you're not kidding," she snapped, then waved her hand. "No point in you even being here. People will just think that you had something to do with this."

"I would hope not to go through that again, but I was

hoping you would be willing to talk to me because it's upsetting everybody that they're all being hauled in and questioned."

"Everybody?" she asked, her eyes wide.

"Of course. We have to get to the bottom of who's been getting the drugs, and that means everybody, which is setting off the entire place."

Joy stared at her, wincing. "God, I really messed up, didn't I?"

Since that was something they had just gone over, Sydney didn't add to it by agreeing. "Now, was it only one person?"

"Yes, of course it was," she said, shocked.

"Hey, I don't know," she murmured. "For all I know, he was giving them to somebody else."

"I don't think so." She frowned, staring at a point behind Sydney's shoulder. "I don't think he would do that."

Of course he would do that, but it wasn't up to Sydney to reinforce that behavior. Anybody who would do whatever to get drugs had a plan, either for his own personal use or for somebody else's. "So, you're saying that you don't dare tell me who it is because you're afraid for your life. Is that it?"

Joy looked at her. "You don't believe me either, do you?"

At this complete change in Joy's demeanor, Sydney stared at her nurse. "It's not a case of me not believing you. It would help me to know who has a drug problem, who may attack me in my own clinic. Also it's a matter of needing to get to the bottom of it. We'll find out, but your cooperation would make it easier on everybody. Unless you really just hate everybody here and think they should all suffer anyway."

Joy flushed at that. "I don't hate anybody," she muttered, "but I can't say I'm particularly interested in turning him in."

"So now everybody is being questioned, about whether they slept with you, whether they had any relationship with you, whether they knew anything about the guys you were sleeping with, and we're, of course, making that investigation very thorough. Therefore, you can imagine better than anyone, I suppose, just how that is going."

Joy stared at her in shock.

Sydney shrugged. "What do you expect them to do? You won't tell, so it will come down to the data gained as these other thirty-odd people here are grilled," she snapped. "Every single one of them has to be questioned."

That appeared to be the wrong thing to say because almost immediately Joy started to bawl, rolling around and crying into her pillow. Waiting for her to calm down somewhat, Sydney went on. "This may seem awful and unfair to you, so you can stop some of that by telling us."

She shook her head. "You don't understand."

"No, I don't understand a nurse handing out drugs to her boyfriend, without going through the proper channels."

Joy raised her head and glared at her. "Sydney, do you even see everything that's going on around here? I mean, you're there in your nice, cushy little spot in the clinic," she stated, abruptly sitting up. "Do you see everything else that's going on? I mean, people are dying here. You really think I'll tell you anything and get killed myself?"

"And why would you telling me anything about your current boyfriend get you killed?" she asked, enunciating clearly and slowly to ensure there was absolutely no misunderstanding, knowing that Magnus stood behind her, listening.

Joy gave a half-laugh, half-cry. "God, you're so naïve. Don't you realize how much it's all connected? This place is tainted," she muttered. "I just want to go back stateside and get away from it all, and, if you don't get me out of here soon, I won't get away at all."

Magnus stepped in at that point. "If it's connected, then help us put a stop to it," he urged. "Making a substantive commitment by providing information could go a long way toward getting some compassion over your role in this whole mess."

Joy stared at him. "Yeah? And, if I do that, it'll just make it worse for me here. I mean, helping you after I'm gone, … that's a different story. However, while I'm here? … No way. That can't happen. I might have been stupid and a fool to wind up in the middle of this, but I still want to see tomorrow."

"Yet the person who could be helping us to detain your drug-addicted boyfriend, somebody who could be giving us information to put a stop to the attacks and the break-ins and the thefts, isn't cooperating." Sydney stared at Joy. "We will be doing our best regardless, but, if another person dies, … that's on you." Sydney spun around and left, Magnus joining her.

One of the things that Joy had mentioned was completely true. With everybody being questioned and scrutinized, they would all look at each other with suspicion, wondering who was involved, how deeply people—those they supposedly knew—might be involved, and who all had been friends with Joy. It was an unpleasant scenario to watch, as all the interpersonal relationships slowly cracked under the strain.

DAY 8, EARLY AFTERNOON

MAGNUS MENTIONED IT to Sydney later that day, and she nodded. "Yes, and I'm sure you'll see an awful lot more people asking to leave, even before their time is up," she murmured. "When something such as this happens, it all falls apart very quickly."

"And it sucks because it is one person's fault. If Joy had just said who it was, then we wouldn't have to waste time looking at everybody."

"And because we're looking at everybody," she added, with a groan, "they're all looking at each other. And there's no real way to get out of it, not until we find out who has been sleeping with her. Do we know for sure that whoever she's been sleeping with is the one she got the drugs for?"

He stopped, looked at her. "Wait. I thought that was the whole deal. If she had a sexual relationship with anybody else here, that will sure muddy the waters." He widened his stance. "I really don't want to think that somebody else is involved."

"Me neither, but I'm also not so foolish to assume that she couldn't have made this mistake more than once. And maybe that's why it got ugly."

Magnus tried to get his head wrapped around what Sydney just shared. "So are you saying that she could have been sleeping with two people?"

"I certainly think it's a possibility, but that's not what I'm bringing up. I'm just wondering if the drug thing got out of hand because another person got involved. Maybe she did it once for her boyfriend. Then he told somebody and so on. That would potentially widen our net and make it that much harder."

"Yeah, so you know, if we had any idea of people who were friends originally but are not now, we might have something to go on. But really, all we have now is everyone looking at each other sideways, trying to figure out what's happened and how bad it really is out there." He hated to think about how big this net might need to widen. "And that doesn't even address whether or not it had anything to do with the deaths," he added quietly. "Because, I hate to say it, that's a bigger issue."

They walked into the cafeteria, dished up dinner, and ate quietly. After dinner, they poured two coffees, then took their mugs and sat down in a corner. Magnus studied Sydney over the rim of his cup. "What do you think about her belief that she's in danger?"

"I think she believes it, but, other than that, I'm not sure what to say," she replied quietly. "It's always a problem because it adds the element of fear, which becomes very irrational and overwhelming," she explained. "And, yes, I get it, and I understand where she's coming from, but I don't know that I believe her. She won't talk about it, … so we don't have anything else to go on, which is also concerning. If she is correct, it would also imply that she thinks somebody would have access to her here."

"I think, considering what's happened so far, everybody believes that access isn't exactly a hardship. They're supposed to be safe here," he said quietly, then tilted his head at her shrug. "I know, from your perspective, that probably sounds foolish." Just then his phone buzzed. He looked down at it and winced. "I have to go for a meeting."

"Let me know what happens."

He got up, hesitated, and looked around.

"I'm fine. I'll just stay here and see if I can visit with some people."

"Might not get too pleasant a reception," he warned.

"I haven't done anything. In fact, due to Joy's actions coloring me, they should be sympathetic to me."

"Or they'll believe that you're responsible." And, with that, he took off with some parting words. "If you go somewhere else, let me know where and when." And then he was gone.

WITH ONE LAST parting look in her direction, Magnus quickly raced to the meeting with Ted and Jerry.

As he walked in, they looked up. "Do you have anything new to offer?"

He shook his head. "No, so far, I'm not getting anything. You guys?"

They shook their heads. "No, we've got lines on a couple men she was sweet on, but we've talked to both of them, and they've denied it."

"But of course they would," Magnus pointed out.

"Absolutely. Too bad we can't do DNA testing."

"We could if the matters were severe enough."

Ted asked, "What would you suggest in the meantime?"

He hesitated and then said, "Her sheets."

Ted looked at him and then nodded. "That's not a bad

idea." He pondered it. "I mean, it might take a little while to get that testing done, but at least we would have some answers."

"She also made it very clear that, as far as she's concerned, talking to us puts her in mortal danger."

At that, Ted snorted. "But she would say that, wouldn't she?"

"She also made comments that the drug thefts would be related to the deaths too."

At that, Ted just stared at him.

Magnus pulled out the recording and prepared to play it for them. "And, yes, I have sent this to you both."

"I saw that. I just haven't had a chance to listen to it." Jerry stared at his cell phone. "I didn't really figure you'd get anything useful." He played the recording, and, as she started talking, Ted shook his head. "She doesn't say very much, does she?"

"Nope, she sure doesn't. Just enough to get herself out of trouble or at least make it sound as if she's getting herself out of trouble."

"And yet she can't, as we all know." Ted listened to the recording again, and he shook his head. "She sounds distraught, but I'm not sure *terrified* is the right word. She does request that she go stateside before she talks about this."

"Yeah, and that's probably just an excuse too," Jerry muttered. "The stupid bitch wants to ruin this for everybody."

Privately Magnus agreed, but these scenarios had been happening since time began, and Joy's lovers played a role as well, so it was hardly anything Magnus was prepared to sit here and single her out over. Would it be nice if it hadn't happened? Yes. Was it muddying waters that didn't need to be muddied? Yes. On the other hand, if Joy had cooperated, Magnus would have a whole lot more respect for her. If she'd spoken up in order to stop this travesty from continuing, Magnus may have defended her himself.

"How's the good doctor doing?" Ted asked, with a smirk.

"She's doing pretty well, considering. She doesn't like any inference that she might have been involved."

"But she very well might have been," Jerry said. "Did you even consider that?"

"For all of the two seconds it took for me to discard it," he murmured quietly, looking over at him. "Are you seriously thinking she is involved?"

"I have to, considering the circumstances we're in."

"What would she gain by it?" he asked curiously.

"I don't know. Why don't you tell me? You're the one who's close to her." And there again was that same sneer.

Then Magnus wondered, was Jerry jealous? "Hey, if you want to take over looking after her, let me know. It would free me up for other things."

"Like she'd let that happen." Jerry laughed. "No, that's fine. You keep your babysitting job, and I'll do the real work. But then, this is our case anyway, and you're just along for the ride." And, with that, he got up and walked out.

Magnus let out his breath slowly and noted Ted watching him closely. "Nice fella," Magnus quipped, pointing to the door that had just been slammed.

"Jerry's okay, and I've worked with him a lot. He does tend to feel strongly about certain things though."

"Apparently including the doctor in this case."

"I think he just doesn't want to let her off the hook too quickly."

"I don't think he wants to let her off the hook at all, but I also think Jerry's invested more emotions in this matter than are probably good for him."

Ted's eyebrows rose slowly as he contemplated that. "What are you thinking?"

"Obviously a component of jealousy is involved. I just don't know if it's dangerous enough to be a problem."

Ted winced. "How about we just don't go there right now? I've only ever known him to be fair, and I'll maintain that position for the duration of our investigation," he added in a cool tone. "If you do hear or see anything to the contrary, let me know." Then he put down his notes and faced Magnus fully. "In the meantime, we'll just forget you said that."

Magnus snorted. "In all investigations, it's important to keep an open mind, to make note of all facts, big and small." And, with that, he got up, and this time it was his turn to walk out.

As he walked into the medical clinic, he was surprised she wasn't here. However, since he had left her at the cafeteria, he headed that way quickly. Sure enough, she was sitting there, having tea, visiting with a group of other people. The moment he got there, the conversation died, like roses in fire.

She sighed. "My bodyguard is here."

"Is it that bad?" one of the other women asked, almost with a playful moan.

Sydney shrugged and the playfulness fell right off the other woman's face. Not only that, all of them looked around sideways, somber. Sydney added, "Nobody knows which way this will break right now, so it's more of a precaution than anything." And, with that, she smiled at him. "Ready to go, I gather?"

He nodded. "Unless you want to stay here and talk for a bit."

She shook her head. "Nope, you pretty well killed the conversation." She got up, and they veered off to the side.

"Was that conversation going anywhere?" he asked curiously.

"I don't know that it would, but it was definitely interesting. They were all talking about being questioned and how nobody really had any idea who Joy was going out with. They knew relationships were happening, but nobody was paying any attention."

"But that's not really normal either," he noted quietly. "When you think about it, somebody's always paying attention to everything."

She smiled. "And you could be right. I don't know. They're all wondering what they missed, and that's got them worried."

"Of course it does. Nothing quite like knowing you missed out on something that's led to such a mess."

"They also don't necessarily blame her. More to the point, it seems as if they feel she might have been manipulated." He stared at her in surprise, as she shrugged. "All I'm telling you is what the conversation was about."

"Good to know," he said, as he thought about it. "We don't want her being hated, but I want her to be safe. However, we need answers from her, and the only way she's prepared to give them is if she gets out of here first."

"Which I would be all for"—Sydney waved to the outside world—"except for the fact that nobody's going anywhere in this weather."

"They managed to get one flight in, so they'll be trying

to get another one in, as soon as the weather breaks. Not to mention we also need supplies. They'll be coming. It's just a matter of when."

DAY 8, LATE AFTERNOON

As they walked into the clinic, he closed the door behind them. “Take a look around. Is anything wrong, amiss, or out of place in some way?”

She hesitated, looked at him carefully. “Why?”

“Because we set a trap earlier.”

She walked over to the drug cabinet. “No, it doesn’t appear to be touched.”

He nodded. “I didn’t think he’d fall for it, but it was worth a try.”

“Why would he try at all, if, … if she’s already been caught. At this point in time, she’s the only one who’s guilty.”

He smiled at her. “That’s good thinking, but people do all kinds of things. So finding out that he’s lost his resource might make him a little more desperate to make one last score and to grab something more.”

“Maybe.” Thoughtfully she looked around. “What kind of trap did you set?”

He smiled. “The cameras and audio are constantly being checked, and, so far, there’s been nothing. I guess that means it won’t be an issue at all. But I’ll leave a little something extra in place, just in case.” He then put something on the edge of the door.

Something that would dislodge if the door was opened.

She frowned at that. "That's not a very reliable test. What if I had dislodged it?"

"Yet I set it up, and you hadn't been back yet, right?"

"No, I haven't been, and it was still there, correct?"

He nodded. "I'll set it up tomorrow morning as well. Are you ready to go to bed or …"

She nodded. "I am really tired. I think it's the rush of adrenaline finally leaving me. I'll make one last trip to the ladies' room, then get to bed." Even as she spoke, a yawn escaped her. With that, she gathered up her clothes and headed back out of the clinic doors again.

"I have apples and cheese and crackers, should you get hungry later," he offered.

She nodded, looked back at him, then the door. "Will you set up the door right now?"

"I might as well."

As she watched him, he left something small in place, maybe a hair or a very thin piece of wire. "And you'll leave it locked?" she asked questioningly.

"Oh, yes." He quickly nodded. "At this point, this door will be locked all the time."

She nodded. "And I suppose, if anybody takes anything now, it will look as if it's me, won't it?"

He smiled. "To a certain extent, yeah. If more drugs go missing, and we don't have a better explanation, then absolutely. Both of us will be under fire for that."

She winced. "*Great*, just what I want right now."

"That's one of the reasons why we're taking as many precautions as we are."

"I appreciate it. I really do." But she groaned. "At the moment it really sucks to be me."

He motioned at her. "Go on. Head on down the hallway. I'll be right behind you."

She hesitated, then nodded. "I'll see you in a few minutes." She walked toward the bathroom. She wasn't alone in there, since it had a group of stalls, with several others getting ready for bed, but the chatter stopped when she walked in. She smiled at them and said, "Good evening, ladies."

They stood silent, almost as if waiting for her to leave.

Sydney didn't say anything, just finished up and walked out, saying good night. A chorus of good nights followed her, but the words didn't sound natural or normal. It sounded as if they were all too glad to be rid of her, as if she were the enemy, one of those people who never quite belonged. Being singled out was nothing new. It was an awkward moment, but, as a doctor, Sidney was often considered to be on that side at times. So she should be used to it, but it still hurt.

She knew most of these people. They had all been in her clinic at least once, if not more the longer she had been here. She could put names to each and every one of them. Maybe they thought she didn't use that bathroom like everybody else, but why would they? She didn't know, but her arrival had most certainly surprised them.

As she headed to the clinic, there was no sign of Magnus. Presumably he'd gone to use the facilities as well, before getting ready for bed, although his nighttime routine was a whole lot different than hers. She stood outside the clinic door, waiting for him, wishing she could lay down, as her head was throbbing again.

That was something else everybody had forgotten about. Nobody thought about Sydney's own injuries and what she went through—or what she had been through after the series of break-ins, the assault by the Russian, the kidnapping, and the betrayal of trust by a nurse under her supervision.

No, they were only thinking about Joy and what Joy had done and whether Sydney herself was involved as well. That was something Sydney didn't appreciate at all, but she knew she wouldn't be rid of that speculation anytime soon. As she turned toward the door, she looked for the tiny wire, the little sign that he had left to verify that no one had entered. When she didn't see it, she stopped and wondered.

She stood here for a long moment. Several other people came by, looking at her questioningly, she just smiled and said she was waiting for somebody. At the knowing looks that crossed their faces, she sighed heavily.

When Magnus appeared, shaved and clean moments later, she whispered in a low voice, "Did you set up the door? It doesn't look as if you did."

He stepped forward, quickly glanced down the hallway, then checked. His face turned to stone. "Yeah, I sure did," he whispered. "How long have you been here?"

"A few minutes. Nobody's been in or out in that time."

He didn't say much, just looked around the hallway again. "I want you to stay here." And, with that, he stepped inside the clinic and closed the door on her.

She waited in the hallway, but presumed that, if somebody had already entered, they were likely gone by now. When Magnus opened up the door, he nodded. "Yeah, somebody was in here, but I'm not sure if they took anything."

"Well, that woke me up." She walked in, headed right to the medications, and checked. "Somebody's been grubbing around in here, but what they were looking for isn't here anyway."

"Meaning, you moved it again?" he asked.

She nodded. "I think I told you that before, and I did it even before we established that it was Joy, but I assumed it was still someone trying to score drugs," she muttered. "Don't know that it's the same one, but—"

"Damn suspicious. Good enough."

When he hesitated, she looked at him and said, "Go on."

"The problem with that is, … they picked the lock, which also means that they can come back in again."

She stared at him. "It's really disconcerting to think that somebody could do that."

He smiled. "The thing is, everybody here has the training and the skills to do that," he said apologetically. "We just don't expect one of us to break into clinics on our own bases, but the reality is, theft on the bases is rampant. We do our best, but …"

She nodded. "Still, you need to let somebody know, so text them, and maybe somebody will show up. I presume one of your cronies."

"Maybe." Then he quickly sent off a text.

She looked at him with one eyebrow raised, and, when Mountain strode in not much later, she smiled. "I wondered if you would be the one to come by."

He stared at her and looked over at Magnus. "How the hell is this continuing to happen? That's a brand-new lock. It's supposed to be much harder to pick."

"Doesn't take long though, does it? What about the digitals or the video camera we set up?"

"So the intruder already saw it, took out the battery, ruined whatever went on inside the camera, and dismantled it." Mountain turned and glared at Sydney.

She held up her hands. "Don't get angry at me. I've done everything you guys have asked."

He nodded. "You have, but somebody seems to think that you still have something that they want, … and they want it bad."

She snorted. "All they want is in the cabinets."

"Yet did they get it?" Mountain asked curiously, as he strode over to study the drugs.

"Nope, the ones stolen last time haven't been restocked, and I hid the others that I may need for people here."

At her use of the word *hid*, he turned and looked at her in surprise.

She shrugged. "Hey, I might need them, and I don't want anybody else coming in here and taking them."

"Where did you hide them?"

She immediately snapped her lips closed and glared at him. He stared at her in shock. "Seriously?"

She shrugged. "If you don't know, then nobody can know."

He groaned, then turned and looked at Magnus to find him grinning. "What are you smirking about?" he snapped at him.

"She does have a mind of her own." Magnus laughed. "Honestly I don't blame her. If nobody knows where they are, then she doesn't need to suspect everybody either."

"Yeah, well, it's hardly anything I'm likely to steal," Mountain muttered, glaring at her still.

"Yeah, maybe not, but this way, you also won't get in trouble."

"So what? You're trying to protect me now?" he asked in astonishment.

"I don't know who I'm trying to protect, honestly," she

snapped. "What I want is for people to stop trying to steal, and that seems to be a problem."

"It means we need a guard here all the time." Magnus looked over at Mountain, who shook his head. "I'll do relief, but I have a lot of other things to be doing too." He sent a warning look at him.

Magnus frowned, nodded. "That's true."

"We're stretched thin right now. So, keeping a guard on both Joy and the clinic would stretch us beyond thin."

"You could send Joy back here," Sydney suggested, "and that guard can keep eyes on both her and the clinic."

The two men considered it, and then Mountain nodded slowly. "That might work. Any chance you could get her to hand over some information?"

"I tried that." Sydney raised her hands in surrender. "And she shut me out both times, as you probably know already. She'll only talk if she's stateside and safe."

"It's that *safe* part that gets me," Mountain noted quietly. "Almost as if she firmly believes she's not."

"Oh, she firmly believes it, but I don't know how much of it is the hysteria of everything else that's gone on," Sydney said flatly.

"Right, and that is where I end up confused."

Just then a team member raced into the clinic. Larry, another of the British team. "We've got two men who didn't return from a snowshoe trip. We're sending out search parties."

"I'm in," Magnus said immediately. He looked at Sydney. "Mountain will stay with you long enough for Joy to be moved here, and then both of you stay put with the guard. I'll be back as soon as I can."

And, with that, he took off down the hallway, leaving

her staring after him.

"WELL, TOBY, THIS is a hell of a deal," Magnus told his favorite sled dog.

Toby barked in response. Magnus walked to the second dog Joe had given him for this skijoring trip. Normally, when skijoring, one dog pulled one man on skis, but, in this case, he had a backup in case of trouble. Beside Benji needed more training, and Toby was always ready to go. Magnus had spent a little time learning how this sport worked, and it amazed him at the speed and at the amount of ground they could cover.

Minutes later they were off. Magnus had a half pack with safety gear, flares for emergency, and a few rations for himself and the dogs, if need be. He was well dressed, providing nightfall temperatures didn't kick his butt. Communication devices were hit and miss out here—mostly miss. He'd been given a designated territory to search.

Four other teams were involved in this search, some on dog sleds and some on skis. Magnus was the only one alone. That was by choice. Mountain had okayed it. There'd be hell to pay if something happened to Magnus on Mountain's watch, but they both knew Magnus needed to see what was going on out here. This could be a simple case of equipment failure—and the team of two missing men were waiting for a rescue—or something worse. It could also just be that they couldn't maintain the grueling pace the two had originally set and were slower on the return than expected.

It didn't matter; these temperatures could be brutal, and rescue had to be fast to keep anyone else from dying. Not something anyone at the camp wanted.

Unless this was a case of foul play. And that was a whole different story.

The pace Toby set was incredible, and Magnus flowed behind him on skis on the packed snow, as they raced across the tundra. It was amazing, exhilarating, and almost mind-boggling that this combination of dog and man in such a way wasn't used more often. It was popular in the Nordic countries. Then they excelled at most winter activities, especially survival and travel.

He kept searching the surroundings, but, so far, he caught no sight of the two missing men. When Magnus had seen in the distance one of the other teams nearing his, he'd turned then and headed toward several of the small rises on his right. He kept moving forward, amazed at the speed. The search teams would have their full area covered in less than ten more minutes. Then the question would be, did Magnus go back or keep looking?

He made it to the closest rise and just over, when Toby started barking. The three of them picked up the pace. When Toby came to a stop, Magnus looked around. The sunlight went quickly. The chill had set in. For all their speed, he needed to turn around and head back before darkness fell. However, if there was any chance he could find the missing men, he would continue on. … The snow cave was close by. The one Terrance had been using. What were the chances these two missing men had gone there for refuge?

Skiing forward, at a much slower pace, he headed toward it. Sensing he was close, but almost impossible to locate in this light, he stopped and studied the terrain.

As he searched, Toby barked, followed by a yelp, and

another yelp—then pain exploded in his head, and he knew nothing more.

MASON LISTENED QUIETLY, as Mountain updated him.

"So, the nurse has been stealing drugs for her boyfriend? How is that a thing?"

"I know. Everybody was vetted before approval to arrive here. Everybody is supposed to be checked before coming up here, but it's not that unusual, even within our own country's missions. You know that." Mountain pinched the bridge of his nose.

"Oh, I know that all too well. So, that explains the break-ins at the clinic, but it doesn't explain the murder of the Russian, the man who was found and airlifted out, or the other missing people."

"No, the strangled Russian's name was Helsky, and apparently the Russian government wants a full investigation. Plus his two teammates are pretty belligerent about what happened to him, and the young man who was airlifted out alive was Terrance." Mountain hesitated. "He's still alive, the last I heard. Do you have an update for us on that?"

"No change in his condition at this point," Mason said quietly. "The young man is alive, tests are being done, but, so far, they haven't found out what's going on."

"Great, so no answers there either. We went over his ice cave thoroughly and found minimal tools or information. We've got the rest of the team here to deal with the thirty-three training members, not including the five of us."

"Five?" Mason asked sharply.

"Yes, five. … That would be Sydney, the doctor, plus

Magnus, myself, Ted, and Jerry."

"Do you consider Jerry to be in the clear, Mountain?" Mason asked.

"No." He snorted. "We also have the colonel, and we would think that one of those two is clear. That makes thirty-nine in total, counting the prisoner, Joy." Mountain hesitated. "I know it's a lot of work, but I'm wondering if Tesla's got a minute or two. We need histories on all these guys to see if there are any prior connections."

Mason whistled at that. "What kind of prior connections are you hoping for?"

"Animosity would be one thing, to give us a chance to figure out what they're doing and why. Such as, did somebody already meet this Russian in the past? Did somebody already meet Terrance in the past? Is any old animosity happening here? Then of course any drug history issues for someone here would be nice to confirm. The whole gamut. We're short on data. And now we're short on time too."

Mason snorted. "And Tesla is pregnant. Remember? Talk about short on time …"

MOUNTAIN HAD JUST finished his call when he was ordered to the colonel's office.

As he stepped inside, several other men were waiting, the atmosphere tense, the men angry, their faces stiff with disapproval.

"Magnus hasn't returned." There. The bald statement hung in the room.

"You sent him out alone," Joe accused Mountain. "He's still got two of my dogs."

"Right, he has Toby and Benji," Mountain confirmed absentmindedly, as he contemplated the news. Magnus was a bit of a lone ranger at the worst of times. He was well trained, beyond competent, and, best yet, he was no one's fool. If he hadn't returned, it was because he couldn't.

"The two missing men are back. They had sled issues. All the search parties are back, except for … Magnus."

Mountain swiveled and headed to the door.

"Where are you going?" the colonel snapped.

"After him."

"No, you're not." The colonel stood and leaned over the desk, so he saw Mountain around the others. "I'm ordering you to stay here. No one else is going out in the blizzard. We don't have any more resources to spare."

Mountain never faltered. He left and never looked back.

DAY 8, LATER AFTERNOON

When Joy showed up with the guard, Sydney looked at her in surprise and then smiled. “This should be much more comfortable.”

Joy looked at her steadily. “Was this your idea?”

“We’re short-staffed.” She shrugged. “The dispensary was broken into again.”

Joy paled, but she didn’t say anything. She walked over to a chair and sat down.

“Obviously you don’t get any access to computers or anything else,” Sydney stated firmly.

“Right, never let it be said that I get any privileges as a prisoner.”

“Nope, you sure don’t.” Sydney huffed and left it at that. She turned toward the guard. “And it’s up to you to ensure she behaves.”

“Not a problem,” he said cheerfully, with a nod.

Sydney got straight to work and then wondered if this was the best of ideas, in case she had patients come to see her. She didn’t keep regular business hours, working whenever she needed. Regardless, not a whole lot of privacy was available within her clinic. She frowned at that, but thankfully the prospect of patients kept her busy. Expecting to see Magnus on each hour that passed, she was disappointed to not have any sign of him. She went for dinner, made it back with something for Joy to eat, and still Sydney saw no sign of him. She sent him several texts and got no answer.

Finally she turned to the guard and asked, "Have you seen Magnus?"

At that, Joy snorted.

He looked at Sydney and shook his head. "Nope, I haven't gone looking though, and I won't either," he said, his tone firm.

"Right." She had Mountain's phone number, so she quickly sent off a text message, asking him.

When he showed up a few minutes later, he motioned at her. "I need to talk to you."

She stepped out into the hallway, and nobody was there, so he murmured, "No, I haven't heard from Magnus."

"As soon as he gets back, let me know, will you?"

"Yeah, I will." And then he was gone.

She stepped back into the clinic and noted a sense of hush in the room. She turned slowly and looked back and forth at the two of them. The guard was standing with his arms crossed, leaning against the wall. Suspicious, she knew something had gone on while she hadn't been here. She thrummed her fingers back and forth on her arm, as she considered her options.

The last thing she wanted was a guard here that might be potentially involved. Yet she didn't have any reason to judge him, except for the fact that whatever conversation had happened was being kept from her.

She walked over to the guard, looking too calm. "What was the conversation I interrupted?" she asked in a firm voice.

He looked at her, then his gaze slid over to Joy, and he shrugged. "She asked if she could do anything to get out of here faster."

She turned and looked at Joy, who glared at her. "Is this what you do when you're a prisoner? Instead of just cooperating, you try to finagle a way out?"

"You expect me to sit here and take whatever's coming my way?" She sneered. "I thought it was my right as a prisoner to try and fight it."

"You can defend yourself all you want," she snapped back. "But let's not forget that you're the one who was stealing drugs from here, a place where you had a position of trust. And right now the guard will be under question if you even talk to him again." She turned to look back at the guard. "Do you understand me?"

He flushed and nodded. "Yes, ma'am."

And, with that, she returned to her desk and worked to catch up on her reports and inventory, sending off as many emails as she could—including a request for a change in guard, as soon as possible, and yet as secretly as she could.

She sighed. She had to work fast, while there was a window of internet. The satellite worked sometimes but not a lot and not reliably. Her cell phone was often better, but much slower to type on, of course. She found that if she got them written at least, she could send them into the queue, ready to send when she had a moment of service.

And, with that done, she also sent off a message to Mason, saying that she hadn't heard from Magnus and was hoping everything was well. Of course with Mason stateside, he couldn't determine anything firsthand, but she felt as if something were wrong. She texted Mountain again. Didn't get an answer. Damn it. She paced her clinic, before sitting down on her bed.

When Mason phoned her a little later, he asked, "Can

you talk?"

She walked over to the guard. "I'll step out into the hallway."

The guard just nodded and opened the door.

She turned to look back at Joy, who just glared at her. When Sydney stepped out into the hallway, she kept the door open. In a low voice, she murmured, "I'm out in the hallway. What's up?"

"Magnus is missing. The other search and rescue teams, including the two missing men, have all returned. Magnus is past his time to return."

Her breath sucked into her chest, and, for a moment, she could hardly breathe. "Dear God," she whispered.

"I know. Compounding the issue is the colonel has suspended any further search for Magnus until morning," he noted in a collected tone. "However, Mountain has ignored that directive and has gone after him. I'm telling you first, so that you can be prepared for, … for when he finds him."

"I'm glad you said *when*," she whispered, her voice hoarse with worry.

"*When* is a given, but I don't have to tell you that the weather is still shitty up there."

"No, you don't. It's also lightened up somewhat, but nowhere near enough for somebody to not get lost."

"*Lost* is the least of my worries. You need to be on your guard and keep an eye on Joy. I don't know how much she's involved, or if any extraneous issues are going on there, but watch your back right now."

"Thanks for that."

She hung up and walked back inside, moving as silently as she could. Thankfully nothing seemed to be going on that she saw between the guard and Joy. But still, she was no longer comfortable around him. When the colonel showed up a little later, she stepped out into the hallway with him and quickly told him about the incident with the guard. She couldn't forget his directive to not search for Magnus, already hating him for it, no matter how logical it was to keep the others safe. Still he was running this compound and needed to be kept in the loop.

He looked in Joy's direction. "I guess that makes sense, if Joy's trying to weasel her way out of here somehow."

"Maybe, but it's left me feeling a little insecure. I don't know if she's working with someone."

"I'll switch him out," he confirmed immediately. "The last thing we want is more issues."

"Considering we're dealing with drugs as well, which may or may not be a surface issue, it can't hurt."

"Done." He stepped into the clinic, where the guard and Joy were at opposite ends. The colonel turned and looked at her, with a quick nod. She smiled, and he told the guard, "You are relieved. You can go get dinner."

The guard looked at him with relief, then quickly bolted. The colonel turned back to Joy. "Try a stunt like that again, and you'll be back in the storage locker."

She shrugged. "What makes you think I can't get to people there?"

"Good point, and you're certainly giving me some insight into your true character." He gave her a clipped nod. "Keep it up. We'll have everything we need to know pretty-damn soon anyway."

And, with that cryptic comment, he was gone.

Sydney walked over and slumped onto her office chair, then pinched the bridge of her nose. All she could think about was Magnus and the fact that he'd gone out on a mission to help somebody else and had been waylaid somehow. She quickly sent Mason a message, asking who else would have been with Magnus and who else would have known where he was going.

He responded. **He went with two dogs and survival gear. It could have been a setup. We don't know. Multiple parties were out there. He shouldn't have gone missing.** And, with that, he signed off.

Of course nobody knew anything because, if you were involved, you wouldn't tell anybody, would you? It was enough to make her fidgety. When she stepped out into the hallway, she almost jumped at the sight of another guard. However, this time, he remained outside. He introduced himself, and she looked up at him and smiled. "Hi. Are you here for the next few hours?"

He nodded and smiled at her. "You're fine here now, Doc. I promise."

"Thank you." She smiled, feeling better already. "I do have to warn you that Joy's tricky."

"I've been warned." He straightened and took his position beside the door.

As she walked back in, Joy stared at her. "Did you really get the other guard in trouble because I talked to him?"

"*You* got him into trouble, not me."

She rolled her shoulders. "God, you're such a bitch."

Sydney stiffened at that but didn't say anything. In the position that Joy was in, it was quite possible she would try all kinds of tactics to get herself into a better circumstance, but Sydney wouldn't listen to it. Joy had already betrayed Sydney's trust once; it wouldn't happen again.

MAGNUS WOKE TO the blowing wind all around him, snow piling up beside him, and yet the cold wasn't quite as bad as he had imagined. He shifted; something was up against him. He reached out a hand and noted one of the dogs was here. He checked him over, but his fingers came back sticky. He swore at that, then sat upright to find both dogs had been shot.

They were both moving and alive, which was even worse, but why the hell would anybody try to kill sled dogs out here? And then he groaned. *To stop Magnus from getting out of here alive himself.* And because he had two injured sled dogs, with no sled, just skis, it would be damn hard for him to carry both animals back to where they could all get help. Yet he was determined to do just that.

Benji had blood on one leg and was limping badly. The cold would set in pretty-damn fast in him though, especially if he were immobile. Toby had been shot along the rump, but it looked as if it had missed anything major. Both dogs looked at him and whined. They'd been well loved and well cared for, but they were also trained for battle, and right now they knew they'd been hit and were down. It was Magnus's job to try and fix it.

At the same time, he didn't know if he'd been shot himself, but his head was killing him. If he had been shot in the head, somebody was damn serious about stopping Magnus—or, at this point, more a case of leaving him and letting Mother Nature do the job. But, if Magnus wasn't shot, well, whoever that asshole was, he would rue the day he'd ever tried to hurt Toby, Benji, and him. Magnus stood up slowly, checking himself out. He was fine but damn cold.

He felt the chill starting to settle in, but, as he looked down at the dogs, he whispered, "It's all right, guys. I'll get you back. I promise."

He didn't know how the hell he would do that but thankfully, off to the side, was a sled. A broken sled. Set up for two dogs, instead of the normal four. Since Magnus has his two dogs, although both were shot, Magnus hoped that meant the two sled dogs that went with this broken sled may have been released. The shots that Toby and Benji sustained were not life threatening. Maybe the shooter couldn't kill the dogs—or Magnus.

As he looked over the dog's injuries again, Magnus decided there was a good chance the shooter had changed his mind and was an animal lover of some kind.

Maybe shooting these two dogs had been more than he could handle. Or the shooter wanted these dogs to die slow and hard, the bastard. Either way, Magnus was left with two injured dogs to get back to base, but he did have skis. And the nearby ice cave, … where Terrance had been.

He reached up to find matted blood on the side of his scalp, then swore. So, he had been shot from a distance, but hadn't even heard it, not with the wind out here, and the bastard had left the three of them for dead. Swearing at that, plus realizing where he was now, and knowing that his chances of getting back to the camp tonight were not great, Magnus wouldn't have the dogs pull him this time.

He realigned his skis toward the cave, noting that any tracks heading there were mostly covered in snow. Some were still visible, so he quickly followed them, for as long as they lasted, while he encouraged the dogs to keep up with him. Then he just kept pushing one ski in front of the other, sliding whenever he could push to slide, and moving as fast as possible to get to a shelter.

He headed for the snow cave, hoping to find somebody

there, but it was empty. If Magnus died here, he'd be the second person to be found at the cave, and that would look beyond odd too. His mind still considered the issues, figuring out what the hell went on with him and the dogs and why somebody would even pull such a stunt. The investigation was a big part of it, he was certain, but there had to be more to it than that.

As he stumbled inside the cave, bringing the dogs one at a time into the small space, he used the lower portion of his shirt to bind the leg wound on Benji, and for Toby? Well, that was a little rougher. Staying warm was the biggest issue, so he pulled them up close and held them against him, while the dogs wagged their tails and licked him.

"I know, pals. I know. Not exactly where we thought we'd spend the night."

But out here, and thankfully away from the cold and the wind, they could make it. He knew no way his communications would work, but surely somebody was out looking for him at this point in time. All he could think about was Sydney and what Magnus being stuck here could mean to her—because if somebody else was trying to hurt her again, this was a hell of a way to go about it. His heart told him that she had to be innocent. Yet no way, with all the investigations he was involved in, would anybody look at his death as anything other than suspicious.

With the cold temperatures, he drifted in and out of sleep, checking on the dogs, pulling them up close, hoping that morning would come and that the storm would abate, that maybe the temperature would even rise. If he were dreaming, he might as well dream bigger and better.

When he heard a shout in the distance, he shifted, and, slowly unwrapping from the dogs, he heard a commotion outside. Cupping his hands around his mouth, he shouted as loud as he could, and he heard excited voices. Then grabbed his pack and shot off a flare.

Next thing he knew, he was surrounded by other dogs, all yelping in joy. He quickly hugged them, thankful that a rescue was at hand. He looked up to see Mountain glaring down on him. Magnus smiled. "I'm pretty-damn glad to see your sorry face."

"What the hell happened?" Mountain asked. "Are you okay?"

He reached up a hand to his head. "I've been shot. Burned along the back of my head. Not sure what else. I've got two injured dogs in here, both with gunshot wounds," he whispered, his tone grim. "I don't think either wound will kill them, but this damn cold surely will."

With that, Mountain made an exclamation, came further inside the cave to check Magnus's wound, and then bent to take a look at the dogs. Lifting one of the dogs, Mountain took him over to his sled, then came back for the second. He reharnessed the six dogs he'd come out with, then helped Magnus up.

"I'm good. I'll be fine." Magnus rubbed his hands together to get them warm, to stir his circulation, as he stepped into the snow. He hated how wobbly his legs were. "I just need to get in out of this cold."

"Yeah. Believe me. I got a lot of guff about coming out as it is."

"I appreciate that. I would think we would have made it through the night, but …" And he left his voice hanging.

"Likely," Mountain agreed, "but I want to get you back now, and I want to get both of these dogs to Joe or Sydney, so they can look at them."

"Yeah, that would be my vote."

With the extra blankets Magnus had come out with, they bundled up the dogs and him, as all three got settled on the sled platform. Magnus was running down quickly. He didn't have anywhere near enough energy to make it all the way back on his own. He put his head down, realizing just how much this trip would zap his energy.

"I don't know who first sounded the alarm, but I can tell you that Sydney started getting uneasy pretty early on. She will be overjoyed to see you." Mountain chuckled. "You lucky dog, you."

"Yeah, maybe. A little early to tell."

Mountain punched Magnus lightly. "That's more than a lot of people get, so nurture it, and you'll be just fine."

"What is this, dating advice coming from you?" he asked in a teasing voice.

Mountain shuddered. "God, no, I'm definitely not anybody you should be taking that kind of advice from."

Magnus chuckled, although it took most of his energy. "I won't argue with that, but I'm damn grateful you came for me."

"Yeah, well, the colonel's pissed at me. I went against direct orders, but my instincts told me to come, so here I am."

It took another forty minutes before they pulled into the camp. When Joe raced out to help, he quickly noticed that the two dogs had been shot. He swore a blue streak that didn't stop, until they got both dogs and Magnus down to the medical clinic. As soon as they approached, the door opened, and Sydney cried out in joy. She raced forward and wrapped Magnus up in her arms.

Mountain immediately called out, "We've got two injured dogs, and Magnus has been shot as well."

"Oh my God," she said, immediately all business. She barked at the guard, "I need Joy out of here."

Mountain looked at the guard and ordered, "Take her back down to the supply quarters."

The guard nodded, and a sleepy Joy was led out, protesting the whole way. Of course the inventory area was nowhere near as comfortable, but she was completely overrun with rejections, as everybody moved, filling the clinic to help the injured.

DAY 8, LATER THAT EVENING

SYDNEY GOT UP for the umpteenth time, walked over, and checked on Magnus. He was sleeping, blankets piled up, trying to get him warm. His temperature was still a little too cool for her liking, but he was here, at least safe under her care.

As she checked his head wound, he grasped her hand. "I'm fine, you know." He pulled her hand toward his mouth and kissed her palm gently.

She leaned over and gave him a hug, whispering in his ear, "I was so damn worried."

He smiled. "I'm glad to hear that. I'd hate to think that you were looking forward to my demise."

She shot him a look; then she turned and walked over and checked on the two dogs, sharing one hospital bed. The one wagged his tail and appeared to absolutely suck up the attention. The other one slept heavily. She checked the wounds that she had cleaned and stitched, then returned to Magnus. "So, you didn't see anything?"

"I heard two yelps, so I think the dogs took the first hits. Then me," he said in disgust.

"Anyway, let's go back to sleep. You'll be fine in the morning."

"I could be warmer."

"Are you still cold?" But she already knew he was because she'd been checking his temperature.

"Yeah, can't say …"

Just then his teeth started to chatter, and she winced. "I don't have any heated blankets for you, but, if you can shift over a bit, I'll wrap around you."

He did as told, and she immediately joined him, getting as close as she could, trying to smother him with her body heat. "I'm so sorry," she whispered.

He tried to answer her, but his teeth were chattering too hard.

She groaned and just waited for it to calm down. Shivering was how the human body naturally raised body temperature, but the shakes could be very uncomfortable when they got this hard and this long. By the time his body finally calmed down, she knew he'd be exhausted.

"I wish you had seen something," she murmured. "It just seems as if everything's going around in circles, and we're not getting anywhere."

"We'll solve one part, and that'll slowly lead to another," he said quietly, when he could.

He shifted in the bed, so that she was wrapped around the front of him; then he pulled her up close. "That's better." And there they laid together, him spooned with her against his chest, and their legs wrapped up together. "It's not how I expected to spend the night."

"Hey, you could still be in the ice cave, curled up with the two dogs," she muttered.

"How are they? I was so pissed when I found out that they'd shot those dogs. Especially Toby. I have to admit I love that dog."

"Yeah, you and me both." She chuckled. "They will be fine, but I don't know about Joe. He seems pissed."

"You didn't expect to look after four-legged critters up here, did you?" he asked in a teasing voice.

"I've looked after quite a few in my time. An animal's an animal, and honestly those are my favorite kind. So I'll do anything I can to keep them safe. If it kills their careers though, that's pretty rough."

"They're Joe's dogs, so I'm not sure that's even a consideration. However, if he ever finds out who shot them, believe me. We will struggle to hold him back."

"I don't doubt that," she murmured. "What about you? Will you ship back stateside now?"

He chuckled. "No, I'm here for the duration," he said, with a clear-cut resolution in his tone. "And, if somebody went after me, what do you want to bet it has something to do with all these investigations?"

"Do people know that you're attached to them?"

"I don't see how they can't be suspicious of it, as I've been very visibly over your medical clinic mess, and, with me questioning everybody as it is, they've got their own suspicions."

"No, that's true. And considering that the last guy in that snow cave is still comatose, and the best medical minds haven't figured out why, that's a whole different story."

"Nobody injected me with anything?"

"I did check, but I couldn't find any injection sites. Do you have a reason to think they did?"

"Not that I'm aware of. I didn't see anyone approach. I don't know if this was a warning or if he would come back."

"I would suspect *come back*," she said thoughtfully. "But the weather's pretty shitty, so they would be taking a chance hanging around. Maybe they decided, if they just left you there long enough, you would have died."

"I can't be killed that easily," he growled.

"And that is a mistake they won't make twice," she warned.

He considered that and then nodded. "You know what? I'm okay with that. If anybody wants to play this game, they just upped the ante, and believe me. I won't take that kindly."

"I won't take kindly anybody who hurt these dogs. That they'll survive isn't the point."

"I'm wondering if he didn't have second thoughts on that."

"That was another point everybody was wondering about. The colonel ordered everyone back, but Mountain? He defied his direct order."

"All's well that ends well."

"Not really. I mean, when you think about it, yes, you're here, and you'll be fine, but did anybody happen to do a headcount? I don't know. I presume everybody else was doing their job, while I was doing mine."

He chuckled at that. "We would think so."

She smiled. "They should have done that, shouldn't they? They should have looked to see who was missing. Although they should have done that part way earlier. Otherwise your shooter could already be back by now."

"And that's what I was wondering, … whether he had already made it back, in which case nobody would know he was missing. He might even have joined the search party."

"And people go to their rooms and hide away for hours at a time, particularly if they're not doing anything—which is the case, with all these storms pushing everything back. So for somebody to disappear for a few hours isn't out of the norm."

He shifted in the bed and then sat up.

"Are you okay?" she asked.

He groaned. "Bladder."

"Can you make it to the bathroom?"

"I can. I just don't want to." He chuckled. "I'm finally warm. Besides, it was lovely having you curled up against me."

"If we can't get you warmed up again, then crawl back under."

"I can't get warmed up again," he stated immediately.

She laughed. "Let's get you to the bathroom first, and, no, you're not going alone."

"If you say so." He pushed back the covers to get up slowly.

She opened the door to find another guard outside; she frowned at him, surprised.

He shrugged. "Nobody's sure what the hell's going on. You're precious goods, Doc."

She snorted. "Or this guy is."

He grinned and nodded. "That could be."

"Now, he needs a hand to the washroom. Are you up for that?"

"Sure can."

"I don't want him to go anywhere alone."

"No, neither do I."

She waited at the open clinic door, and, when the guard helped Magnus get back to her, he was walking a little bit better, looking a little bit stronger. She smiled. "Seems every step you take that you're getting better," she said, when she finally got him into the clinic, thanking the guard and closing the door behind her.

He leaned over and gave her a kiss on her temple.

"That's because I'm walking back to you."

She rolled her eyes. "A little cliché." But it warmed her heart anyway. "Get back into bed." She motioned him to the closest hospital bed.

He cast her a look. "Are you coming in with me?"

She snorted at that. "Nice to know that you're feeling better."

"Yep, absolutely." He grinned. "How about you have a nap, and then you come join me."

"How about you get into bed, and we'll see how you do."

He stopped to look at her, then waited. "And then?"

She rolled her eyes. "Then you better get your ass in there."

She walked over to the dogs, smiling. Something was so endearing about that young boy persona of Magnus. She was seeing a whole different side to Magnus, and it was definitely appealing. Checking on both dogs, she realized that their bladders were also likely full.

When the one stiffly got up and walked around, heading to the door, Sydney looked at Magnus. "I need you to wait here, while I get the dog outside."

He immediately sat up. "I'll take him."

She glared at him. "That cold wind out there will hit you and send you right back into shivers."

"The dog needs to go out," he suggested, "so the guard and I could take him."

She hesitated. "We'll all go."

And, with that, she called out to the guard outside, and, as she opened the door, saw him crumpled on the floor in front of her. She cried out and bent down to deal with him, as a shot rang out. She flattened to the floor, as Magnus charged out of the room at full speed, giving chase down the hallway.

She called Mountain on her phone but he was out of breath. "I'm already on the run, heading your way."

"The guard's been hurt. Magnus has gone after a shooter," she cried out. "And I've got dogs that need to go out to the bathroom," she added, as an afterthought.

She heard Mountain's startled exclamation. "We'll handle that part later." And he clicked off.

By the time she had the guard stabilized out in the hallway, a crowd of people had collected. Utilizing two men, they picked up the injured man and laid him out on Magnus's empty bed in the clinic. She went to work, checking his vitals and the wound in his shoulder—high up, which was a relief.

The two men who had helped to carry him in, then asked her, "What the hell's going on?"

She shook her head. "Whoever attacked Magnus earlier came in after him, apparently for a second attempt tonight," she said, her tone grim.

The two men looked at each other. "We'll stand here—in case you're next in the line of fire."

"I appreciate the help. I know several people have gone after the shooter, but I don't know …" She looked over at them. "Could one of you check on the guard standing watch over Joy in the supply area?"

The two men exchanged looks, and they nodded. "One of us will stay here, and the other is going." And, with that, the second man quickly disappeared down the hallway.

She looked at the first. "Not exactly the training we thought we would have, *huh*?" she said, as she worked steadily on the guard.

She found a bullet wound. When she had the bleeding stabilized, and his vitals were calm, she sent a message to the colonel, who showed up at her door almost immediately. He glared at her, as she motioned him in and shut the door, asking the guard to stand outside. With him outside, she explained what happened. The colonel harrumphed several times, but it was obvious he was pissed.

When he took off in a rush, she said, "I need this guard picked up as soon as possible. He is stable, and the bullet went clean through, but this isn't the place for him to recover, particularly now."

When the colonel left, she sat down on a chair, trying to just relax a little bit, and, when the door opened, she looked up to see somebody that she recognized but barely. "Hey, are you in need of assistance?"

"Yeah, I am," he said, holding up a gun and pointing it at her.

She stared at it. "Well, shit."

"Yeah, you're not kidding. All this crap for a few drugs."

"Did you shoot Magnus and the dogs?" she asked.

He stared at her and shook his head. "I don't know what the hell you're talking about. I just want the drugs."

"Right, the drugs that Joy gave you."

He nodded. "Yeah. It's hard enough dealing with people you don't want to be with, but, when she's got the drugs, it's … torture."

Sydney took two steps forward, when the door slammed open behind the gunman. The second guard came in and slammed his fist into his jaw, then wrestled him to the floor. She kicked away the gun, then stood over the prisoner and stared at him. "Stealing drugs is one thing," she said quietly, "but did you have anything to do with any of the killings or the other shootings?"

The guy cried out in frustration, obviously having withdrawals. Hence his poor attempt to steal more drugs.

Once the guard secured him, they sat him in a chair, waiting for the others to show up.

"I didn't have anything to do with it. It was her, that stupid bitch," he cried out.

"What do you mean? What stupid bitch?" Sydney asked, a horrible feeling sinking in her heart.

"Joy. She got me hooked on these damn things. I told her that I'd been off them, but that I had a weakness for them. She brought them to me, as if it were candy, as if a gift from her." He snorted. "And, once I took the first one, I was lost down that stupid rabbit hole again."

Sydney winced. "Did you have anything to do with the rest of the nightmare going on here?"

He looked over at her slyly, and she watched the calculating look in his eyes, as he tried to figure out how to make this work in his favor.

Sydney shook her head. "Believe me. The colonel is on his way here, and he won't be very impressed with you at all."

He winced. "There goes my career." And then he glared at her. "You need to talk to Joy. She knows more than she's saying."

"Do you also know more than you're saying?" she murmured, looking down at him.

He shook his head. "No, but she kept saying that she knew something that would get her out of this mess. Get her out of this hellhole and out of the military. She said she had great blackmail material, and that was all there was to it."

Sydney exchanged a sharp glance with the guard and

then motioned at the door. "Go check on your guards," she said urgently. He winced and looked down at the guy they had secured to the chair. She waved him off. "I've got the gun. He's tied up. Go."

And, with that, he raced out. She quickly pulled out her phone, sent a message to Magnus, Mountain, and the colonel, and then she sat and waited. She didn't have to wait long when the door opened, and Joy slipped in, looked at her, and smiled.

"Look at that. You found him." She sneered at the prisoner. "You just couldn't resist, could you?"

He stared at her. "If it wasn't for you, I wouldn't be here in the first place."

She just rolled her eyes. "Once a druggie, always a druggie."

And he snapped right back, "Once a narcissist, always a narcissist."

Sydney stared at him, then back at Joy and wondered. Maybe Sydney had been all wrong about it. She'd noticed that Joy had always been super-aware of her surroundings and of the people, almost in a manipulative way, but Sydney hadn't known her well enough to see it at that level. "Did you guys know each other stateside?"

He nodded glumly. "Yeah, Joy knew me, when I was full-on into drugs." He started to shiver. "She likes to control people that way."

Sydney frowned at Joy. "What are you doing here now?"

"I can't have him testifying against me, can I?" She sneered again. "I mean, so far, it's just my word against anything he says, and he's a druggie, so he will say anything he wants."

With that, she pulled a handgun from her back pocket.

"What the hell? Is everybody here walking around with weapons?" Sydney asked.

Joy laughed. "Weapons are all over this place, and we all know how to use them."

Sydney sighed, nodded. "Yeah, we do, and, if you don't put that sucker away, somebody will use one on you."

Joy shrugged. "No, I don't think so." She waved the gun in Sydney's direction.

She took a deep breath and tried to sidetrack her. "So, what's this about you knowing a whole lot more about what's going on here than anybody else?"

She smiled a knowing, cocky, arrogant smile that set Sydney's teeth on edge.

"Yeah, you're right. I do, but no way I'm telling you guys anything. I want a free pass out of here, and I'll only talk when I'm out and away from that killer you've got running loose."

"So, you're not the killer?" Sydney asked, trying for a derisive note to see if she could get Joy to open up.

Joy immediately shook her head. "Drugs are easy. Controlling people is easy. All they want is sex. They're either addicted to one or the other." Joy waved the gun. "Women? We're just an addiction in itself." She snorted. "Not that you would ever know. You wouldn't even bed that bloody idiot Magnus. I'd have jumped his bones in seconds," she muttered, staring at Sydney, almost as if she were some foreign bug.

"Maybe so," Sydney replied quietly, "but jumping his bones isn't what I would consider the priority or what I'd care to do right now."

"Yeah, that's because something is wrong with you," Joy said, with a shrug. "Men are to have fun with, drugs are to use, and the world is to make your oyster." She gave Sydney a feral grin. "You sit here in this little clinic, all prim and proper, friendly enough with everybody, but not close to anybody. You have no real friends, and nobody knows a thing about you." Joy stared at Sydney. "I've worked with you for almost four weeks now, and I don't even know where you're from. I don't know anything about you."

"And why is that important?" Sydney asked, trying hard to keep Joy talking. "What difference does it make?"

"See? That's the thing. You don't open up. You keep to yourself in here, when, for all we know, you and Magnus have been having this hot affair, and no one would even know."

"What? Is that what this is all about? You wanted Magnus for yourself?" she asked in a moment of shock. "I don't think he's even looked at you twice."

Oops, maybe not the best thing to say, as Joy turned the handgun and raised it, but her hand wasn't tightening. The look on her face was sheer fury.

"I've already bedded at least six guys here, and I really don't give a shit about Magnus, and you shouldn't either. That mighty holier-than-thou bullshit doesn't go very far around here. Besides, something's off about him."

"Yeah, what's off?" Sydney asked.

"I don't know. I haven't figured it out yet, but definitely something is off."

As far as Sydney was concerned, it was the fact that he was involved in all these investigations, but, hey, she'd take Magnus over this bitch any day.

She got up from her chair, when Joy pointed the gun at her again. "Don't move."

"What will you do? Just shoot us here? Do you really

think you'll get out of this place? What will you do? Run out in the middle of this storm? You do know you'll freeze within twenty minutes."

"Not if I go carefully and if I take the dogs." She laughed. "I do have an in with the dogs."

"Oh, God, you're not screwing Joe, are you?"

At that, Joy curled her lip and screeched, "God, no, not him, but his helper, Tony? Now that's a good lay." She smirked. "He also told me that, if things got ugly, he could take me out of here, if I was really terrified. He's the one who set up the listening devices. Particularly after I told him that you were doing something illegal with drugs. And of course"—she pretended to shiver and to look afraid—"I'm terrified."

"Maybe you should be," Sydney snapped in disbelief. "People like you, they tend to end up at the bottom of the heap. They climb to the top any way they can, and then they slide all the way down and never get back up again."

Joy glared at her. "No, but you want to know what will happen here? Your prisoner will shoot you, and then, realizing what he's done and that there's no getting out of it, … and no drugs are available, he will shoot himself." Joy laughed with glee, as she walked closer to study the angles of her possible shots.

"I don't think that will work so well." Sydney kept her own handgun hidden in her pocket. "Besides, if you have information on what's going on around here, why the hell aren't you helping?"

"Because nothing's in it for me, and I'm trying to get out of here. If I stay here, I'm likely to become a target because somebody might know what I'm up to," she murmured. "But getting out of here? … That gets me a free pass, and, if

I'm lucky, this guy's got money."

She started to laugh, stepped around behind the prisoner—who was tied up—and quickly cut the bonds on his right hand. She grabbed his hand, then crouched, raised the gun. Sydney didn't wait. She pivoted, dropped to the floor, and fired.

Joy pitched to the ground headfirst, with a bullet in her forehead. The prisoner stared at her in shock, then immediately started screaming. Sydney stood, placed the handgun on her tray of tools, then walked over to Joy, as the door burst open, and several people tumbled in. At the head of the pack was the colonel and Magnus. They both stopped at the doorway.

She turned and looked at them. "Are the guards okay out there?"

At that, Magnus stepped forward. "No, two are coming your way right now, and they need medical, stat."

She nodded. "You might want to take this bitch out of here then." She turned and looked at the colonel, temper still driving through her.

"She was planning on making it appear that the prisoner shot me, then turned the gun on himself, because she got him hooked on drugs. She's the one who's been stealing from the medicine cabinet and feeding him drugs, but he didn't have anything to do with any shootings or killings supposedly. She did know more and said that she had this plan to blackmail the killer, but only once she was safely back home."

She quickly filled in the colonel on the rest of the details, as she sat down on a chair, exhausted.

The colonel faced her. "There will be an investigation."

She snorted. "Yeah, there sure will." She glared at him.

"Like why the hell is your doctor being targeted? Constantly," she added, snapping at him.

"Yet you sent your guards away."

"I did. To make sure the other guards were okay and that Joy was still in custody," she cried out. "This gunman was tied up here, under control, but Joy came in with her own weapon." She pointed to it on the floor, and the prisoner immediately started to speak, vouching for what she'd said. Sydney continued. "Plus, you need a chat with Joe's helper, as Tony was ready to take Joy out of here, if it came down to that. She was sleeping with him too. And he gave her the listening devices found here in my clinic."

The colonel shook his head. "Damn."

"My laptop has a voice recorder app that I initiated after my guard outside my clinic was downed. So, with any luck, it's all been recorded. I'll send that to you, Mason, Magnus, and Mountain."

With that, the colonel tore out of here.

She turned to Magnus. "The dogs still need to go outside."

Magnus nodded. "I'll text Joe. I bet he wants to take possession of both his dogs."

And shortly thereafter, Joe did just that.

It took about thirty minutes for the rest of the mess to get cleaned up, for prisoners to get shuffled, and for new patients to be brought in. One of the guards was ambulatory, and she quickly checked out the nasty head wound where Joy had slammed him with a huge can of vegetables. It bled freely, and Sydney quickly cleaned it, stitched it, put a bandage on it, and sent him to his bed with painkillers, after finding no signs of concussion.

As for the other guard, he was unconscious and stretched

out on one of her hospital beds. She checked him over, but his vitals were strong, and he should be just fine too. She checked his wound, which wasn't bleeding as hard, but it was at the back of his head, not exactly a great spot for it. She covered him up, then turned and looked at Magnus, sitting there, watching her. "Am I in trouble?" she asked finally.

"Because of Joy?" he clarified.

She nodded.

He shrugged. "You do have the audio recording. Too bad the video cam in here was already destroyed. The prisoner certainly backed up your story, and Joy's the one who attacked the other guards, so I would say that you were fully justified, as it was self-defense. There will be a formal process to review what occurred, of course, but, no, you're not in trouble."

She let out a hard breath and finally relaxed.

He got up, walked over, wrapped his arms around her. "Sorry, I should have told you that earlier."

She shook her head. "It's not as if there's been time."

"Did Joy say anything else?"

"A lot actually. Including something about, if she were me, she would have jumped your bones in no time."

He stared at her and then grinned. "In other circumstances, … I might have jumped yours too."

"Hey, in different circumstances I might go for it, but, right now, I'm tired, worn out, and definitely cranky. Joy also said something about this person having money," she said, suddenly remembering that phrase. "She would blackmail him when she got stateside because he had money."

Magnus narrowed his gaze at Sydney, then nodded.

"You should check all the histories of everybody here and on a financial level too."

"We will."

Just then Ted knocked and stepped in. She looked at him and smiled. "Yeah, I know. Now I'm part of another investigation. Get on with it."

He winced and nodded. "All accounts corroborate a good shooting, but still paperwork must be done."

"Tomorrow?" she asked hopefully.

"Tomorrow," he agreed with a nod, as he looked over at Magnus. "How's your head?"

He shrugged. "Better than this guy's."

At that they both turned to look at the second and last guard lying on the hospital bed. "At least he's sleeping now." She walked over and checked on him again.

At that, the guard mumbled, his eyelids opened, and he stared at her. When he started to move, he winced at the pain, and she immediately eased him back down again. She looked over at Ted. "You want to help him back to his bunk? This guy just needs to sleep off his injury. I stitched up the other guard, and, as I'm short on space, I've already sent him back to his bed. I'll check on everybody in the morning."

"Sounds as if you need a good night's sleep too."

"I haven't had one of those in quite a while," she murmured. "So, yeah, that would be nice."

When Ted and the second guard were gone, she arranged for someone to check on him in a few hours. Then she turned to Magnus. "Are you up for bed?"

He nodded. "Absolutely, come on."

He escorted her back to her room. She looked at her room versus the clinic and nodded. "A real bed would be better than a hospital bed. Besides, it was a little busy in there."

After she finished her nightly routines, she stretched out on her bed. He pulled the blankets up over her shoulders and tucked her in, and she smiled. "That's a very fatherly gesture."

"Nope, it's a caring one. Any other time, I'd crawl in there with you and show you just how caring," he said, his voice thick. "I can't believe how close I came to losing you tonight."

She nodded. "Believe me. I know, and I've been avoiding thinking about it. Joy was intent on taking me out. But to think that we'd worked together just fine and that I had absolutely no idea she was like that still bothers me."

"I'm not sure we ever know who people really are, not until something such as this happens," he said. "The good news is that it's over and that you're fine. From now on, we'll change tactics on this bloody case and see what comes next."

"Are you staying here tonight?" she murmured.

He hesitated, looked at her. "Are you offering something?"

She smiled and nodded. "Maybe."

"Then maybe I'll stay. However, you should know that I've also asked the colonel to move me in here."

She stared at him, then a flush worked its way up her cheeks. "I'm sure he thought that was a hell of an idea."

"I think he actually thought it was a good idea," he said, with a smile. "Particularly considering I've spent the last few nights looking after you anyway."

She nodded, then smiled, flipped back the blankets. "So, you might as well get in and cuddle tonight too."

He hesitated. "You know what? I'm not sure I have

enough control to make it just a cuddle."

"Nobody said it would be just that either," she corrected, with a laugh.

"I'll be back in a few minutes." When he returned, his face had been washed, and he looked a whole lot better.

She smiled at him. "If you'd taken any longer, I would have been asleep."

"Good thing I wasn't then." He crawled into bed and quickly wrapped his arms around her and tucked her up close. "But you need some sleep."

"I do need sleep, but I'm also far too wound up for it. So, maybe a little distraction to take my mind off everything would be a great idea."

He leaned over, kissed her gently. "Only as far as you want to go."

She smirked and held him close. "I'm totally okay with all of it. Honestly it would be nice to be held and to know that not everybody out there is gunning for me."

His arms tightened around her, and he nuzzled her neck and whispered, "Believe me. When I knew that Joy was gone and that the guards had been attacked, … I knew she was heading after you."

"After me and her druggie boyfriend," Sydney noted.

"I'm sorry for that."

"Apparently they knew each other before, and she kept him supplied with drugs all the time. After that, he took a long time to get off them and managed to get himself clean. However, as soon as she saw him, she immediately got him hooked again."

Magnus shook his head; then he gently kissed Sydney on the nose, pulling back her hair, so he could look into her eyes. "But now she's gone, and her druggie boyfriend, as you call him, will get a chance to recover yet again."

She gently brushed the hair off his face. "We have to remember that you're still recovering from a head wound."

He snorted at that. "It will take a whole lot more than that to keep me down."

He nudged his hips toward hers, making her fully aware of the erection pressing between them. She chuckled and shifted. "As long as we go slow and steady, I don't think it'll hurt you."

He lifted his head and grinned. "I'm always happy to follow doctor's orders."

She rolled her eyes at that, but, within minutes, she was moaning softly, as he followed her instructions of slow and steady—gently caressing her skin, moving up one side and down the other, until she was a bundle of jelly in his grasp.

When he finally lifted himself up over her and slid inside, she quivered mindlessly. He whispered, "What do you think, Doc? Is that slow enough and steady enough for you?"

She wrapped her arms around him, pulled him down tight, then whispered, "Yeah, it's definitely time to pick up the pace."

He chuckled and did as she wanted, driving into her time and time again. When she came apart in his arms, he followed in a moment. They lay on the bed, cuddling gently, at peace on the inside.

"I didn't expect to find somebody up here. I've always maintained that relationships at these training bases just weren't for me. Being a doctor always changed things."

"I can't say I've ever done this before either." He nuzzled her neck. "So why don't we just say it's a first for both of us?"

"And the last." She chuckled.

"I wouldn't go as far as all that," he murmured. "We'll be up here for weeks yet. I'm pretty sure, by that time, this whole scenario will be shut down, and we'll be back to wherever we're supposed to be," He frowned. "We might want a whole lot more than to be living in two different countries."

She nodded. "I may be part of the British team here, but I was heading stateside. I have an apartment in Redding, California."

His eyebrows shot up, and he grinned. "California it is then, and that's where I would be going anyway."

She nodded. "Sounds like a good idea to me. And in the interim"—she waggled her eyebrows—"we are sharing a room for more than a few weeks up here, aren't we?"

He laughed. "And, when the storms are raging outside, not really a whole lot more to do inside, than get to know you better." He lowered his head and kissed her yet again. When he finally came up for air, he whispered, "It will be dicey for the next few weeks. You know that, right? Until we find out all that is really going on here."

"Yeah, I do know that. Another reason why I'm not at all against having you move in. But don't ever think I want you just for protection. I've had my eye on you right from the beginning."

"That's good to know because I sure as hell have felt the same way. But, like you, I didn't think it was appropriate. Now I have a damn good excuse for being at your side, and that's where I plan to stay."

"What about getting somebody else to come help?" she asked.

He nodded. "Apparently somebody else is on the team that nobody's really been aware of. You'll meet them tomorrow."

"I'll meet *them*?"

He laughed. "Yep, whether you knew it or not, you're now part of the insider track as to what's going on here," he murmured. "So, when Ted comes back tomorrow, you'll find him with another man. That other man is part of the secret team that's been investigating here."

She frowned. "I need more info than just *another man*."

He nodded. "That's fine. His name's Rogan."

"Rogan?" She frowned. "I think I saw him at dinner last night. Big guy, short hair, beefy, seems to be a big weightlifter?"

"Yeah, that's what he may seem to be, but it's not his deal. He just comes by it naturally. He was a cop for a few years, before he went into service, and then he went immediately into investigative work as well."

"Good, sounds as if we need that. Military or navy?"

"Navy, and he has a lot of survival training experience."

"That's good," she said. "I'm hoping for a new nurse too. There is somebody here who I can use to some degree, but I haven't needed to call on her yet."

"I think that's being taken care of as well. However, I don't know if she'll be reassigned tomorrow or not."

"Good enough," she whispered, wrapping her arms around him, and then she yawned.

He nodded, tucked her up close. "Yes, Doc, definitely time for bed." He kissed her on the forehead. "Tomorrow's a whole new day."

And, with that, they closed their eyes and slept.

EPILOGUE

ROGAN WALKED INTO the medical clinic to introduce himself and found Magnus there in one of the hospital beds, sitting up, a cup of coffee in his hand, talking to the doctor. Rogan stepped up and shook hands with Magnus, who looked at him, his gaze intent. Rogan just let him look. Then he turned to face Sydney and smiled.

"Hi, Sydney. I'm Rogan."

She beamed, reached out, and shook his hand. "Am I glad you are on board."

He chuckled. "Yeah, I've heard a bit about the hellish nightmare going on here right now."

"You're not kidding. And I'm getting a new nurse today as well, but I have yet to see her."

"She's been here during training, so she's been tapped to come in and to help you with your short-staffing issue."

At that came a knock on the door. A woman entered, smiling as she stepped forward, and looked at Sydney intently. "Hey, apparently I've been reassigned as your nurse. I'm Lisa."

Sydney studied her. "That's interesting. I didn't even realize you were here. I thought I was getting someone else."

"I came in a couple days ago on one of the flights where patients were airlifted out," she said quietly. "I've done some sledding myself, quite a bit actually, but I wanted an opportunity to do it within the military's parameters, only now I have been reassigned here." She turned and looked around. "Apparently this is the most dangerous place in the whole damn base."

Sydney winced. "You could be right. But it's a pretty large base, with multiple outbuildings in this little military village, so I wouldn't count on it. Anyway, this is Rogan, and this is Magnus."

Lisa looked at Magnus, smiled, shook his hand, then turned to Rogan. "I already know Rogan." She acknowledged him, with another laugh.

"Yeah, last time I went out with you on a dog sled, you dumped me, the dogs took off, and I was left stranded in that lovely blizzard."

She smirked. "That was your own fault."

"If you say so." He shook his head. "I'm glad to hear that you're getting some training. Maybe by the time you're done here, you'll know how to mush a team."

She rolled her eyes. "Don't be such a baby. If you hadn't screamed like a little kid, the dogs wouldn't have been afraid in the first place."

He snorted. "Screamed like a little kid? You jumped a crevasse."

She shrugged. "Stopping wasn't really an option, and, hey, at least you got dumped on the far side."

Magnus and Sydney watched this exchange in fascination, as Rogan and Lisa volleyed barbs back and forth. Sydney reached out a hand to Magnus, who stepped forward and wrapped an arm around her shoulders.

Rogan turned his attention to them. "Don't worry. Lisa and I know each other from way back, so all is good."

Sydney smiled and chuckled. "I'm glad to hear that. It

sounds as if you do have a thing going on."

He looked at her. "Oh no, that we do not. She was married to my best friend. That's all there is to it." Then he nodded in goodbye and walked out.

Lisa looked after him, and then turned to the two of them and smiled. "He's right. I was married to his best friend, but that was a long time ago. And the marriage itself? Well, it didn't last more than ten months," she shared, with a sad smile. "Teenage pregnancy, teenage marriage, lost the baby, lost the husband, and, hey, life is not what you think it's going to be anymore," she murmured.

"And Rogan?" Sydney asked.

"I think in a way he blames me for the baby and for his friend. I was just as heartbroken. We were both so damn young." She shrugged. "Anyway, Rogan and I have stayed in touch over the years, mostly because of the work we do. And surprise, surprise. Here we are. Let the world bring what it may, I'm up for it."

And, with that, she smiled and asked, "Where's my desk?"

Sydney pointed.

Then Lisa nodded, headed over, and declared, "Okay, let's get to work."

This concludes Book 1 of Shadow Recon: Magnus.

Read about Rogan: Shadow Recon, Book 2

Shadow Recon: Rogan (Book #2)

Rogan arrives at the arctic training camp in the midst of chaos and suspicion. Missing men, fires in the kitchen, Magnus still recovering… and Mountain tearing across the tundra searching for his brother…

Lisa was brought in to assist Dr. Sydney in the medical clinic and is only just now catching up on the horrific events that's plagued the camp. She's trying to ignore the distrustful gazes as the only newcomer allowed in, even as everyone is trying to leave.

And yet through it all, the team investigating find some answers and yet a dozen more questions arise. Adding to the confusion, the science center is having unexplained issues with their generator. But with several scientists gone missing their problems are just starting. And those problems spill over to the training center upping the ante for both groups…

Find Book 2 here!

To find out more visit Dale Mayer's website.

https://geni.us/DMSSRRogan

Author's Note

Thank you for reading Magnus: Shadow Recon, Book 1! If you enjoyed the book, please take a moment and leave a short review.

Dear reader,

I love to hear from readers, and you can contact me at my website: www.dalemayer.com or at my Facebook author page. To be informed of new releases and special offers, sign up for my newsletter or follow me on BookBub. And if you are interested in joining Dale Mayer's Reader Group, here is the Facebook sign up page.
http://geni.us/DaleMayerFBGroup

Cheers,
Dale Mayer

About the Author

Dale Mayer is a *USA Today* best-selling author, best known for her SEALs military romances, her Psychic Visions series, and her Lovely Lethal Garden cozy series. Her contemporary romances are raw and full of passion and emotion (Broken But … Mending, Hathaway House series). Her thrillers will keep you guessing (Kate Morgan, By Death series), and her romantic comedies will keep you giggling (*It's a Dog's Life*, a stand-alone novella; and the Broken Protocols series, starring Charming Marvin, the cat).

Dale honors the stories that come to her—and some of them are crazy, break all the rules and cross multiple genres!

To go with her fiction, she also writes nonfiction in many different fields, with books available on résumé writing, companion gardening, and the US mortgage system. All her books are available in print and ebook format.

Connect with Dale Mayer Online

Dale's Website – www.dalemayer.com

Twitter – @DaleMayer

Facebook Page – geni.us/DaleMayerFBFanPage

Facebook Group – geni.us/DaleMayerFBGroup

BookBub – geni.us/DaleMayerBookbub

Instagram – geni.us/DaleMayerInstagram

Goodreads – geni.us/DaleMayerGoodreads

Newsletter – geni.us/DaleNews

Also by Dale Mayer

Published Adult Books:

Shadow Recon

Magnus, Book 1
Rogan, Book 2

Bullard's Battle

Ryland's Reach, Book 1
Cain's Cross, Book 2
Eton's Escape, Book 3
Garret's Gambit, Book 4
Kano's Keep, Book 5
Fallon's Flaw, Book 6
Quinn's Quest, Book 7
Bullard's Beauty, Book 8
Bullard's Best, Book 9
Bullard's Battle, Books 1–2
Bullard's Battle, Books 3–4
Bullard's Battle, Books 5–6
Bullard's Battle, Books 7–8

Terkel's Team

Damon's Deal, Book 1
Wade's War, Book 2
Gage's Goal, Book 3
Calum's Contact, Book 4

Rick's Road, Book 5
Scott's Summit, Book 6
Brody's Beast, Book 7
Terkel's Twist, Book 8
Terkel's Triumph, Book 9

Terkel's Guardian

Radar, Book 1

Kate Morgan

Simon Says… Hide, Book 1
Simon Says… Jump, Book 2
Simon Says… Ride, Book 3
Simon Says… Scream, Book 4
Simon Says… Run, Book 5
Simon Says… Walk, Book 6

Hathaway House

Aaron, Book 1
Brock, Book 2
Cole, Book 3
Denton, Book 4
Elliot, Book 5
Finn, Book 6
Gregory, Book 7
Heath, Book 8
Iain, Book 9
Jaden, Book 10
Keith, Book 11
Lance, Book 12
Melissa, Book 13
Nash, Book 14

Owen, Book 15
Percy, Book 16
Quinton, Book 17
Ryatt, Book 18
Spencer, Book 19
Hathaway House, Books 1–3
Hathaway House, Books 4–6
Hathaway House, Books 7–9

The K9 Files

Ethan, Book 1
Pierce, Book 2
Zane, Book 3
Blaze, Book 4
Lucas, Book 5
Parker, Book 6
Carter, Book 7
Weston, Book 8
Greyson, Book 9
Rowan, Book 10
Caleb, Book 11
Kurt, Book 12
Tucker, Book 13
Harley, Book 14
Kyron, Book 15
Jenner, Book 16
Rhys, Book 17
Landon, Book 18
Harper, Book 19
Kascius, Book 20
The K9 Files, Books 1–2
The K9 Files, Books 3–4

The K9 Files, Books 5–6
The K9 Files, Books 7–8
The K9 Files, Books 9–10
The K9 Files, Books 11–12

Lovely Lethal Gardens

Arsenic in the Azaleas, Book 1
Bones in the Begonias, Book 2
Corpse in the Carnations, Book 3
Daggers in the Dahlias, Book 4
Evidence in the Echinacea, Book 5
Footprints in the Ferns, Book 6
Gun in the Gardenias, Book 7
Handcuffs in the Heather, Book 8
Ice Pick in the Ivy, Book 9
Jewels in the Juniper, Book 10
Killer in the Kiwis, Book 11
Lifeless in the Lilies, Book 12
Murder in the Marigolds, Book 13
Nabbed in the Nasturtiums, Book 14
Offed in the Orchids, Book 15
Poison in the Pansies, Book 16
Quarry in the Quince, Book 17
Revenge in the Roses, Book 18
Silenced in the Sunflowers, Book 19
Toes up in the Tulips, Book 20
Uzi in the Urn, Book 21
Lovely Lethal Gardens, Books 1–2
Lovely Lethal Gardens, Books 3–4
Lovely Lethal Gardens, Books 5–6
Lovely Lethal Gardens, Books 7–8
Lovely Lethal Gardens, Books 9–10

Psychic Visions Series

Tuesday's Child
Hide 'n Go Seek
Maddy's Floor
Garden of Sorrow
Knock Knock...
Rare Find
Eyes to the Soul
Now You See Her
Shattered
Into the Abyss
Seeds of Malice
Eye of the Falcon
Itsy-Bitsy Spider
Unmasked
Deep Beneath
From the Ashes
Stroke of Death
Ice Maiden
Snap, Crackle...
What If...
Talking Bones
String of Tears
Inked Forever
Psychic Visions Books 1–3
Psychic Visions Books 4–6
Psychic Visions Books 7–9

By Death Series

Touched by Death
Haunted by Death
Chilled by Death

By Death Books 1–3

Broken Protocols – Romantic Comedy Series

Cat's Meow

Cat's Pajamas

Cat's Cradle

Cat's Claus

Broken Protocols 1-4

Broken and... Mending

Skin

Scars

Scales (of Justice)

Broken but… Mending 1-3

Glory

Genesis

Tori

Celeste

Glory Trilogy

Biker Blues

Morgan: Biker Blues, Volume 1

Cash: Biker Blues, Volume 2

SEALs of Honor

Mason: SEALs of Honor, Book 1

Hawk: SEALs of Honor, Book 2

Dane: SEALs of Honor, Book 3

Swede: SEALs of Honor, Book 4

Shadow: SEALs of Honor, Book 5

Cooper: SEALs of Honor, Book 6

Markus: SEALs of Honor, Book 7

Evan: SEALs of Honor, Book 8
Mason's Wish: SEALs of Honor, Book 9
Chase: SEALs of Honor, Book 10
Brett: SEALs of Honor, Book 11
Devlin: SEALs of Honor, Book 12
Easton: SEALs of Honor, Book 13
Ryder: SEALs of Honor, Book 14
Macklin: SEALs of Honor, Book 15
Corey: SEALs of Honor, Book 16
Warrick: SEALs of Honor, Book 17
Tanner: SEALs of Honor, Book 18
Jackson: SEALs of Honor, Book 19
Kanen: SEALs of Honor, Book 20
Nelson: SEALs of Honor, Book 21
Taylor: SEALs of Honor, Book 22
Colton: SEALs of Honor, Book 23
Troy: SEALs of Honor, Book 24
Axel: SEALs of Honor, Book 25
Baylor: SEALs of Honor, Book 26
Hudson: SEALs of Honor, Book 27
Lachlan: SEALs of Honor, Book 28
Paxton: SEALs of Honor, Book 29
Bronson: SEALs of Honor, Book 30
Hale: SEALs of Honor, Book 31
SEALs of Honor, Books 1–3
SEALs of Honor, Books 4–6
SEALs of Honor, Books 7–10
SEALs of Honor, Books 11–13
SEALs of Honor, Books 14–16
SEALs of Honor, Books 17–19
SEALs of Honor, Books 20–22
SEALs of Honor, Books 23–25

Heroes for Hire

Levi's Legend: Heroes for Hire, Book 1
Stone's Surrender: Heroes for Hire, Book 2
Merk's Mistake: Heroes for Hire, Book 3
Rhodes's Reward: Heroes for Hire, Book 4
Flynn's Firecracker: Heroes for Hire, Book 5
Logan's Light: Heroes for Hire, Book 6
Harrison's Heart: Heroes for Hire, Book 7
Saul's Sweetheart: Heroes for Hire, Book 8
Dakota's Delight: Heroes for Hire, Book 9
Tyson's Treasure: Heroes for Hire, Book 10
Jace's Jewel: Heroes for Hire, Book 11
Rory's Rose: Heroes for Hire, Book 12
Brandon's Bliss: Heroes for Hire, Book 13
Liam's Lily: Heroes for Hire, Book 14
North's Nikki: Heroes for Hire, Book 15
Anders's Angel: Heroes for Hire, Book 16
Reyes's Raina: Heroes for Hire, Book 17
Dezi's Diamond: Heroes for Hire, Book 18
Vince's Vixen: Heroes for Hire, Book 19
Ice's Icing: Heroes for Hire, Book 20
Johan's Joy: Heroes for Hire, Book 21
Galen's Gemma: Heroes for Hire, Book 22
Zack's Zest: Heroes for Hire, Book 23
Bonaparte's Belle: Heroes for Hire, Book 24
Noah's Nemesis: Heroes for Hire, Book 25
Tomas's Trials: Heroes for Hire, Book 26
Carson's Choice: Heroes for Hire, Book 27
Dante's Decision: Heroes for Hire, Book 28
Steve's Solace: Heroes for Hire, Book 29
Heroes for Hire, Books 1–3
Heroes for Hire, Books 4–6

Heroes for Hire, Books 7–9
Heroes for Hire, Books 10–12
Heroes for Hire, Books 13–15
Heroes for Hire, Books 16–18
Heroes for Hire, Books 19–21
Heroes for Hire, Books 22–24

SEALs of Steel

Badger: SEALs of Steel, Book 1
Erick: SEALs of Steel, Book 2
Cade: SEALs of Steel, Book 3
Talon: SEALs of Steel, Book 4
Laszlo: SEALs of Steel, Book 5
Geir: SEALs of Steel, Book 6
Jager: SEALs of Steel, Book 7
The Final Reveal: SEALs of Steel, Book 8
SEALs of Steel, Books 1–4
SEALs of Steel, Books 5–8
SEALs of Steel, Books 1–8

The Mavericks

Kerrick, Book 1
Griffin, Book 2
Jax, Book 3
Beau, Book 4
Asher, Book 5
Ryker, Book 6
Miles, Book 7
Nico, Book 8
Keane, Book 9
Lennox, Book 10
Gavin, Book 11

Shane, Book 12
Diesel, Book 13
Jerricho, Book 14
Killian, Book 15
Hatch, Book 16
Corbin, Book 17
Aiden, Book 18
The Mavericks, Books 1–2
The Mavericks, Books 3–4
The Mavericks, Books 5–6
The Mavericks, Books 7–8
The Mavericks, Books 9–10
The Mavericks, Books 11–12

Standalone Novellas

It's a Dog's Life
Riana's Revenge
Second Chances

Published Young Adult Books:

Family Blood Ties Series

Vampire in Denial
Vampire in Distress
Vampire in Design
Vampire in Deceit
Vampire in Defiance
Vampire in Conflict
Vampire in Chaos
Vampire in Crisis
Vampire in Control
Vampire in Charge

Family Blood Ties Set 1–3
Family Blood Ties Set 1–5
Family Blood Ties Set 4–6
Family Blood Ties Set 7–9
Sian's Solution, A Family Blood Ties Series Prequel Novelette

Design series

Dangerous Designs
Deadly Designs
Darkest Designs
Design Series Trilogy

Standalone

In Cassie's Corner
Gem Stone (a Gemma Stone Mystery)
Time Thieves

Published Non-Fiction Books:

Career Essentials

Career Essentials: The Résumé
Career Essentials: The Cover Letter
Career Essentials: The Interview
Career Essentials: 3 in 1

Manufactured by Amazon.ca
Acheson, AB